When Secrets Become Lies

D1521575

Molly O'Connor

TotalRecall Publications, Inc.
1103 Middlecreek
Friendswood, Texas 77546
281-992-3131 281-482-5390 Fax
www.totalrecallpress.com

Copyright © 2020 by Molly O'Connor
Background Cover Graphic: Shutterstock
First Published (February 14, 2015)

ISBN: 978-1-59095-430-0
UPC: 6-43977-44300-7

Printed in the United States of America with simultaneous printings in Australia, Canada, and United Kingdom.

SECOND EDITION
1 2 3 4 5 6 7 8 9 10

To my children and
grandchildren, my many friends
near and far, you bring me joy
each and every day.

To

Heather

Best Wishes

Molly

Once you draw a breath and let it go, you can never get it back. A life altered cannot return to what it was. A split second can draw the line between what is and what will be. It takes but one breath.

Chapter 1

March 7, 2003

She was in chemistry class when Mr. Swan, the Principal arrived at the door and beckoned Philippa. "Oooh, you're in trouble" and "What did you do, Flip?" followed her into the hallway.

Mike Styles, her closest friend stood in the hallway with his parents, solemn expressions on their faces. Philippa felt chills crawl up her neck.

"What's wrong?"

Mrs. Styles grasped Philippa by the upper arms, looked her in the eye and in a soft emotion choked voice said—"honey, there's been an accident."

"Accident—what accident?"

Mike stepped forward. "Flip, your parents were in a car accident. We're going to the police station."

"Is that where they are? Are we going there to pick them up? Are they hurt? Do we need to take them to the hospital?"

At the police station they were ushered into a small room with a sitting area and a coffee machine. A police officer stood by the window. Constable Mabel Eaton, a senior Trauma Specialist introduced herself. "I'm afraid I have very disturbing news …" and that is how Philippa learned her life would never be the same again.

"Dead! They can't be dead."

Her screams were muffled by the closed door—the reality was posted like a billboard on the face of a stranger who spoke the dreaded words.

March 10, 2003

Silhouetted against the setting sun, Philippa stood motionless. Two white caskets, side-by-side, stood suspended over gaping holes ready to be lowered into the ground. They blushed pink in the afterglow. Like a choreographed chasse, shadows of scattered clouds glided over them—the final number in the dance of death.

Head bowed, the teen twisted a sodden wad of tissue and chewed her bottom lip. Tear-stained, her face was obscured by a curtain of soft brown hair shot with glints of gold. She lifted her hand and pushed wayward strands off her shoulders, shuddered and dabbed at her eyes, eyes that darted back and forth like a frightened bird.

Philippa stepped forward and placed her hands on her parents' caskets. She sought some response to say it wasn't so. But it was. Elaine and Patrick Snelling's lives were ripped away in a devastating moment. Philippa hunched her shoulders and clasped her elbows tight to her small frame, the full realization of her parent's death sliding over her like quicksilver, cold and elusive. Her center, her anchor, her parents lay inside coffins shrouded in mauve silk.

Philippa's Aunt Helen, her only living relative, had rushed to Ottawa from Montreal as soon as the news reached her. Too young and too shattered, Philippa stood aside and let her aunt deal efficiently with arranging the funeral details. Helen's hasty efforts at providing comfort hung unheard as Philippa cowered in a prenatal position in the depths of the sofa. Devastated and disassociated she hardly registered that her aunt also grieved. Helen lost her only brother—her big brother. During the two days prior to the funeral, Philippa repeatedly flared into angry tirades against the truck driver responsible for the accident.

"He's the one that should have died—he's the one that was speeding and couldn't stop on the ice-slicked road."

Now, standing in the graveyard in the cool of a late March afternoon, unaware of the earthy scent of freshly dug gardens or the beauty of marshmallow clouds, Philippa searched through her troubled thoughts reaching for one comforting memory. One that would give her enough strength to walk away and leave her mother and father behind. Helen had suggested that Philippa concentrate on happier times. Tragic as it was, her parents would be with her always. "Think about your last birthday."

Philippa's sixteenth birthday on June 28th of the previous year, had been a special celebration—a milestone marked in style, a happy time. Sixteen coral roses, delivered at breakfast, dominated the center of the kitchen table. She was hugged and kissed by both parents before she left for school. Good-natured teasing from peers followed her throughout the day with "sweet sixteen and never been kissed". A celebratory dinner at the Westin Hotel in Ottawa was full of laughter and good conversation. They were seated beside one of the gigantic windows overlooking the lazy water of the Rideau Canal that reflected white fairy lights from the National Arts Centre that twinkled like stars on the surface of the water. The mirrored flag of the Peace Tower played lazily in the ripples.

The in-house pianist played "Happy Birthday" and all the diners sang as the moon settled over Capital Hill. A tenor's voice rose from the back of the room sending his greeting to the rafters with virtuosic fervor. Ceremoniously carried to the table, a three-tiered black forest cake glowed with sixteen pink candles. Her closest friend, Mike, wearing a white shirt and tie, navy blazer, and grey flannels, sat directly opposite Philippa. He cheered and clapped, as did all the diners as the cake was paraded toward the birthday girl. When the cake was served, Mike stood, cleared his throat, his tall swimmer's body commanding attention, and raised his Coke in a toast.

"To Flip," he said in his raspy teenage voice. "May we all share in celebrating her next sixteen. Here's to my best friend." He bent over, clinked her glass, winked, and blew a kiss.

*****

She would never celebrate another birthday with her parents. The coffins' surfaces appeared to turn from white to shades of pink dulling to grey-white as the sunset slipped below the horizon. Philippa still stood with her hands pressed on top of each as she recalled how her mother and father fawned over her with gifts when they returned home from the birthday dinner party. She had assumed after receiving so many gifts that all her presents were opened when Patrick grasped her shoulders and squeezed them affectionately.

"Just one more, Flip." He walked away and disappeared into his den shouting back across his shoulder. "Your mother and I knew it was time for this one."

Flushed and smiling, he was the picture of a proud father, dark eyes sparkled as he smoothed wayward strands of graying hair that had escaped his ponytail. Youthful for a man in his mid fifties, he gave her a roguish grin before he disappeared into the next room. He returned holding a slim box. Philippa eyed the size and shape and knew it was just right for a laptop computer. She ripped off the paper festooned with brightly coloured balloons. Patrick ceremoniously plopped the elaborate bow on top of her head. Blinded by camera flashes Philippa blinked then laughed, happy tears trickling down her cheeks. A streamlined silver Mac lay on her lap.

"Oh, my God, Oh, my god! Thank you. Thank you."

"Start it up," her mother ordered.

The monitor came to life. Patrick and Elaine exchanged knowing glances. A montage of family pictures filled the monitor, faded to black then one-by-one they slid onto the screen. The slide show depicted Philippa from infant days to one taken a few days before accompanied by "Yes, sir, she's my baby."

"Wow! Cool!" chorused her friends.

Later after her other friends left, she sat with Mike on the front steps of the wrap-around veranda, of the two-story house clutching her new computer. The soft June air was filled with the smell of lilacs. Dew glowed like silver gauze spread over the lawn. Mike removed his tie and propped himself on his elbows letting his long legs dangle down three steps. Philippa played with the ends of a colourful silk scarf that matched her sky-blue sweater and skirt. No words were needed the night was full of happy thoughts.

She remembered sitting there, her prized computer on her lap. Now, she stood beside the bodies of her father and mother ready to be lowered to their final resting place. The computer was at home on her desk.

A wayward breeze lifted strands of hair from her neck sending cold chills down her spine. Blinded by tears, she stumbled backward—strong hands caught her. Mike appeared silently beside her and wrapped his arms securely around her shoulders.

"Steady, Flip. It's time to go." She leaned into him letting him lead her away along a winding path past rows of names engraved in stone to a waiting car. Budding trees lined the pathway, a promise of new life. Philippa turned and whispered, "Goodbye, Elaine and Patrick, you will be with me always."

Frank Styles, Mike's father, watched the teens approach. He stepped away from the fender he was leaning on and opened the back door of a silver-coloured Toyota Camry. His stocky frame lent an appearance of strength. "She'll need us all. Bless her." Frank spoke to the car fender.

"Careful you don't bang your head." Mike guided Philippa into the back seat and eased in beside her.

They sped along city streets passing people walking along the sidewalks chatting with animated gestures. Hurried shoppers ran to catch their buses and teens were slumped against telephone poles smoking—outside everyday life continued. Inside the car, death delivered silence.

The drive took less than thirty minutes. They turned down a divided avenue to Philippa's house, through a sub division, built in the late 1970s. The avenue was lined by mature maple trees laden with swollen buds and well-cared-for detached homes of middle income families. Hers was a clapboard two-story, painted yellow with white trim, the colour of sunshine that gave no indication of the heavy hearts within. Cars parked one behind the other lined the curb. Dark-clad people filed up Philippa's front walk. There had been no church service, only graveside prayers. Mourners were gathering at the house to offer condolences.

Mike grasped Philippa's hand to stop her trembling. She slid across the leather seat and raised her hazel, red rimmed eyes to Mike's clear blue. Mike gave a warm supporting nod.

Stepping out of the car, Mike placed his hand firmly on the small of her back and directed her forward and up the steps to the front door. "If I can get through the day with my Adam's apple rubbing on this collar, you'll get through this too." He squeezed Philippa's hand. His efforts to lighten the tension brought a weak return squeeze.

In the hallway, Mike took Philippa's coat and tilted his head to indicate she should join her aunt who was standing in the middle of the living room greeting guests. Swallowing a deep breath, Philippa stepped hesitantly forward, stopped, straightened her back, and moved on to join her Aunt Helen who was dressed in a black bell skirt topped by a trim wide-lapelled jacket nipped tight to the waist.

Helen, tall and slim, wore an expression of warm tolerance as she listened to strangers, neighbours and friends of her brother and sister-in-law's. Her crimson lips were formed into a forced smile, her head nodding. Philippa moved beside Helen and stood woodenly as people took her hand, hugged her, and stroked her arms offering awkward comforting words. "Thank you for coming—you're so kind." Helen's words floated to Philippa in a vacuum.

Sable, the family cocker spaniel lay at Philippa's feet. There were only three receiving condolences, Philippa, her Aunt Helen and Sable. Every now and again, Philippa bent over to touch Sable's familiar silky black fur. Soft dark eyes flashed adoration followed by a swish of his tail.

Mr. Petry, her next door neighbour who she had taught to use his computer, stood holding both her hands in his, as if in prayer. When she had set up his internet he talked non-stop about his family, his cat and his garden. Today there were no words—his firm grip and passionate eyes said everything. Philippa nodded, she understood. Other mourners sputtered awkward clichés then sorted themselves around the living room and engaged in hushed conversations talking endlessly of the tragedy and Philippa's bleak future.

Helen, with her arms across Philippa's back, guided her from person to person through the living room. Plates of half eaten sandwiches and scrunched napkins lay on tables and the mantelpiece. Together, they spoke to everyone repeatedly expressing their appreciation for their support. Guests told stories of happier times hoping to push back the tragic reason they were gathered.

"I remember when they returned from their year away with a new baby. No one had any idea that Elaine was pregnant. Philippa became their total focus. Elaine seldom was depressed anymore."

Their words played like a far away echo in Philippa's head. She had always wondered why her parents had kept the pregnancy a secret, probably because they were so afraid of a miscarriage or stillbirth. When she had asked her parents about her birth the pat answers were always the old fables—she was found under a bush—she was delivered by a stork.

Eventually, the house emptied and the cars drove away.

Philippa slumped to the living room floor beside Sable. She twisted her pet's ears and buried her face in his fur. Sounds of her Aunt Helen directing a few remaining helpful neighbours gathering soiled napkins and plates drifted to her. She half smiled as she thought of her mother's description of Helen—the organizer. She heard the dishwasher start, her Aunt bidding goodbyes and final words of "Thank you. You were a big help."

Joining Philippa and Sable on the floor Helen gathered her niece in her arms. Together they rocked and rocked taking comfort in each other. Eventually they moved to the kitchen. There was little evidence that soiled plates had recently covered the gleaming white-tiled counters. Damp tea towels hung over the oven handle and the backs of chairs. Serving platters and utensils had been cleaned and returned to their rightful place in the cherry-wood cabinets.

"I put the kettle on for a cup of hot chocolate." Helen handed a mug to Philippa, then poured boiled water over a packet of green tea.

"This is my mother's favourite mug." Philippa held it as if she held a precious delicate art piece.

Helen silently nodded and took a chair across from her niece. "I'll stay here for as long as it takes to finalize the legal stuff." Helen said. "We've a lot of decisions to make, like selling the house and deciding where you'll live."

"What do you mean sell the house? I want to stay here. It's my home." Philippa cried out in alarm.

"But baby, you're too young to be on your own, and I live in Montreal so wouldn't be here if you needed me."

"No! I won't move."

"Philippa, dear, I'm all you have now. Decisions have to be made."

"Aunt Helen, I can't leave school. I have to stay here."

"No, the best solution would be for you to move to Montreal and live with your Uncle Elliot and me. Of course we'll have to find a home for Sable since your uncle's allergic to dogs."

Philippa stared at her aunt in disbelief, anger flashing like golden darts from her eyes. She stood too quickly and toppled her chair, ignored it and ran to her room. She slammed the door behind her and threw herself on her bed. "There's no way I'm going to live with my uncle. He hates me and I hate him." Philippa punched her fist into a pillow. "Why did this have to happen? It's not fair. Uncle Elliot didn't approve of my mother and father and he dislikes me. I don't want to move and I don't want to lose Sable. I don't want to live without my parents."

She reached for a photograph she kept on her bed-side table. Smiling faces appeared out of focus through her tears. She reached for a corner of the counterpane to wipe her eyes. Patrick and Elaine stood arms around each other, both, tall, fit and *alive*. Philippa ran a finger over Patrick's swarthy face, a contrast to Elaine's milky white. They were a handsome couple known to live for the moment—spontaneous and unpredictable. If she favoured either, it was her mother. Philippa had similar pale skin, hazel eyes and glints of gold in her mousy-brown hair, but other than that there was little resemblance in looks or personality. Philippa was studious and thoughtful. She barely reached 5'2", was not the least athletic and had a prominent dimple in her left cheek. She was far from beautiful in the Hollywood sense. Her most redeeming feature was a smile that managed to captivate everybody. Her Aunt Helen often went on and on about her brother not telling her that Elaine was pregnant. They simply arrived back in Ottawa after a year-long cross-Canada trip with a new-born, Philippa.

Helen shook her head at her niece's sudden departure. "I hope the legal matters aren't too complicated. Elliot and I should be compensated for Philippa's care but regardless, she's my only niece so I'll make sure she's taken care of no matter how Elliot feels." She muttered to the white, ceramic coffee cup cradled in her hands; her crimson manicured nails gripped the sides. "Patrick and Elaine's lawyer, Don Evans, agreed to meet me tomorrow morning. There is a will. He insisted that Philippa be there and that's a good thing. She's going to have to learn to deal with what life has handed her. At least, we'll know what-is-what once the will is read."

A fine drizzle fell during the night leaving the morning air sweet with ozone. Grey clouds were breaking apart to reveal a promise of a clear blue sky. Hustling about the house Helen brewed coffee, unloaded the dishwasher and let Sable out into the fenced yard before calling up the stairs to Philippa. "Time to get up, dear, we have to be on our way in a half hour." When Philippa came downstairs her eyes were red from lack of sleep and bouts of crying. She let Sable in the back door, wiped his paws, reveled in his nuzzling and fed him. "I'm never going to let you go." She whispered in his ear.

Helen grabbed her car keys, summoned Philippa and they set off for downtown. Morose and silent in the passenger seat, Philippa cast nervous glances at her aunt. The conversation of the previous night was still tormenting her. As they merged onto the expressway toward the center of Ottawa, Philippa thought about her Aunt Helen. She was Patrick's younger sister and like him was tall, had dark hair, dark eyes and olive skin. She knew Helen coveted the latest fashions so readily available at affordable prices in the garment district of Montreal. Of course she had an *in* since her company, Turn of Events, was highly sought after for organizing designer fashion shows.

Helen's perfectly-shaped eyebrows furrowed as she concentrated on the traffic and watched for the right exit.

"I don't want to move to Montreal. I don't want to leave my school. What about my friends?"

Philippa's outburst caused her aunt to grip the steering wheel tighter and purse her lips.

"Frankly, Aunt Helen, the thought of losing my home's bad enough, but living in the same house with Uncle Elliot would be unbearable—you know he and I don't get along." Her voice started to rise from a mere whisper until she was near shouting. Her tone did not convey that she openly adored her aunt but not Elliot, her husband. He was selfish and whiny. "And I won't part with Sable he's...."

Helen interrupted Philippa. "Honey, I'm sorry I upset you so much last night, but you simply have to face reality. I know you've more than enough to deal with right now. But facts are facts. Believe me, baby, if there was another solution, I'd be the first to embrace it."

"I don't want to move."

"It would be preferable to let you stay at your high school until the year is out, but I see no alternative. Let's see what happens at the lawyers. Perhaps, we can make some interim arrangement."

"Do you think so?" Philippa's voice was flat and disbelieving.

"I don't know. We'll see. You know your uncle Elliot arrives home from India tomorrow and he's had another bad turn."

Her aunt told Philippa that Elliot had suffered a bout of depression which was always the case when he left India.

"He is not easy to live with, as you can well imagine. He'll need to make some personal sacrifices as well."

"He won't allow it."

"He won't be happy at the thought of a teenager in the house nor the additional expense. That'll upset him even more. But you're my family so he'll just have to accept it." Helen patted her niece's knee.

Philippa quietly grunted.

"Oh, dear, I do hope your parents made some workable arrangements." Helen changed lanes. "They tended to live life in such a haphazard way. Frankly, I don't know what we'll learn at the lawyers."

"What can lawyers do?"

"Well, we do know there's a will and hopefully that's a good thing. Lawyers make sure the terms of the will are honoured. When it was drawn up or what it contains, I've no idea. Your parents were far from the most organized people. Why when they returned to Ottawa with you, they hadn't even arranged a place to live and here they were with a new baby! I had no idea you were on the way. It's as if you appeared out of nowhere. However, I was in India and your mother lived in fear of never having a child, so maybe it was understandable that they kept the news of you quiet until they were positive you arrived safely and were healthy."

Philippa slunk down in her seat offering no comment. She indicated with a pointed finger that the next exit was the one to take.

Pulling into the right turn lane, Helen followed the signs to Main Street and eased the car into a side parking lot of an imposing, two-storey, late 1800s red brick house that stood behind a discrete gold-lettered sign labeled *Evans, Sands and Forester.*

Stepping from the car, Helen smoothed her black, tailored pant suit—not her usual fashion style, but appropriate for the occasion. She wore it buttoned with no blouse, a simple strand of pearls gleamed against her dark skin accenting a modest glimpse of cleavage.

"Come along, Philippa."

Toting a sleek black handbag, her long strides ate up the walk as she easily balanced on five-inch heels. They were met by a smiling receptionist when they entered the plush receiving area.

"Good morning, Mrs. Ravi, Philippa. Please come right in. Allow me to say how sorry I am at your tragic loss." She spoke as she rose from her desk and walked around to meet them. She led them down a hallway, lined with certificates displayed on the walls, to a conference room. She and Helen chatted about the weather and the drive into town. Philippa rubbed her sweating palms dry on her blue jeans and pulled down her navy over-sized sweat shirt, as she followed closely behind. Her runners left tread marks on the hardwood floors from the damp grass she had cut across. With downcast eyes she bit her bottom lip to control the tears that constantly threatened.

"Mr. Evans will be right with you. Can I get you a drink, coffee, juice?" The receptionist cheerfully asked. Both indicated "no" as they seated themselves mid-table in high-backed navy leather chairs. The rosewood paneling and heavy furniture made the dark room imposing and threatening.

Don Evans filled the doorway as he strode into the room. At 6'3" and weighing over 250 pounds, he portrayed the image of the rugby player he had once been. A warm smile spread across his face when he saw Philippa slouched as deeply into her chair as humanly possible. Even in mourning she was the picture of a typical teenager. He approached the conference table patting Philippa on the head as he reached to shake Helen's hand.

This patronizing move alerted every nerve in Philippa's body. She folded her arms tight across her chest and managed to slump even lower into the leather.

"Mrs. Ravi, I'm so sorry we meet under these circumstances. Patrick spoke of you often. Philippa, I can't begin to find words to express how devastated I am for your loss. I'm sorry I was not there yesterday for support but I just returned from England late last night. I spoke with your aunt before my flight home. Your parents will be missed not only by their family but by the community as well."

Philippa glanced up and forced a weak smile.

"No one ever wants to deal with moments like this, but life and death have a way of shifting our center of gravity, and when it does, it helps somewhat if affairs are in good order. Philippa, I met with your parents late last year and drew up their wills. Hopefully, this will be some consolation and make matters a whole lot easier for you. I'll quickly outline the general overview and we'll deal with the details later. But first, I want to tell you we have undertaken to proceed with civil action against the truck driver and the trucking firm."

Helen nodded her approval and leaned forward to hear every word.

Speaking directly to Philippa, Evans continued. "There is every reason to expect a fairly substantial settlement that will help compensate for your loss."

"I don't want money. I want my mother and father back." Philippa's voice was high and strained.

"Philippa, I know this is difficult. Time will heal, but I am obligated to outline and follow your parents' wishes. They wanted what is best for you."

Slowly, she raised her head, bit her bottom lip and forced back threatening tears.

"Regardless of any settlement, I want you to know that you were left in good stead. Since you're the only heir, the house, vehicles, and all chattels go to you. There're some substantial investments and an insurance policy that'll provide for your education, living expenses and incidentals. However, given your age, all funds will be placed in trust and administered by our firm as directed by your parents. We'll act as your guardians."

"You mean, I have to report to you like a parole officer?"

"Nothing of the kind." Don released a slight chuckle. "We only manage the financials. A monthly allowance will be determined and since your father served in the army you qualify for a pension and the same goes for the Canada Pension Plan."

"What do you mean, Canada Pension Plan? I'm not old."

"Yes, right. But CPP has a special mandate to fund orphans and under the circumstances we'll apply for that allowance."

Philippa had not thought of herself as an orphan but here was the reality thrown right at her. She *was* an orphan.

"The army pension is approximately $935 per month and the CCP is around $250. This, too, will be administered by our firm. I have notified Harvey White, the district manager for Farly Insurance and he's ready to expedite the file as soon as he receives the proper documents."

"Those would be the ones you said were in a safety deposit box?" Helen was rustling through her purse.

"Quite. There are also documents that we'll need for the pension funds. It's my understanding that those, too, will be in that box at Central Trust on Bank Street. I'll provide you with the letter of introduction that you'll need to access the box. Did you find the key after our conversation yesterday?"

Helen nodded. She produced a small brass key from her purse. After much searching she finally had found it in an envelope in Patrick's desk drawer. "I'm surprised that Patrick and Elaine made these arrangements they were so scatter-brained."

"Not in this case. Often, when we think we know someone a total contradiction happens. I know their lifestyle was somewhat contemporary but they always made sure their finances were in good order and that their wills were current. As trustee, our firm will receive a fee for our services and review the file annually with Philippa."

"I expected to act as guardian. This is so unexpected."

"Mrs. Ravi, although Patrick and Elaine did not choose you as Philippa's guardian, they did mention you as the only family contact."

Philippa noticed her aunt flinch. It was a deliberate slight by her brother. Helen glanced at Philippa then nodded to Don Evans to continue. Philippa resumed her sullen posture.

"We welcome your scrutiny as well, if you so choose. There's one caveat though; Patrick and Elaine stipulated that should their demise precede Philippa's eighteenth birthday, arrangements will be made for her to stay in the family home should she so wish. Once she's of age, she can determine herself what she wants to keep, or sell. In the meantime, Philippa, they insisted they didn't want you to bear any more disruption in your life."

Philippa had been chewing on a strand of wayward hair, concentrating on an invisible spot on her knee and rubbing her left hand along the arm of the chair. When she heard she would be allowed to remain in the house, she looked up with interest.

"I have" continued Evans, "as per instructions set out in the will, taken the liberty of finding a suitable person to act as chaperone and housekeeper."

"Who"? Philippa let the hair drop from her mouth.

"I have two individuals who come highly recommended and are willing to move into the house with you. I can arrange for interviews as early as this afternoon, if this suits. Mrs. Ravi." Don turned his attention to Helen. "I hope and assume you'll want to be a part of this decision."

Helen nodded. "Frankly, this makes things a great deal easier."

"I understand you're anxious to return to Montreal, so these arrangements should be made as quickly as possible."

"Yes."

"Philippa, I know this is a terribly difficult time for you but please believe me when I say, we're acting in your best interest and following your parents' wishes."

Philippa managed a small smile. "I'd rather this than moving away, I didn't want to lose Sable."

Don shot her a questioning look but thought better of taking it any further. The meeting took less than an hour as they went over the details of the will and Don outlined the legal process.

"We'll go directly to the bank," Helen said rising. "Can you ask the applicants for the housekeeper position to come to the house this afternoon allowing each about an hour with us? I'll get back to you later."

She shook Don Evans hand and turned to Philippa. "Do you understand what has transpired here?"

Philippa indicated a 'yes', pulled another strand of hair into her mouth as she rose and headed for the door.

"Mr. Evans, I'm sorry," Helen indicated with a toss of her head toward the petite slender figure slouching away. "Philippa has had to deal with so much in the last few days and the future won't be easy either. We've no choice but to move forward, she is going to have to bear up and get on with life. Thank you for all you've done."

In the car, Helen asked Philippa if she was all right.

"I'm glad I can keep Sable and stay at my school. Oh, Aunt Helen, I miss Elaine and Patrick so much. I don't understand why this happened." The tears rushed to the surface and streamed down her face.

Helen drove silently. Philippa had regained some composure by the time they reached the bank but chose to wait in the car while Helen took care of the safety deposit box business.

Alone in the car, Philippa thought about the day her parents were killed.

A transport truck had careened down a hill and broadsided Patrick's prized red Miata. Death had been swift. The truck driver escaped uninjured.

Numbly staring out the breath-fogged car window she watched the ghostly image of her aunt returning, carrying the contents of the safety deposit box in a large white envelope.

Once on the road, Helen avoided driving anywhere near the intersection where the accident happened and instead chose another route. She parked her black Sentra next to Elaine's muddy Dodge Caravan and hastened into the house. Philippa followed. Sable greeted them both with agitated wiggles and quick scurrying around their feet. Philippa knew the signals and reached for Sable's leash. A walk around the block was what they both needed.

Later, seated at the kitchen table, Helen, now wearing tight red stretch pants and a colour-coordinated cashmere blouse-over, pored over the documents matching them to the list Don Evans had given her: Patrick's birth certificate, Elaine's birth certificate, Patrick's military discharge papers, social insurance and CPP numbers, marriage certificate, deed, insurance policy and a baptismal certificate for Philippa. A pair of first booties and a lock of fine baby hair wrapped in tissue paper in a velvet jewelry box were also among the contents. Helen held the booties and shook her head. So like Patrick and Elaine to treasure them as much as legal documents.

"Sweetie," Helen spoke to Philippa seated across the table from her, "there's no birth certificate for you."

"So what does that mean? I wasn't born? Patrick used to tease me that they found me in a cabbage patch and other silly places. Knowing Elaine it probably got stashed it with a mess of papers or was accidentally thrown away," said Philippa.

Reaching for the phone, Helen dialed the direct line for Don Evans. He was quick to answer and pleased when Helen told him they had found most of the documents on the list.

"All the papers are here except Philippa's birth certificate. There's a baptismal one and that's all."

"Not a problem. I expect that'll be enough for the insurance company, but the government will want proof of birth before releasing the pension funds. No matter, we'll simply apply for one. I'll need the place of birth and date. If you can drop by with the other papers later today, I'll start processing them. I've contacted Florry Waters and Rachael Fin, the ladies I mentioned."

"Ladies?"

"The ones applying for the chaperone position; Florry'll come by at one this afternoon and Rachael at three. I do hope one of them will meet your approval.

"Oh, quite—thanks."

"Can I expect the documents sometime after your interviews?"

"I'll arrange to send them by local courier," Helen answered, "and I'll include the information on Philippa's birth date and where she was born. Thanks for all your help. I'll call later today or early tomorrow morning regarding the interviews."

"Is the birth certificate a problem?" Philippa asked.

Chapter 2

Florry Waters moved the car mirror until she could see her reflection. Turning her head from side to side, she scrutinized her high cheek bones and sharp chin. She twisted a stray strand of hair and forced it into the fat tidy roll skewered to the back of her head. Once soft amber it was now a wiry yellow-grey. Running a finger over the deep blue eye shadow layered above her soft hazel eyes, she examined her dark eye liner and nodded approval. Taking a lipstick tube from deep within a red patent purse, she touched up her bright pink lipstick, put it back, readjusted the mirror and stepped out of the car. A beige woolen suit, several sizes too large, hung on her slender frame. Ruffles of her scarlet blouse spilled over the jacket lapels. Holding her head high, she stepped purposely up the walk in sensible brown flat loafers. A doorbell chimed from deep within when she pressed the button. She could hear footsteps approaching from the other side of the forest green door.

"Hello. You must be Florry. Please, come in."

Florry followed Helen through an archway on their right into a large bright sitting room. Off-white furniture hugged soft green walls offset by densely abstract-patterned drapery. Helen indicated the sectional sofa and leaned over the back of an armchair facing it. Florry smoothed her skirt discretely over her knees as she sat.

"Can I get you a cup of tea or coffee, Miss Waters."

"Thank you, tea would be nice."

While Helen went to prepare the tea, Florry inspected the

mantelpiece above the beige brick fireplace and admired an array of carved birds and animals displayed on it. Turning to take in the rest of the room, she wrinkled her nose in distaste at several unusual sculptures. "Must be some form of modern art," she muttered. Two twisted formations, easily two feet tall, stood on the beige carpet beside the fireplace. Several smaller, equally contemporary pieces, sat on teak side tables and a credenza under the large front window. The Scandinavian-styled furniture with its sleek simplistic lines was a decided contrast to the wildly elaborate art work. Florry turned to look at two boldly coloured abstract paintings hanging on the wall behind the sofa. "My, my—different tastes than mine." She resettled facing the archway to await Helen's return.

"Do you take cream and sugar? Please help yourself." Helen had placed a tray on the teak coffee table. Philippa following behind her aunt introduced herself before sitting apart in a dark green rocker beside the credenza.

Holding her cup in her right hand and her saucer securely grasped in her left hand, Florry took a sip of her clear black tea and prepared to answer questions.

"Have we met before?" Helen asked. "You look vaguely familiar."

"I don't recall ever meeting you Mrs. Ravi." Florry answered. "But it's possible we've passed on the street."

"Possibly, or you simply remind me of someone." Helen nodded then proceeded to explain the position. She asked a number of questions about house management. Florry responded clearly and without hesitation.

"I live in Montreal and it's important that Philippa has as normal a life as possible under the circumstances. We're looking for someone who can manage the household, prepare meals and be a companion for Philippa. She's a bit old for a chaperone but still needs a responsible adult to be available for her." Helen went on to outline the duties and asked questions about Florry's former positions.

Philippa was leafing through Florry's letters-of-reference and employment history. "Excuse me Ms. Waters, I see that the last time you did this kind of work was over sixteen years ago. Why's that"?

Florry carefully set her saucer on the coffee table. With a slightly quivering left hand she steadied it by putting her right firmly on top of the cup. She had hoped this would not be noticed.

"There was a tragedy. I sincerely hope you'll understand, I haven't been able to bring myself to work with children since. I was with a family in Quebec, an engineer at the local mining company. His wife suffered from severe depression so I was hired to manage the house and see to her needs." Florry shifted and pulled at her skirt.

"There were sad circumstances involving the loss of a baby. It was a dreadful time. I was overly affected by it and could never bring myself to look after an infant again." She paused and took a moment to compose herself. "I thought this position with a teenager, not a wee one, might be something I could handle. I've done house cleaning jobs over the years and that's how I heard about this job. I work for Mrs. Evans, the lawyer's wife, and I overheard them talking. I asked Mr. Evans to recommend me."

Florry spoke more and more rapidly. "Believe me, I understand the pain of losing a loved one, I've lived with it every day of my life. I promise, I promise I'll be supportive but never intrusive. I do hope we can develop a mutual respect for one another, one adult to another, right Philippa?" She raised her head and smiled weakly at the teenager. "I really think we could make this work."

As she talked her hand reached to stroke Sable who had settled his dark head on Florry's lap. This did not go unnoticed by Philippa—he used to do that with Elaine.

The interview included a walk through the house with quick explanations in each room. Florry noticed that the furniture was not extravagant but in good taste with yet more art objects scattered throughout the house. "Oh, my goodness!" She started when faced by a sculpture beside the kitchen table. It depicted a grotesque beast with its mouth twisted and wide open, tears running down its cheeks and a butterfly perched on its nose.

Upon seeing Florry's shocked expression Philippa explained with a little laugh, "Everyone's taken aback by this. It's not my mother's usual style but it was a statement to my dad, the beast, not to growl or upset the butterfly, my mother, before she had her morning coffee. It's a family joke. Patrick, my father had a habit of over-reacting to situations in a totally unexpected ways—often unacceptable."

"Your mother made these statues?"

"My brother, Patrick, and his wife, Elaine, were artists. They worked in different media," Helen answered. "Elaine tended to do rather way-out abstract sculptures using any material at hand. Some are pretty startling. Elaine was specific that they all made a political statement. It's hard for me to grasp why they were so coveted. She won many awards and her works is highly appraised. Patrick carved birds and animals. Frankly, I don't consider any form of visual interpretation other than paintings qualify as art."

"Well, I must say, I like the wood carvings." Florry said. "Those little creatures are so life-like."

The trio returned to the sitting room. A few more questions completed the interview. Helen led Florry to the front door. "Thank you, Florry. Don Evans will let you know one way or the other."

"Thank you, Mrs. Ravi, Philippa." Florry reached to pat Sable before she opened the front door.

Helen and Philippa watched Florry drive away. "I wonder what the other applicant is like. She should be here any minute." Helen closed the door behind them and went into the sitting room to collect the cups and saucers. Philippa made no comment and sat deep in thought on the edge of the sofa.

Rachael Fin arrived by taxi, and rushed up the walk to the front door fifteen minutes late. "Mrs. Ravi, I'm so sorry" she uttered breathlessly. "I'd one of those mornin's when nothing works right. Just as I's heading out the door the phone rang. Doesn't it always? Just when you need it least... Well, it t'was my mom and she wouldn't get off the phone. So I do apologize."

Her slight Ottawa Valley accent was a contrast to Florry's carefully spoken English. Rachael wore black slacks, sling-back pumps, a simple, tailored lemon-yellow blouse and carried an enormous black plastic purse. Her makeup, artfully applied, accented her fair features and large dark eyes. Short curly brown hair looked professionally coiffed. A radiant smile showed even, whitened teeth. She obviously cared about her appearance.

Helen and Philippa followed the same process for the interview with Rachel as they had with Florry. Rachael was divorced but childless and had served with the same family for seven years looking after, first their son then two years later, their newly arrived daughter. Treated as an extended member of the family, her references were glowing. The reason for changing jobs was due to the fact that both children were in school and the mother had been able to adjust her hours to be home with them. A baby-sitter, housekeeper was no longer needed.

"Would you have any objection if the children came to visit?" Rachel asked.

Philippa smiled. "Of course not, you obviously miss them."

"I thought that looking after a house with a teenager would be a good change," said Rachael, "I certainly need to find a new position."

"With these glowing references, I'm sure you will have no problem" Helen said.

During the house tour, Rachael listened and said little as she followed along. She made no comments about the décor or the art work but did express her approval of the large screen television.

The interview was completed and as Rachel was leaving she turned and asked Philippa if she was dating or had a steady boyfriend.

"I tend to move in a group, we've not paired off."

"I just want you to know, Mrs. Ravi, I'll be diligent when it comes to making sure Philippa keeps to her hours and I expect to meet and approve her friends." Rachael announced. "I may not've been in charge of a teenager before but she might as well know, I can spot drugs a mile away."

✽✽✽✽✽

Florry drove along Woodroffe Avenue deep in thought. She

had moved to the Ottawa area in November, 1999 and with a small inheritance bought a single-wide mobile home south of the city. Her 1990 Toyota Corolla, though it was a "rusty bucket", as she called it, was reliable and her principle mode of transportation. Turning south, Florry thought back to her interview:

My heart goes out to that young lady. Right now, I think she's way too composed and will hit the wall before too long. The Aunt's definitely self centered but loves her niece desperately so she's very torn. If I get this position, I'll have to make sure she's kept informed and happy. That's one beautiful house, a far cry from my single-wide. Now what'll I do with it if I get the job? Lease it out? Perhaps. No, I think it'll be my get-away. I own it free and clear so it makes sense to hold on to it. Besides, Aunt Helen Ravi is bound to come to Ottawa often and that'll give me time on my own. Oh, that poor wee dear, how dreadful to lose both her parents in such a tragic way. She's a sad little thing but has a sweet smile. My first impression is that she's a good kid but time'll tell. I might do some discrete investigating through her school. Yes, I'll give the principal a call if I get the job. Good idea to know what I'm up against and then he'll need to know who I am. Of course the neighbours'll fill me in; of that, I am sure.

Florry turned left toward the village of Manotick and eased the Blue Corolla into a parking spot at the strip mall. She avoided shopping in the city and preferred supporting local merchants. She went to the pharmacy to pick up a few items on her list. Florry was a list maker and always carried a small notebook and pen in her purse. She strolled up and down the aisles itemizing things she'd have to do if she got the Snelling job.

I'll have to notify all my clients. Of course Mrs. Evans will know from her husband. After all, I've been doing housework for the Evans's now for four years. Mr. Evans was kind to recommend me for this job. I must remember to write a thank you note. Maybe Joyce, my neighbour'll take my other clients. I'll check. It would be better if I can offer them a replacement. And I'll ask Joyce if she'll keep an eye on my place. I'll have to cancel the newspaper. What'll I do about the services and the satellite TV? Oh, my, there's a lot more to this than I thought. Yes, I can cancel the newspaper but I'll need the other things if I'm to spend any time at home. Besides, I'll have a nice salary and can manage. I should go over to the hardware store and pick up light timers—no, silly, you haven't got the job yet!

With the items she needed in her basket, Florry waited in line at the cashier still deep in thought. When she left the store, bag in hand, she stepped off the curb right into the path of a maroon SUV. The blast of its horn made her jump back onto the curb and jolted her to the moment. "Stupid me, I should watch where I'm going."

When she arrived home, she threw her jacket over a kitchen chair and plugged in the kettle. No sooner was it sizzling than her back door flew open and Joyce appeared in the opening.

"Flo, where've you been? And where'd you get this thing?" she asked as she picked up the suit jacket from the chair holding it away from her as if it had a foul odour.

"Joyce, good God, can't a gal keep a few secrets?" Florry was itching to share her news but not without being coaxed. "I picked it up at the Thrift Shoppe. I needed it for an occasion."

"Yeah, well, you and me's best friends and best friends don't have secrets. What kind of occasion would've made you wear that moth-eaten thing?" Perfectly at home in Florry's place, Joyce went to the cupboard and took out two mugs, sat them on the table then turned to the refrigerator and pulled out a carton of 1% milk. "When're you go'en to buy decent milk? This 1% crap is nothing but white water!"

"It's my house and my choice. It sure doesn't stop you from helping yourself, does it?" Florry spat back. "Besides, it's not moth eaten, it's just a little out of date."

Friendly arguments opened their conversations nearly every day. As they sat across from one another, Florry pondered about how much she should tell her friend at this time. If she didn't get the job she wouldn't have to share the disappointment and could continue as before. But of course she would reveal all and hovered over her cup as she started. "I went for a job interview...."

*****

Rachel waited on the front sidewalk for the taxi she ordered. Glancing back at the large, well maintained home she smiled, "this would be one sweet gig," she muttered out loud. Seeing the taxi coming around the corner she waved it to the curb and got in when it stopped beside her. Settled in the back seat, she took one last look at the house with its sweeping veranda and neat gardens.

Yes, sweet. Miss Rachael, you'd be just like a queen in a palace. Sure beats my crummy apartment. And the girl, Philippa, she didn't seem like a bad sort, a bit spoiled but what kids aren't these day? She'd be in school all day so I'd have the place to myself—peachy. Have to make sure Johnny doesn't think he can just drop in whenever he pleases. Time I dumped him anyway. He's getting to be a bore. Gosh, I forgot to ask about days off. Shelly and the gals might have to get another bowling team member. Philippa's a cute kid, a little plain, but a few highlights in her hair and a little makeup would go a long way. Too bad about her parents, though.

The cab pulled over outside a triplex. Rachael paid the driver giving him a meager tip. She shouldered her over-sized purse and jangled her keys as she strolled up the walk. Glancing at her watch, she realized that it was time for *Turn of The Night*, her late afternoon soap opera. She threw her purse on the sofa and grabbing the remote plopped down.

Yeah, it's definitely time I dumped Johnny. He's getting on my nerves and I don't like that he snorts coke and smokes cheroots. I'm real careful not to use drugs or smoke cigarettes. You just need to make one bad impression on an employer and the next thing you know—wham—you're out of a job without a recommendation for another. I was real lucky to be with the Millers for seven years—and little Kyle and Krista, just like they was my own kids. It'll sure be different looking out for a teenager. Well, she better watch herself, she won't put anything over me. I can spot drugs and booze a mile away especially since my brother was sent up for dealing.

Rachael went to the refrigerator during the commercials and poured a glass of iced tea and grabbed an apple. From her galley kitchen she kept an eye on the screen. In the small sitting room, a soft grey pull-out couch, laminate grey coffee table, two fold-away chairs and a 42″ TV set left little floor space. A door opened off the hallway to a tidy bedroom with a queen-sized bed smothered in pillows and plush toys. Another door off the entrance hall led to a compact bathroom. Cosmetics cluttered shelves over the toilet and down one wall. Rachel couldn't resist the newest washes, moisturizers, makeup and hair products on the market.

As soon as Turn of the Night's over, I'm going to call Johnny and tell him about the Snelling job. Maybe he'll come over and we can go for a drive then grab a burger and a beer.

Chapter 3

Helen and Philippa sorted through the two applications at the kitchen table, buff folders lay open on the blue melamine, photo copies of letters and documents were separated for each candidate. Helen got up and poured a glass of Chardonnay for herself and a cup of chocolate milk for Philippa then sat beside her niece.

Philippa, her hazel eyes intent, looked up at her aunt. "You first, Aunt Helen, who do you think?"

Helen sipped her wine, bit her bottom lip in concentration, and leaning closer to Philippa, drew a few pages closer. She studied them, glanced over at her niece who was chewing a strand of hair and twisting her sleeve.

"Philippa, for God's sake stop that filthy habit!"

"Um, oh, sorry, I wasn't thinking."

"Frankly, I'm not smitten with either," said Helen. "I'd rather have someone a little more cultured, but I guess the quality of person I'd rather have wouldn't be looking for this kind of work, so that's not really important. Both have excellent references but neither has done anything equivalent to this job. Rachael seemed more interested in the television set than what she's supposed to do—makes me wonder if she's going to attend to detail and keep up with her duties. Her experience is with caring for small children not running a household so she tends to be a bit controlling. Your input mightn't be something she'd readily accept. You've never been treated that way. Your parents consulted you on all family decisions. I have to say, something I didn't always approve of."

"They respected my opinion."

"Well, it seemed patronizing to me, but I have to admit that now, under the circumstances, you'll cope better. You're very aware of the everyday running of the house."

"Don't forget, Aunt Helen," interrupted Philippa, "I'm almost an adult. I'll be seventeen soon."

"True. But you're still naïve about many aspects of life. Oh God, Philippa, did your parents even talk to you about the birds and the bees?"

"Hey, I may not've had many boyfriends but I do know what's what. Besides, it's 2003 and they teach all that in school."

Helen shot her niece a questioning look then returned to reading the resumes. "Florry's quite the opposite of Rachael. I think she's always been told what to do and'll need direction from you, me and Don Evans. She certainly showed interest in your well being though and asked sensible questions about managing the house."

"Sable sure took a liking to her."

"I got the feeling she was rather guarded and didn't tell us everything. Did you notice how fidgety she got when you asked her about the last time she worked with children."

"Hey! I'm not a child. But you're right. I think she was hiding something but it seemed to me that it was something personal. She obviously loved that woman's baby and when it died she took it very hard. I don't think it has anything to do with this job."

"She's certainly a queer duck, wears rather peculiar clothing …"

"Oh, my God," interjected Philippa, "did you get a load of her outfit? Straight out of a rag bag—and that…"

"Well, now," countered Helen with a sly grin. "You've got to admit that the blouse was a *niiice* touch—red satin with ruffles." Helen started to snicker and held her hand over her mouth to suppress a laugh.

"Oh, yeah," exclaimed Philippa, "did you check out the pink lipstick with the red blouse, clashy classy!"

Helen glanced at her niece about to chastise her for being unkind. They had always had a mutual and distinct sense of fashion. It was one of their shared passions. "Perhaps she just needs..."

She noticed the glint in Philippa's eyes—the smile sliding across her lips, her dimple deepened as she continued. "—and the bag of a suit, holy cow, I expected moths to come flying out at any time!"

Unable to contain herself, Helen started to chuckle. Simultaneously the two of them burst into spontaneous laughter and continued until tears rolled down their cheeks. They ended up holding aching sides trying to catch their breath. Helen waved a hand in the air as if to call a truce, but it only served to send them into further fits of laughter. Finally, sucking in short breaths, the odd snigger escaping, they settled down. Helen draped over the table and Philippa sprawled out full length in her chair. Spent and flushed, they wiped away laughter tears. All the tension from the difficult week they had both endured eased. Aunt and niece smiled and for the first time in days.

"I don't intend to be mean by criticizing her. I like her. I don't know why, but I like Florry. I like her better than Rachael."

"You know what?" Helen spoke while getting her breath. "So do I. Clothes do not make the person, she seemed really sincere."

*****

The serious business of arranging the running of the house and deciding where responsibilities lay occupied all their time for the following week. Helen stayed in Ottawa even though Elliot had returned from India to Montreal and phoned every day to ask when Helen was 'coming home'.

"For God's sake, Elliot, can't you stop thinking about yourself for just this week? My niece lost her parents and has to deal with a new person in the house and I've buried my only brother. You'll just have to manage till I get home on Monday. What?"

Helen drummed her fingers on the counter as she listened. "Oh, the porridge's in the top left-hand cupboard. Just follow the instructions on the package. What, you don't know how to work the stove? For God's sake, Elliot, buy some cold cereal to get you through this week."

Helen stabbed 'end call' and mulled over the conversation. Elliot was so dependent that he was like having a spoiled child. His parents in Delhi doted on their only son, wailing and carrying on every time he left to return to Montreal. When he visited them he always came back depressed and morose. He had had no choice but to leave India when he graduated from university, there were no decent jobs there and he couldn't earn a sustainable living. His parents refused to consider moving to Canada but never let up about being deprived of their only son. They made no secret of how they thought Helen had stolen him away.

Elliot and Helen had been married for seventeen years, and for the most part, it proved a workable relationship. Elliot now owned his own accounting firm and Helen, an event planning company, both successful. It was low season for Turn Of Events, and Helen competently managed her agency during her absence through telephone conferencing. Every one of her employees was carrying an extra work load to enable Helen to stay in Ottawa, deal with her loss and help Philippa work through the legal issues and daily household concerns.

✸✸✸✸✸

Don Evans sat rapping his pen on the top of his burled maple desk. He had all the information he needed and now, knowing that Philippa had been born in Nova Scotia on June 28, 1986, he arranged for one of his staff to get the necessary documents and prepare the rest of the details. Of all his clients, Patrick and Elaine were the ones who never ceased to surprise him.

Don and Patrick had a special client-lawyer relationship, with Patrick oft times relying on Don for personal advice and guidance. He thought back to how they became clients. Elaine was an only child. Her mother succumbed to colon cancer when Elaine was eighteen and her father, Roger, suffered a massive stroke fifteen years later. Roger named Don Evans as executor of his estate which included a tidy inheritance to Elaine.

He knew that Elaine was distraught over losing her father and refused to benefit financially from Roger's death. The money was placed in a trust fund and managed capably by Evans' firm had increased significantly over the years. Later, Elaine and Patrick went on a year-long cross-country trek, returning with their new-born, Philippa. Elaine, then, wanted a home and used a portion of her inheritance to buy it. Don continued to handle their legal work.

He recalled that Elaine and Patrick lived a rather unusual life style, blending into the contemporary arts community yet perfectly at home in a suburban neighbourhood. They attended art shows whenever and wherever possible. They appeared carefree, Elaine in her signature long flowing colourful gypsy skirts and Patrick with his hair long tied in a ponytail, but when it came to dealing with finances, they kept their accounts in order and were meticulous about making sure that if anything happened to them, Philippa would be financially secure. Did they have a premonition? Who knows?

Don reached for the dark oak owl that Patrick had carved and presented to him the previous Christmas. He admired the quality of the craftsmanship and how Patrick incorporated the wood grain to emphasize the feather detail. Setting it back on his desk, he let out a deep sigh and picked up the ringing phone.

"Mr. Evans, Helen Ravi here."

"Mrs. Ravi, I was just thinking about your situation. Did the applicants arrive?"

"Yes. We have decided that Florry will fill the bill. Do you know how soon she can start?"

He smiled. "I'm pleased. I know she will do a very good job. I am pretty sure she can start immediately."

*****

Helen stayed in Ottawa to settle affairs and give Florry instructions. At the end of each day, Florry went home to her trailer. She couldn't wait to tell all to Joyce as they sipped green tea.

"They're really nice people. That poor wee Philippa's trying so hard to bear up. I just know she'll fall apart before long. I guess I'll get used to the weird sculptures her mother made. They're all over the house; some are even hanging from the ceiling going up the stairs. To me they just look like a bunch of recycled junk thrown together. It's going to be a real challenge to keep the dust off those things."

"Who'd ever buy that kind of stuff?"

"Don't know, but from what Helen tells me she had her art in some real fancy galleries and corporate offices."

"So now it's Helen, is it?"

"Yep, I'm to be treated like a member of the family. How do you like that? That'll take some getting used to."

"Didn't you say the dad was an artist too?"

"Patrick—carved beautiful birds and animals. Now those, I like. The family room has a shelf with nothing but his work, there's a fox curled in sleep that I just love to run my hands over, it is so life-like. There's one with three cats curled up in a snow-covered doorway that you would swear was real. It's small but so lifelike."

"Don't know as I could sleep with all that artsy junk around."

"Oh, I've my own room with a lovely double bed and my own TV, if you please. I even have my own washroom. I'm in the basement so it's like having my own apartment. However, I'm included in the family activities so don't have to stay in my room. I've complete run of the house."

In the evenings during the week, Florry took Joyce to meet her house cleaning clients and everyone wished Florry well in her new job and agreed to hire Joyce. Florry returned to the work at the Snelling's during the day.

*****

Arranging scheduling needs, determining budgets, and getting to know each other made the days fly by. Once the Thrift

Shoppe suit was hung at the back of her closet, Florry appeared in elastic-waist jeans and flat loafers ready to tackle housecleaning and gardening; the makeup had disappeared.

Elaine hadn't been a fastidious housekeeper so Florry had lot's to keep her busy as she made it her crusade to attack every room and scrub every corner. Philippa asked that her parent's bedroom remain as it was for the time being, she was not ready to deal with it. A knowing look passed between Helen and Florry.

Mike and a couple of friends dropped in most days after school. They brought gossipy news and, at Philippa's request, study material. Philippa, not ready to return to class yet, knew she must come to terms with it sooner or later. Mid-term exams were fast approaching.

"Gosh, Flip, are you going to be okay?" asked one of her friends giving her a hug. "We miss you something terrible. In Computer Science class, Mr. Hagman doesn't know half as much about programming as you do."

"Well, no wonder." Mike let the straw drop into the can of Pepsi he was holding. "Flip and her dad spent hours delving into the latest computer stuff and hanging out with the geeks while her mom was schmoozing potential clients at art galleries."

Mike Styles's family had known the Snellings for years. Mike and Philippa grew up together and considered each other best buddies. They shared the love of computers and were avid gamers. Mike was a keen competitive swimmer and, even though Philippa had little interest in sports she attended local meets and cheered him on.

The Styles, Susan and Frank invited Helen and Philippa to dinner the night before Helen was to return to Montreal. They lived two blocks away so Helen and Philippa walked. Sable went too, straining at his leash the whole way. They were greeted warmly and ushered into the family room and served drinks, the adults wine, the teens soft drinks. Much of the conversation was about how life had changed, descriptions of Florry and how Patrick and Elaine had arranged things. Talking about everything with Mike's family eased Philippa's apprehensions. After all, Mike's parents were very close friends of Patrick and Elaine and both Helen and Philippa knew they could rely on them if needed.

"Helen, you can rest assured we are here if Florry or Philippa need us."

"That's good to know. Thanks." Helen smiled at her hosts and took a sip of her wine as she followed the group to the table. She still wore black but now her pantsuit jacket was open and a violet crepe blouse draped softly to reveal a decided cleavage. "It seems that Philippa and Florry quickly bonded. I now feel I can return to Montreal without worrying about our girl. My, this Chardonnay is delightful."

After dinner, Mike and Philippa excused themselves to play computer games in the office.

"Will you still be able to go to computer camp in July?" asked Mike.

"Oh, my god, I so totally forgot about that."

"Gosh, Flip, you've gotta go. It's the opportunity of a lifetime."

"I think the fees are all paid up Mike. I don't know, I'll have to check."

"Well, it's coming up fast. And you know how tough it was to get into that camp."

"I'll have to think about it. Right now, I'm trying to get up the nerve to return to school. I dread all the sympathetic looks and hugs I'll get. I'm terrified I'll turn to mush and make a fool of myself."

"Nonsense, you wouldn't make a fool of yourself," said Mike. "Nobody expects you to be cheerful. And don't forget that all our friends will be there so you won't be by yourself. You just have to deal with it, the sooner the better. Why don't we all hook up Monday morning then you won't have to walk to school alone. And think about the camp—it might be just what you need right now."

Early Monday, Philippa slung her backpack over her shoulders. Helen was returning to Montreal so said her goodbyes and made sure Philippa understood that she could reach her on her cell any time of the day or night. She gave Philippa a big hug and waved at Mike who was patiently waiting on the sidewalk. Helen watched the long lanky youth walk protectively beside Philippa. She was wearing denim cut-offs and he was in cargo pants—each wore a school t-shirt.

"She'll be all right. I hope." Helen muttered to herself then called to the kitchen, "Florry, come on let's get going."

Helen and Florry took one final run to the shopping center to pick up some last minute items. They arrived home with much more than they intended. "I simply cannot stick to what's on a list." Helen reached for the ringing phone as she opened the refrigerator to set a jug of milk on the shelf.

"Hello. Yes, you caught me just before I headed off to Montreal."

Don Evans inquired how Florry was coping.

"Florry is working out very well." She nodded at Florry who discretely vanished out the kitchen door to gather up more grocery bags. "In fact, we are more than pleased."

"I'm not surprised. Mrs. Evans and I are chastising ourselves for letting her go. In fact, Mrs. Evans was wondering if you could spare her one day a week, nobody knows our house and routine like her."

"We'll discuss it but I see no reason why not. Is that why you called?"

"Well, not exactly. There seems to be a small problem. There's no registration of Philippa's birth in the Nova Scotia records. Do you know the name of the hospital where she was born?"

"Honestly, true to Elaine and Patrick's lifestyle they inferred they used a mid-wife. Knowing their *laissez faire* take on life, they probably didn't do the paperwork."

"That is quite unlikely. If the mid-wife was a registered practitioner, she would have been obligated to report any and all births."

"Well, God knows if they used a licensed person, probably some old native on a reservation. They had a thing about the 'system' controlling their lives. Now what do we do?"

"We'll continue making inquiries but in the meantime the release of the insurance policy money has been approved and the deposit should be here within a week, it'll then be partly invested in mutual funds with the rest going into an interest bearing trust account," answered Don. "I'll keep you and Philippa advised. I have your cell number so will give you a call when we know anything further. The lawyers for the trucking firm are undercutting our demands but I have a gut feeling they do not want this to go to court. I wouldn't be surprised if we get a substantial offer shortly."

"Thanks for all your help. Please keep me informed."

"Have a safe trip home. Cheers."

After Helen left, Florry busied herself rearranging the kitchen cupboards. If she was going to run this house efficiently, there was much organizing to do. Peering into this cupboard and that, she sorted pots and pans, noted what was available and what was not. She washed everything and lined the shelves. She made a list of things she needed to add before setting about baking chocolate chip cookies and blueberry pies.

Philippa arrived home from school, rushed through the front door indifferent to the smells of fresh baking, and dropped her backpack on the floor. Florry went to greet her but Philippa had vanished. Florry quickly searched all the downstairs rooms before going upstairs. Her first thought was Philippa's bedroom, but the door was open with no Philippa in sight. Then she heard a faint mewling and found Philippa stretched across her parent's bed with her face buried in her father's bathrobe, sobbing uncontrollably. Florry pulled the door closed and sat on the top step waiting.

Chapter 4

May, 1985

Patrick leaned forward, his long back bent over his work bench, his dark eyes peering through protective glasses. Concentrating on every minute detail he guided a slender stick sander that hummed as it lightly caressing the thin legs of a heron. Dust powdered his already salt and peppered hair. His nose and mouth were masked. He flipped a small switch on the handle and the sander fell silent. Patrick raised the bird to the light turning it left to right to check for any flaws. Satisfied, he set the tool aside and prepared the piece for the next step. Each carving Patrick created was life in miniature, scaled to perfection and coloured skillfully using natural pigments, then polished to a fine luster. As he examined the model, he recalled watching the heron stride around the perimeter of a pond, doing its slow dance, then with the speed of a heartbeat its beak struck the water's edge and raised a struggling frog. Real life, real creatures were the models for his work. The frog captured in the wooden beak did not struggle. The moment was caught by his camera while holidaying in Algonquin Park. The picture was pinned to the wall in front of him.

Weekend trips to the park not only provided Patrick with subject matter but were his and Elaine's regular escape from the pressures of daily life. They started camping long before he retired from the Canadian Forces.

Patrick enlisted in the army the week he turned eighteen and was assigned to Personnel Services. By the end of his career he had reached the rank of Quartermaster. He retired from the forces shortly after turning forty-seven with a full service record and a comfortable pension.

While stationed in Ottawa at National Defense Headquarters, Patrick befriended an old sergeant in food services who whittled while on his break. Fascinated how this chipping away at wood produced amazing images he, under the tutelage of the sergeant, soon was deep into learning the craft. He had a natural ability for carving. He developed a passion for it and before long realized he hungered to learn more. His craft became art. He studied woods, felt their heart and knew their every grain and texture. He sought out wood carvers at craft and art shows in Ottawa and beyond. That was how he met Elaine eleven years ago.

The annual Artisan Craft Show at Lansdowne Park in Ottawa featured a renowned expert that Patrick was eager to meet. He was determined to improve his skills and learn new techniques. Elaine had a booth immediately beside the master carver Patrick wanted to interview. Her display caught his attention. Standing in front of it, one hand cupping his chin the other his upper arm, he puzzled over several outlandish contemporary sculptures. They incorporated everything from soda cans to plastic bags. Yet this *garbage* had been transformed into masterful shapes with a certain beauty and flow. A head of flaming red curls along a bent back at the back of the stall was all he could see of the booth's owner.

"I'm intrigued with your work." Patrick leaned over the display and shouted to the hair. "Not sure I like it but it has certain magnetism. Can I ask what you are trying to say?"

Tossing the unruly mane off her face, Elaine answered briskly as she stood and turned to face him. Her sharp tone cut the air. "It's about finding beauty in the most innocuous things. It's about excessive packaging ending up in careless hands. It is about telling people there's no need to waste. It's all about saving the environment."

Patrick watched her long body unfold like a colourful cartouche. A deep voice, brightly coloured skirts and layers of jewelry made Patrick believe he was speaking to a gypsy, a gypsy with a brittle attitude. He turned to walk away but she stepped out in front of him. She picked up a sculpture made from plastic bottles and held it out for him to consider. The symmetry was outstanding.

"I'm trying to send a message to stop destroying nature by littering it with garbage. I know I can't save the world but if I can convince a few influential people, then I'll have accomplished something." There was a passion in her voice.

Patrick hesitated, intrigued.

"All my work is created from articles carelessly thrown into pristine wilderness. Packaging has become the number one curse of the twentieth century. All of this garbage used in my work was putting wildlife at risk. I gathered them in Algonquin Park. Oh.." Elaine caught herself. "Sorry, I didn't mean to sound argumentative. I get so caught up I could go on for hours..."

"Then why don't you? When do you close your booth? Are you up for a walk along the canal?"

Patrick still wondered how he convinced this long slip of a girl with strong opinions and a temperament that matched her flaming hair, a girl some twelve years younger than him to become his wife.

He set the heron on the counter and started to clean his tools.

The door burst open. Elaine rushed into the warehouse workshop waving a letter in her hand held high over her head.

"Paddy, I've just been accepted for the Victoria Art Show. Can you believe it? It's the most prestigious show in the west, barring none. What an opportunity! Oh, my god when I submitted the photos and descriptions of my work, I had little hope of getting past the selection committee. You know that people can judge my work rather harshly. Oh, my god, I'll have to call the packers…"

"Hold on there—not so fast. Congratulations. I'm so very proud of my talented wife." Patrick stood up from his work table shed his goggles and mask. He wrapped his arms around her in a bear hug and planted a kiss on her forehead. "When's the show?"

"August twelfth to the seventeenth—that only gives me six weeks to prepare. All the pieces will have to be crated and shipped to arrive on the ninth. I'll have to be there to make sure they're properly unpacked and displayed. Damn, Paddy, look at me, thanks to you, I'm sawdust all over." Elaine's rapid discourse was cut short.

"What do you mean 'I'? I'm going too, aren't I?"

"Of course, silly, I was just thinking in the first person—of course you'll go, I couldn't imagine doing a show without your help."

"Oh, it's just my help you want, eh? Ha, well you'll probably find a strong hulk cheaper—make sure he's an ugly one. I'll just stay here all by myself."

"Damn it Paddy, you just love to twist my words. I can't imagine being away from you. You know I need you and want you and …."

"Mm, I like the 'want' part," whispered Patrick as he lifted away a mass of curls and nuzzled Elaine's long neck taking little teasing nips at her skin savouring the smell of apricot lotion. He slipped his hands under her bulky lime green sweater and walked his fingertips up her spine.

Elaine's body sparked and she arched to welcome his advances, his arousal apparent. Their love making was long and slow. Patrick's muscular body responded as she stroked and massaged his back. She inhaled the subtle wood smells drifting from his hair, felt the rhythm of his body and she snuggled as deep into him as possible.

Patrick lay stretched out with Elaine cradled in the crook of his arm after their spontaneous love making. The workshop was strewn with discarded clothes and the air, normally permeated with smells of clay, heated metal and sawdust, was heady with musky sex odours.

Patrick and Elaine shared a rented work space in an artist cooperative. It was an 'L' shaped room consisting of a large open area jammed with bin after bin of what appeared to be assorted garbage. This was where and what Elaine sculpted.

A rectangular smaller wing to the left was neat by contrast. Patrick's wood carving tools were hung above counters running the length and breadth of the area, each labeled and orderly. With the exception of new dust, the counters held only tidy containers. This was where they worked but they were both passionate spontaneous lovers so lusty behavior wasn't restricted to outside the studio.

Patrick smiled and silently congratulated himself that he had had the common sense to lock the studio door. Their love making had on occasion put them in embarrassing situations. Particularly the time, when Elaine's father Roger, had walked into the studio unannounced. Roger had quickly done an about-face, grinning from ear to ear as he headed outside for a smoke, returning only after Patrick, smiling sheepishly, beckoned him. It was less than a year ago that he died. Elaine, who, her entire life, struggled with bouts of depression was inconsolable at losing her father.

Thinking about Elaine's news, Patrick was sure the show in Victoria would keep her busy and her mind occupied. *"Hmmm, I might just take some time to slip away and do a little detective work,"* he thought. A discovery he made when helping Elaine go through Rogers effects warranted some sleuth work.

Three days later, Patrick poured two glasses of wine, handed one to Elaine and slipped in beside her on the hide-a-bed couch in their small apartment. Raising his glass, he examined the colour of the Merlot, placed it under his nose and sniffed the bouquet.

"Oh, you phony." Elaine gently backhanded Patrick on the leg. "Ceremony—for an eight dollar bottle of wine?"

"Well, I want to make a very special proposition," said Patrick, "so I'm setting the mood." He leaned over and pecked Elaine on the cheek. "I propose that we take the whole year off and do a cross-country tour hitting as many art shows as we can." The words tumbled out, and Patrick, glass still raised, watched Elaine.

She started to speak but Patrick held his finger to her mouth, signaling a 'shh', and placed a sheaf of papers in front of her.

"What's this?"

"A list of shows—west to east from August to July. What do you think?"

"God Paddy, have you gone crazy? Where did this idea come from? We can't just pack up and head off to the great open spaces…"

"Why not? The lease on the apartment is up for renewal and the workshop equipment can be stored in a rental container. We have no kids, no pets and no obligations except to each other. What better time? And think what a wonderful creative experience it will be."

"Don't blame me for not having a family. Paddy, you know I would do anything to have a baby." With that Elaine burst into tears and rushed into the bathroom.

"Oh, God, here we go again," shouted Patrick. "All I have to do is mention children and you go off half-cocked. Damn it, Elaine, I thought you'd be thrilled to spend a year on the road."

Standing at the bathroom door clad only in navy boxer shorts, Patrick ripped up the list of artisan shows he had so painstakingly compiled. "Come on now, Sweet Shanks, you're letting your glass of wine sit all alone, not to mention me. You know I love you with all my heart and only want what makes you happy—I thought that after the dreadful year you just went through, this would be a good idea."

Blowing her nose, Elaine came out of the bathroom, stuffed the damp tissue in her pajama top pocket and melted into Patrick's waiting arms.

"I'm sorry. I just feel so incomplete. I want babies. My poor daddy died without ever having a grandchild and I am going to die without ever being a mother." She retrieved the kleenex, blew her nose, looked into Patrick's concerned eyes and nodded her agreement —"I think your idea is brilliant—we'll go."

Patrick held up the shards of the document.

"Patrick! You always over-react and do stupid impulsive things."

The rest of the evening was spent piecing together the torn

bits of paper to resurrect the list between sips of wine and furtive kisses.

*****

Roger Frost, Elaine's father, had taken a long time to die. He suffered one stroke after another leaving him debilitated and wheelchair bound. Elaine hovered over him, nurtured him, read to him and spent eight months crying nightly in Patrick's comforting arms. Roger had been a doting parent, bending to his daughter's every need, always 'there', and now, he wasn't. Roger often told Patrick that, as Elaine's father, he knew Patrick was the best thing to happen to Elaine. He knew she would always be well cared for regardless.

Patrick wasn't so sure. He certainly hadn't provided a lavish life style with his military income and he had been away for months at a time. Now that he was retired, he earned even less. However, he knew that Roger wasn't measuring Patrick's worth in monetary terms.

Roger lived in a small low-income rental apartment for seniors and it came as a complete surprise that he had made a will. Don Evans had been Roger's attorney and executor. Through dealing with Don handling Roger's will, Don became Elaine's and Patrick's lawyer.

Roger left a substantial insurance policy and some bonds as well as cash. Elaine, in her grief, could not handle benefiting financially from her father's death. She rejected any mention of using her inheritance for personal reasons. At Don Evan's suggestion, the funds were held in trust and managed by Evans, Sands and Forester.

Going through Roger's effects was another issue. Elaine broke

down again and again. She had difficulty discarding anything—
to her it meant throwing away her father. Patrick handled as
much as he could without upsetting Elaine. That's how he
discovered a file of old papers in Roger's desk. At first the
documents seemed to relate only to Shirley, Roger's wife and
Elaine's mother. Leafing through the file, Patrick found Shirley's
death certificate, social insurance information, diplomas from
various courses she took and correspondence between Roger and
her. He was about to close the file and hand it over to Elaine when
he noticed a handwritten page.

It was creased as if it had been crumpled up to throw away
then smoothed out. It showed a poorly drawn family tree; not
complete, but obviously Shirley's. It went back four generations.
Elaine already had a generation tree her mother had given her,
beautifully drawn with calligraphy edging. Elaine prized it.

Patrick was puzzled by this crumpled copy in Roger's files
and he scanned the entries. His eyes fell on the last one. In 1946,
Barbara Lynn Ewer was written in a box below Shirley's name.
What? There was no Barbara Lynn Ewer to the best of his
knowledge. It was impossible. Unless Shirley had another child,
a child out of wedlock—she would've only been sixteen years
old.

Patrick sat still trying to understand what he was seeing
wondered if it could be true. If Barbara Lynn existed, Elaine then
had an older sister, a half-sister. If Barbara Lynn was born where
was she? Was she put up for adoption? The possibility raced
through Patrick's thoughts. How would Elaine react to this
news? He knew she was fragile enough at the best of times and
he always protected her from anything that might affect her
emotionally. He decided against telling her. The timing was all

wrong. But he had to know if this Barbara existed and what happened to her. He would do some investigating then decide what to tell Elaine.

Shirley Frost's maiden name was Ewer and she lived in Saanich, British Columbia until she and Roger moved to Ottawa in 1950. Barbara Lynn Ewer must have been born while Shirley lived in Saanich. If Elaine had a half-sister, Patrick intended to find out. This trip to Victoria gave him the perfect opportunity to do some investigative snooping while Elaine was busy at the art show. However, right now, he had little time to think about this as preparations to spend a whole year on the road took every waking minute.

*****

"Elaine," Patrick called out when he came in after being out all afternoon. "I cashed in a Savings Bond. And guess what—I found and purchased a seven passenger Dodge Caravan. If we take out the extra seats it will hold all our stuff and more. I got such a great deal. It has low mileage and with the exception of a scratch above the rear wheel is in excellent condition. Its midnight blue with grey interior automatic 6-cylinder and sweetheart, she handles like a dream. You'll just love it."

"Well, I think it's going to be your love affair but I'm delighted. It's just what we need. It saves the worry of having to ship my sculptures."

"I contacted the art shows you listed and more," said Elaine. "I booked us into as many as I could. We are incredibly scheduled the whole while we are trekking across country. You can show at most of them too. I came up with fifteen possibilities: two are juried and the rest open."

Elaine decided she would need at least 10 additional pieces and drove herself to exhaustion to create them. Patrick carved a collection of birds for quick sale and some additional contemporary pieces so he could get feedback from fellow carvers. They spent long hours in the workroom but the energy was highly charged and creative. The results were outstanding.

Elaine hoped to receive some critical acclaim at the juried shows. Art shows are not only opportunities to sell but a hub for artists to critique and help each other and to network. Patrons for the Arts were always on the lookout for the next great artist.

Patrick expected to take full advantage of these shows as well. It would be a year for personal growth for both of them and one of healing for Elaine.

Elaine's work was accepted for both juried shows so their itinerary was sketched out with plenty of in-between time to explore Canada. They planned to take three weeks to travel west. They reserved a week-long horse-back adventure out of Jasper, Alberta to hike the Rockies and camp in the wilderness. On their return east, they would explore art galleries at every stop. Patrick often spoke of soaring mountain peaks and now he would see them. They both enrolled to take art courses at Banff Centre for the Arts having found ideal ones in early September. Elaine touched base with her graduate school, The Ontario College of Art, to see what was happening while they were in the Toronto area. She got a reply by return mail asking if she would consider teaching a six-week course in January and February. With no scheduled shows during that time it was an opportunity to earn welcome money in case sales were slow at the shows. They arranged to stay with artist friends in Quebec City for two weeks and soak up the culture of that historic city. They investigated finding adventure on the high seas while in the Maritimes. The trip plans fell into place much more readily than they expected, each month except January and February, taking them to a different province.

"Can you believe that we have planned our whole year in just a few short weeks? I can't imagine that everything is crated, insured and our destinations booked," exclaimed Elaine. She and Patrick were tucking the last few items to be stored into cartons. The van was packed and they would be on the road before noon and, if all went well, they would be in Parry Sound for dinner.

Elated, Elaine chatted constantly. As they were driving through Algonquin Park she snuggled into her comfy pillow and fell into a sound sleep. Patrick selected a Leonard Cohen CD and with it playing softly in the background, thought about his discovery of the past few days. He had made phone calls to the registry office and the hospital in Saanich. He learned no records available to the general public listed Shirley Ewer as having given birth. Needing professional assistance, he went to Don Evans, swore him to secrecy, and enlisted his help to determine if there was any way of finding old adoption records. Don hired a researcher in Victoria who had a reputation for getting access to private documents. Patrick was to connect with her, a Miss Hopper, when they arrived in Victoria. She already had learned that Shirley was absent from high school in her third year so was delayed in graduating. Hopper intended to find former classmates who might provide more information.

Patrick turned his attention to the scenic landscape of Algonquin Park where he and Elaine had hiked and camped in some of its most remote areas. Algonquin Park, only a few hours from Ottawa, stretches across thousands of square kilometers covering an area larger than Connecticut. Wild and beautiful lakes, forests, bogs and rivers, cliffs and beaches make it a canoer's and camper's paradise. Rocky ridges, spruce bogs, and hundreds of lakes, ponds and streams offered Patrick and Elaine many carefree days. Patrick, ever alert to birds and animals, carried his Olympus camera always at-the-ready. He stored numerous files of photos to use as reference when carving.

The lonely call of a loon drifted through the open window and blended with the sultry voice of Cohen. Patrick imagined a loon gliding across the cool spring-fed water, its call echoing from rocky shores. He envisioned beavers rippling through the water, fish arching into the air, or a moose, near shore, raising its massive head; these were the subjects that yielded to his knife. This time, however, highway #60 was a long grey ribbon to follow to Parry Sound.

Chapter 5

Hugging the shores of Georgian Bay, the Town of Parry Sound sits on an isthmus between the Bay and Lake Rosseau. A former school chum of Elaine's from Art College, Robin Chalders, lived there and had invited Elaine and Patrick to be her guests for the week.

"Isn't this a great way to start our adventure?" Elaine was wide awake as the van rolled into Parry Sound. "Look at that lake, it just sparkles. I'm so pleased we have the chance to visit with Robin and her husband, Alberto. They've got tickets to attend the Festival of Sound."

"What the dickens is a Festival of Sound?" Patrick gave Elaine a quizzical look.

"A music festival dummy - it's known all over the world. Parry Sound's a hub for arts, culture and heritage. Just you wait and see. Robin arranged for us to meet with fellow artists as well."

"All I want to do is laze around on those sandy beaches. Maybe take a cruise through the islands; maybe get my new fishing rod wet."

"Well, I'm sure you'll spend time wandering through the many art galleries and stuff yourself with delicious food at the farmer's market too. Turn here, Paddy – this is the address."

Patrick swung into a long lane and pulled up to a large beam-and-post log house. As Patrick parked the van in the driveway he saw someone he guessed to be Robin race down the driveway to meet them. Elaine and Robin hadn't seen each other since before both were married. They kept in touch by letter and occasionally a phone call. After the girls hugged, Elaine introduced her husband and friend. Patrick wrapped Robin in a warm embrace. Chatting non-stop Robin escorted them to a guest cottage nestled in the woods. She talked through a bejeweled cigarette holder that remarkably managed to stay in her mouth. Clad in white from head to toe, her tight spandex capris emphasized long legs and an angular body giving the impression of a landlocked egret. Speaking with a decidedly boarding school accent, she told them how delighted she was to have them. Elaine noticed a few grey strands among her warm brown straight shoulder-length hair. But her youthful round face was free of makeup with the exception of light pink lipstick.

Robin ushered her guests along a pathway through a pine woods to a picturesque log cabin. The small cottage stood on a rise with a rustic veranda overlooking the Bay, its square log construction blended with the surrounding pines. Woven wall hangings and overstuffed cushions scattered on the chairs and sofa brightened the interior logs of the living area that was furnished in wicker and willow. A large bearskin rug lay on the floor in front of a fieldstone fireplace that was prepped with logs ready to light. A wall of windows framed the scenic bay capturing rippling waves dancing across the water. Robin opened the door to a surprisingly large bedroom, tastefully decorated in autumn shades.

Elaine pointed to examples of Robin's intricate weaving that hung on two of the log walls. "Oh, Robin your work is exquisite. You have become an impressive artist."

Robin waved away the compliment and went on to talk about the décor. "I try to capture the ruggedness of Muskoka, while creating a welcoming space for my guests."

"Your talents go far beyond weaving. Each room reflects your decorating ability."

Elaine's praise drew a broad smile from Robin who, then said she had to return to the main house. "You should find everything you need. As soon as you dump your bags and get settled, come on up to the house for a before-dinner drink. Alberto is barbecuing steaks."

"Thank you for having us." Elaine gave her friend a big hug. "We'll be up shortly."

Patrick smiled suggestively at Elaine as she closed the door behind Robin. "We might want to delay just a wee bit!" He grabbed Elaine playfully and pinned her down on the deep fur of the bearskin rug. Struggling free, Elaine shot him a not-now look and set about unpacking their suitcases.

"Alberto must rake in the big bucks. This shack and the main house are over the top." said Patrick. "Maybe we should just postpone our trip and stay here permanently."

Elaine called from the bedroom. "Alberto is a builder, I told you that, but typical of you, you weren't listening. He specializes in post-and-beam log homes. Georgian Bay and the Muskoka region are a primary recreation destination for well-heeled business people from Toronto and upper New York State. He built the house and cabin as a showplace and was able to write off the expense." Elaine emerged wearing a bright orange sweater and crisp white jeans. She fiddled with dangling tangerine earrings and straightened three strings of multi-coloured beads. "This cottage is used to host prospective clients. Robin and he work as a team and not only build elite holiday retreats, but provide decorating services as well. The buyer gets a complete package. They arrived here at the right time, just as this area became popular with tourists and have more work than they can handle."

Patrick wolf-whistled at Elaine and went to get dressed shedding his faded denims and donning a similar pair. In the bathroom, he dashed some hot water on his face, threw on an 'Ottawa Valley Boy' sweat shirt and pulled his ponytail free of the crew neck while striding across the length of the cottage. He opened the front door and bowing gallantly ushered Elaine forward with a swoop of his arm. Giving her an affectionate pat on the rear he reached for her hand. They sauntered along another treed path that followed the shoreline to the main house exclaiming over the panorama of the ever-changing bay dotted with dozens of small islands. Early evening air, moist and pine-scented, filled their lungs. Fallen needles blanketed the path bordered with granite rocks spackled with mica chips. They caught the waning light appearing to be studded with precious jewels.

"Look at *that* deck, Elaine."

The house stood out over a rocky promontory, its wrap-around deck hanging in mid-air. Waving arms drew them forward.

Alberto greeted his guests with chilled Margaritas. Elaine scrutinized her friend's husband with approval. He was the picture perfect advertisement for Eddie Bauer, wearing khaki cotton shorts and a simple knit shirt a few shades lighter. Elaine noticed the high-end leather sandals and smiled. Her friend, Robin, had a stylish charming husband. Nursing their drinks while seated in Adirondack chairs on the massive deck, they watched a boat, with fuchsia-coloured sails tacking in the evening breeze, skillfully wending its way along the inlets.

"Oh, whatever is cooking smells absolutely wonderful!" Elaine sniffed deeply, the smells of garlic and spices mixed with the crisp evening air completed the perfect setting.

"No Mexican cooks without adding plenty of spices." Alberto said in his soft accent. "Ah, here's Robin."

Smiling broadly and carrying a swaddled bundle, she approached Alberto and laid it on his lap, then turned to her guests.

"A new addition," she explained. "Lionel came into our lives in May. The pregnancy was at-risk. He arrived prematurely and frail so we didn't make a big announcement for fear of losing him. It was touch-and-go for weeks. But six days ago, we got the all-clear and he's a thriving baby boy. I know he's a surprise, but had we told you, you might not have come." Robin reached for the baby. "I enjoy houseguests and have plenty of help, so it's no extra work. We tried for years to have a family and finally succeeded. Here, Elaine, you can hold him." Robin gently lifted her son and handed him to Elaine. Patrick tensed.

Elaine peered down into soft, dark unblinking eyes that swallowed her whole. With the back of her forefinger she stroked Lionel's smooth cheek and was rewarded with a radiant smile and a gleeful kick.

"He's absolutely beautiful! How wonderful for you. Congratulations. No, Robin, don't take him away. Can I just hold him?"

Patrick knew what lay ahead. Every time Elaine held a baby she went into withdrawal and curled up for hours on end sobbing and sobbing with knees clasped tightly to her chest and her head buried deep in a pillow. But that would be after they returned to the guest house; she could always maintain her composure until she and Patrick were alone, then her defenses broke down. Their perfect week in this hide-away among the pines was going to be one miserable time, cursed by a baby. There would be no romp on the bearskin rug.

The dinner, good wine and great company was not enough to prevent Elaine from going into depths of despair and self loathing as soon as they were alone. Patrick, as usual did his best to comfort her but she cried and berated herself over and over again until she finally fell asleep, rigid and spent.

Patrick carefully eased his arms from around her and slipped on sandals and an oversize t-shirt. Quietly he edged out the door and walked to the bay. Standing on the shore he drank in the clear sweet air and watched the shimmering stars reflected on the still water. A fallen pine log invited him to sit. His chin cupped in his hands, elbows balanced on his knees he inhaled deep breaths trying to relax and thought about Elaine's bouts of depression.

Many times Elaine had thought she was pregnant, only to be disappointed. To her it was a personal failure. How many times had he been on this emotional roller coaster? Too many.

They had been to several fertility specialists and were told by the latest one, their last hope, a renowned doctor in Toronto, that there was no possibility of Elaine conceiving. Patrick had desperately prayed for the opposite, hoping that the promise of having a family would help Elaine through the final days of her father's failing health. But life doesn't always work the way one wants it to. The following week Roger died.

Impulsively, Patrick jumped up, threw off his clothes and dived into the water. He swam through the silence until he washed away the anguish. He returned to the cabin and fell into a deep sleep.

The morning calm was shattered as Elaine screamed at Patrick. "You did what! What if you drowned? Nobody knew you were out in the bay swimming! Patrick, you always go off half-cocked and do the stupidest things without a thought in your head. When'll you ever start thinking before you leap? You have done some really stupid things in your life but this takes the cake!"

Elaine lectured Patrick as he calmly poked at the glowing fire. The swim had had the desired effect and he slept like a stone, wakening to the fragrant smell of brewing coffee and the sound of snapping sparks from the fireplace.

He watched Elaine. Her depression had turned to rage. No longer wallowing in self-pity, she was now bent on berating him. She needed only one small reason and she could rant for hours on his impulsive nature. He hadn't thought that it might be dangerous, he just gave in to what the moment dictated; it *had* been a stupid and impulsive act but, then he was known for that trait.

Doing his best to change the subject, it didn't take much persuading for Patrick to convince Elaine that a quick skinny dip before eating would be refreshing and the perfect start to their day. They could, then return to the warmth of the fire and a leisurely breakfast. Patrick eyed the rug with renewed hope.

The brisk morning air was veiled in a misty haze above the warmer water. Loons called across the bay and scattered fishing boats, with lines dangling, appeared like ghosts, then slipped into the mist again. Patrick and Elaine stroked easily out from shore and back. They emerged into the chilly morning air, invigorated. Patrick raced ahead and greeted Elaine at the door minutes later. He tore off her wet towel and wrapped her in a Hudson Bay blanket. Holding a corner, he encircled them both and eased toward the fireplace where two cups of steaming coffee awaited them. Huddled together, soft sighs of contentment escaped between sips of the strong dark liquid. Patrick stroked the bearskin rug and slipped his hand up Elaine's inner thigh. He smiled when there was no resistance.

"Was everything to your satisfaction?" Robin asked when they arrived at the house.

Knowing glances passed between the two lovers as they assured Robin it was.

"I thought, seeing as its Friday, you might enjoy the market," announced Robin. "We have to get there early as it's such a tourist attraction. I want to pick up fresh produce before it's all picked over." Robin jangled her car keys to hurry them. "Visitors love the First Nation's crafts. But you'll also find hand made clothing, folk art, stained glass, baskets, jewelry, soaps and creams, silk painting, butterfly bowls and whatever new vendors bring each day." Robin paused. "Oh, my, I sound like a promotional. Sorry."

"Elaine read about it and filled me in," said Patrick. "Isn't there street entertainment too?"

"Yes, and there's live entertainment at the gazebo – it features up-and-coming artists from the city and across the province. Just flop down on the grass, listen to the performers and look out over our sandy beaches. Not hard to take." Robin smiled. "You might want to take a cruise on Lake Rosseau. The Idyllwood, a reproduction of a 1920's era private yacht, runs one-hour trips from the dock. The commentator, Mike, is very good and mixes history with humorous stories. But you'll find lots to do. Be sure to take your camera, there're subjects galore."

True to Robin's description, the market bustled with tourists, colourful vendors and attractive merchandise. Patrick spied a booth with exquisite wood carvings and Elaine, knowing he would talk to the artisan for some time, wandered into a gallery.

The morning sped by. They booked an early afternoon cruise, found a little café that featured French crepes and ate on the outdoor patio. Sounds of laughter and music from the park drifted to them. Patrick watched Elaine tense when a couple walked by with a sleeping baby in a Snuggly. However, the moment passed and she became intrigued by the changing scene before her.

Tourists and locals wearing all sorts of holiday attire wandered along the boardwalk. Girls in skimpy shorts with skimpier halters walked beside young bronzed men. Women decked out in brightly decorated t-shirts with quaint sayings often sported ridiculous hats. A family followed in step behind a woman in a saree, their far Eastern language blended with others from different parts of the world. Nearly all had cameras slung around their necks.

"Those crepes were to die for," Elaine dropped her napkin on her bare plate. "Finish up Paddy. The boat leaves soon. We need to get a hustle on."

The Idyllwood was everything the brochures and Robin had claimed. White birch trees luminous against dark pines forested the many islands. Loons, completely at ease with the lake traffic, floated in still bays with babies on their backs. Patrick shot a whole roll of film before they returned to shore, wind-blown and rosy-cheeked, happily recounting the humorous stories of

Captain Mike. They strolled along the boardwalk as day turned to evening.

"Elaine. Patrick," Robin called to them. "Come. We have tickets for tonight's concert." Elaine and Patrick, Robin and Alberto nudged through the festival crowd to the VIP seating. Alberto was a patron and Robin a member of the board so they enjoyed special privileges, choice seating and a service bar close at hand. Alberto took everyone's order and headed to get drinks.

"Oh, my! What a treat! Patrick look," Elaine pointed to her program." Can you believe this? The Prague Chamber Music Orchestra is going to play 'The New World Symphony' by Antonín Dvořák."

The music and the setting held them captive. When the concert was over they sat admiring a night filled with stars their heads filled with wonderful sounds.

"What an incredible evening, and we still have rest of the week ahead of us." Elaine commented.

In the following days, Patrick took full advantage of the outdoors while Elaine and Robin visited galleries and artists. He slipped out early in the mornings and captured photos of ducks on the water, herons in various stages of flight and a northern pelican trying to swallow a large bass. A saucy chipmunk became his favourite subject and he shot far too many pictures of his furry friend, who he named Chippy. The little creature waited on the front porch railing every morning expecting the peanuts that Patrick was only too happy to provide.

On Wednesday, Alberto took Patrick on an all-day fishing expedition while the gals did the spa thing. The grand finale of their visit, the 'catch', was prepared and cooked in a charcoal pit as Alberto's family had done in the Yucatan Peninsula in Mexico.

Elaine and Patrick claimed they had never before enjoyed such a feast.

"This has been a great week," said Robin. "Why don't you stay on for a few extra days?"

"Love to, but we can't," answered Elaine. "We booked a horse-back trek for the twenty-ninth out of Jasper." The week ended with promises of 'keeping in touch' and hugs goodbye.

Elaine, after her initial meltdown, dealt far better than Patrick had expected with seeing, touching and holding Lionel. Perhaps she had begun to accept that she would never have her own children and could simply enjoy other people's. As they loaded the van at daybreak, he noted how bronzed and relaxed she seemed. Yes, this trip was a good decision.

They bent over the Rand and McNally for a few minutes before heading off to follow the Trans-Canada highway across the top of Lake Superior. They hummed along to the radio, commented on rock outcroppings, farm lands and the scenery in general. The miles fell behind.

Chapter 6

Knee-deep in long grasses bordering a marshy area minutes off the road, Patrick held his camera steady bringing a bull moose into focus. His lens zoomed in on the very separation of its hairs, the scrapes on its antlers and the glint in its eye. Legs apart, knees slightly bent, Patrick angled his body to the right keeping his eye to the viewfinder to capture the perfect shot of the animal in stride. Once positioned, he yelled loudly. The moose raised its massive head lifting a rack of majestic antlers, saw nothing threatening and resumed sucking up muddy water to extract succulent pond weeds. Determined to get the great beast in motion Patrick tried once again to startle the impressive animal. Easing his right leg to a nearby moss-covered rock, Patrick shifted his weight as did the rock. One hand gripping the camera for fear of the worst and waving the other trying to balance, his foot slid off and he landed bum first on soggy grass. He fumbled to his feet and brushed his jeans only to smear mud across the leg.

"Damn it to Hell!"

Still a little off kilter, Patrick dared a glance in the direction of the moose. It was gone. He shoved his camera, thankfully still dry, into his bag and stomped back to find Elaine.

"I can't see him," Elaine sat on a culvert at the side of the road, her body curled in a fetal position tears smearing her dusty cheeks. "I can't see Roger any more. I've lost him. I can't remember what he looks like."

Patrick hurried to her side.

"What kind of a daughter am I when I can't remember my own father?"

Never Dad, always Roger, Patrick adopted the same informality. He eased himself down beside Elaine and cradled her, picking a leaf out of her tangled curls. "It's what happens. Its how life goes on, it's a coping mechanism, our minds let go of the past and visual memories fade. Sweetheart, it's okay, it's natural. You won't forget him. That's why families treasure photographs because the mental pictures grow dim."

"He's gone and I can't ever have him with me again," Elaine sobbed. She lifted the hem of her tie-dyed shirt and rubbed at her watery eyes.

"Look out there." Patrick raised his arm and pointed to the vast waters of Lake Superior. "Roger would have sat here with you and talked about the sparkle of the water and asked you to count the diamonds. He would have shown you the horizon where the grey of the sky blends into the grey of the water, yet remains separate. Your life with Roger's like that, you'll always be together, yet separate. Your love will always sparkle. It's not how his face looked that matters, it's the shared moments. They'll come back to you time and time again."

Elaine wiped her red-rimmed eyes again and blew into the tissue Patrick handed her. When she went into depths of depression Patrick was the only person outside of her father who knew what to say, who knew she desperately needed assurance. She reached up and stroked his afternoon stubble, rose slowly, walked to the van, got in and curled up against the passenger door. Dealing with the loss of her father added to the constant pain she felt by the fact she could neither conceive a child nor could they adopt.

Patrick was well versed in the psychological effects of infertility. Significant negative emotions included loss of self-esteem - similar to mourning. Sexual distress, depression, guilt and anxiety were all possible reactions - and Elaine exhibited them all. Doctors and psychologists told him that her inability to control her feelings resulted in a failure to adapt to the complexities of simple everyday occurrences turning them into desperate, unrealistic neuroses and unbalanced behavior. He looked at her pressed against the door of the van. Although she appeared to be resting, her jaw was rigid and her mouth drawn tight.

Deep within her own thoughts, Elaine remembered her mother firmly pulling her mass of curls straight as she forced them into tight braids. Shirley would slick down a stray hair by spitting on her fingers and pushing the damp strand into place.

"I certainly pray that your babies don't inherit this mess. It's a fact that God put women on earth to bring babies into the world but why he allowed the devil to snarl your head, I'll never know." Shirley seldom missed an opportunity to preach to Elaine that it was her duty in life to bring babies into the world.

The cool metal of the van eased Elaine's aching head but she couldn't shake how she felt. She was a failure as a daughter, as a wife and as God's servant. The van passed miles of scenic shoreline and forests but Elaine paid little attention.

"I hope we reach Marathon." Patrick prattled trying to lighten the weighted air in the van. "It's still some miles west of here. It's taking much longer than I thought. Maybe we should've stopped in Sault Saint Marie. It well could be dark before we arrive. This stretch of highway's sure desolate."

With dusk falling around ten o'clock they decided to continue to drive into the evening. They had not realized that this section of the Trans Canada highway stretched for miles through desolate wilderness of pine forests and craggy cliffs. Pulling over the crest of a steep hill Patrick watched the sun slide toward the horizon painting the sky crimson and rimming clouds orange and gold. Within minutes the panorama spread before them blazed scarlet and pink.

Elaine raised her head. "Look Paddy. It's a Tom Thompson sky. I thought they were figments of his imagination. I thought he exaggerated. He didn't. Pull over. I don't want to miss a minute of it."

Relieved to see Elaine jolt out of her depression, Patrick turned the van onto a dirt lane and stopped near the top of the hill. Arms around each other, they stood leaning backs against the warm hood of the van. Brilliant shades of red, pink, coral and purple spread across the horizon. Even after the vivid colours dulled and the clouds turned dusky gray, they remained committing the vision to memory. They returned to the van with a northern sunset stored in their minds forever.

"Damn, Elaine, can you believe I didn't take a single photo?

"When we get back to Ottawa, I'll buy you a copy of Thompson's painting."

Day darkened to night in a very short time and their headlights barely pierced the black. Tired from the long day of driving, they cheered when they finally saw a road sign 'Terry Fox Highway' where Terry had ended his run at Marathon. All the motels near the highway were full but, fortunately, they found the last remaining room in the village, nothing fancy but clean. They set out for a quick walk to stretch their legs. The main street, a long straight road, shot through stark wooden buildings, tired and in need of paint. A waning moon cast ghostly shadows down alleyways its silver crescent mirrored in Terrace Bay to the west. A cool breeze found its way through Elaine's shirt. She shivered.

"Paddy, let's go back to our room."

In bed with a glass of wine and the TV playing softly, it did not take long before Patrick set the drained glasses on the night table, clicked the 'off' button on the remote and turned out the light.

They rose early, refreshed and eager to continue their journey. They walked from their unit to the diner along the bay side of the motel. Elaine stopped, grabbed Patrick's sleeve and pointed out over the water.

"Look, Paddy. See those two small iron grey islands with sharp rock profiles, the shimmering water, the silver sky," Elaine pointed toward the bay. "Notice how severe, dense and stark, yet commanding, they look? Does it remind you of anything?

Patrick shrugged and shook his head.

"Lauren Harris," stated Elaine. "Can you believe it? Within hours, I've seen the very scenes of two of Canada's most famous artists. Can't you see Harris' canvasses, the strong commanding images?"

Patrick shrugged again.

"God, Paddy, open your eyes. That's the exact subject matter and light he captured. I studied his work. Like Thompson's, I never imagined that what he painted was anything near realistic, but it is. Just look, it's real! Oh, I'll remember Marathon, not only as the place where Terry Fox ended his brave campaign, but where I rediscovered Lauren Harris."

They continued to the diner to find it unappealingly smelled of grease and fried food so opted for a late breakfast in Thunder Bay. Armed with take-away coffees they returned to the motel, got in the van and heading west. In Thunder Bay they found a bakery, bought fresh sweet rolls and more coffee. A near-by grocery had fresh strawberries. Nibbling and sipping, they strolled along the bayside admiring the 'Sleeping Giant'.

Patrick leaned over a description tabloid and read aloud:

"The panoramic Sibley Peninsula is a formation of mesas and sills that juts out on Lake Superior. This remarkable peninsula resembles a reclining man so became known as the Sleeping Giant. The largest, deepest, and most northerly of the Great Lakes, Lake Superior has been home to the Ojibwe people for over 500 years. An Ojibway legend identifies the Sleeping Giant as Nanabijou, who was turned to stone when the secret location of a rich silver mine was disclosed."

"A friend of mine wrote a children's book about the giant," Elaine commented. "The giant woke up thirsty and drank all the water in Lake Superior. It caused quite a kerfuffle."

"God help him when he needed a bathroom," Patrick quipped. They continued along the lakefront. Elaine kicked off her sandals and walked into the water and raced back. "That is the coldest water on earth!"

Patrick laughed. They strolled farther and talked about their trip.

"You know, Sweetheart, the Lake of the Woods area is noted for its stellar fishing. What say we stop for a couple of days and I put my rod to good use? I always wanted to land a giant northern pike."

"Sure, I need some down time too, while you're fishing I can do some domestic chores and spoil myself."

After a few inquiries they located a guide, who not only was available but had a cabin vacancy. Patrick followed the directions to Rabbit Lake, turned off the highway onto a gravel road between a rock cut and followed it through steep walls of pink granite. They broke out of the cool shadows into bright sun illuminating a small bay and a tidy fishing camp.

Dave, their guide and host waved the van to a parking spot beside a cabin painted white with dark green trim. He hastily rubbed deeply lined palms clean on weathered jeans and shook hands with Patrick. He nodded at Elaine. Life spent in the sun made his taut weathered skin shine like polished oak. Deep creases around intelligent dark eyes hooded by heavy black brows gave him the appearance of a sage woodsman.

"Let the misses deal with the gear, the boat's packed and ready to go," Dave said. "If we want to get any sort o' catch today we better get on the water." With that he strode off toward the dock.

"Now, that man's all business." Elaine raised her eyebrows and watched Patrick drop the box he was holding, grab his fishing gear and tear off after Dave. She watched them set off in a paint-deprived boat sporting a gleaming outboard that purred to life when Dave pulled the cord. Elaine waved. An all-knowing smile crept across her face as she turned away from the waterfront to unload what they needed from the van and put a few supplies in the refrigerator. She would take advantage of this leisure time to wash her hair and lose herself in a good mystery book. She didn't even have to think about making supper. Dave had guaranteed them a fish feast regardless of the catch.

With her hair wrapped in a towel, clad in a pink halter top and navy Adidas shorts, she padded in bare feet, a book clutched in her hand to settle into a chaise lounge in front of their cabin.

Soon, totally absorbed in the suspense of her novel, she was swept to another time and place.

Something warm touched her arm. Startled, she turned her head to encounter the smiling face of a small girl. The child held out a fist clutching drooping daisies.

"For you," she said proudly.

"Why, thank you." Elaine blinked, smiled and took the flowers. "And what's your name, sweetheart?"

"Candy."

"Well, Candy, I think we need to give these flowers a drink. Do you want to help me?"

Nodding her head, Candy reached for Elaine's hand and toddled along beside her to the cabin. Elaine looked down at the small unkempt child in dirt streaked denim shorts and a faded blue t-shirt. Her straight black hair hung dull and lifeless. She had pudgy cheeks, stout legs and a bright red purse hanging from her shoulder. Large trusting dark eyes studied Elaine's face.

"What're you reading?" Candy asked.

"Oh, not something a little girl like you would like; a murder mystery."

"My mummy was murdered and my daddy's in prison 'cause he did it," Candy blurted.

Elaine gasped, then squatted and stared at this cherub in front of her. "How awful! Who looks after you? When did this happen?"

Candy looked Elaine straight in the eye. "I was just a baby and now I'm almost four so I don't remember it. My Uncle Dave takes care of me – he's my new daddy. He took your daddy fishing."

Elaine forced a grin. "Well, he's not my daddy, he's my

husband. Are you here alone?

"Yes, I can stay by myself. I'm a big girl now pretty soon I'll be four. I like lemonade. Do you have any?"

Elaine smiled, happy she did.

"Do you play 'Fish'? I've got some cards in my purse." Candy reached into her purse and withdrew a well-used deck of cards.

They spent the afternoon sitting on the chaise beneath a towering pine tree playing 'fish', 'I Spy' and singing "There's a Bump on a Log" and She'll be Comin' Round The Mountain between sips of sweet lemonade. At dusk, Candy jumped up and started to run for shore.

"Where're you going?" Elaine called after her.

"Uncle Dave's back."

"I don't see a boat." Shading her eyes, Elaine strained to see far out on the water. "There's nothing there. I don't even hear a motor. Why do you think they are coming?"

Watching Candy at the shoreline, Elaine talked to herself. "It's not fair for this wee tyke to have been forced into a life where she became a miniature adult at less than four years old. She needs a mother. Her hair's dirty as is the rest of her. She certainly speaks well for a toddler and appears old beyond her years. Whatever will become of her?" When Elaine reached Candy's side she still couldn't see a boat anywhere on the water.

"Sweety, I don't see them."

Candy reached for Elaine's hand and moved it to indicate a treed point to the east. "There, see - they're rounding the point"

Elaine squinted and finally saw a small dark form growing larger as she watched. Two figures, silhouetted against a gray sky, waved.

"That's the signal," said Candy. "They caught fish. We have

to gather wood for the fire. Come on."

Elaine followed her chore-focused friend to a wood pile stacked nearly to the roof behind the main cabin. Candy carefully selected what they needed and heaped Elaine's arms with logs. She reached into a barrel of water and took out a wet plank.

"Cedar," she explained, "the fish're cooked on it to taste special. Uncle Dave's the best cook. They caught a big one so I have to phone Three Claws so they can share the feast."

"How do you know they caught fish and that it's a big one?" Elaine asked as she dropped her load of wood beside a fire pit.

"I know" was the only explanation given as Candy rushed into the cabin. Elaine looked to shore to see the boat approaching the half-sunken wooden dock. It eased to a perfect stop. She headed across the lawn to meet them.

Patrick held a catch of fish high in triumph, a grin spread from ear to ear. Always short on conversation, Dave grunted, but shaded beneath a sun-bleached peaked cap of indiscriminative colour his expressive eyes shone and spoke of pride.

The roar of an off-road 4-wheeler entering the camp drew their attention. They watched Candy run to meet it.

"My brother Bert, also called Three Claws," Dave answered the unasked question.

Patrick talked nonstop all the way to the cabin. Without missing a word he uncapped two Molsens' light ale, "you should've seen the fight that small mouth bass put up – and the pike – did you see him? - Fourteen pounds - Dave weighed him."

Elaine half listened. She was looking out the window intent on the small child who was skipping around the main cabin. Elaine watched two teen-age boys arrive behind Three Claws, each with his own vehicle. Bert and Dave busied themselves at the gutting table and prepared a deep-pit fire. The boys chased Candy, caught her and threw her in the air, twirled her around at arms length and bounced her on their knees. Her laughter filled the camp.

In less than an hour, Dave signaled his guests to dinner. Armed with the remaining chilled beer, Elaine and Patrick headed for the large picnic table set for seven. The small-mouth bass lay on the slab of cedar in the center, a tribute to the day's success. Another board held fresh baked bannock and two large bowls steamed beside it. Patrick licked his lips and settled beside Elaine. The fine textured meat, sweet with a woody under-flavour, accompanied by flat bread, wild rice and fresh peas completed the meal. Patrick, still excited about his catch, talked on and on as the rest silently nodded and ate. The simple fare, a gourmet delight, was the perfect meal to share in the wilderness of Northern Ontario. Later, as they sat around a camp fire, Bert and the boys told fishing stories that got wilder and more far fetched as the beer disappeared. Candy fell asleep on Dave's lap.

Elaine leaned over to Dave and pointed at Candy. "How did she know you were coming when you were not in sight and that you had a big catch?"

"Old spirit in a young body."

Patrick watched Elaine but saw no signs of depression even though her eyes concentrated on the small sleeping form illuminated by the light of scarlet flames flickering across her face. Patrick hoped for the perfect ending to his day. He eased his hand over Elaine's leg to stroke her inner thigh. She tensed.

The campfire burned low and the evening came to a close. Patrick and Elaine returned to their cabin after thanking their host and bidding everyone goodnight.

"She's all alone." Elaine burst into tears as soon as Patrick closed the cabin door. "Her mother was murdered – murdered - by her father. Oh, God, she's such a darling, she needs a mother. Why in the name of saints can people like that have a beautiful baby and we, who can give one a good home, love ……..?"

And so it went until Patrick managed to rock Elaine to sleep. He stared up at the ceiling thinking of the miserable demons that haunted Elaine. *I can't continue to live with them. They shatter the happiest moments and turn a bright day dark. If only it were in my power to chase away the doubts and insecurities Elaine deals with – oh, how I wish I could.* He lived in desperate fear that she would disappear into her dark side. *If only her mother hadn't brainwashed her… if there are any gods out there listening to me, please… make her see it doesn't matter.* He would tell Dave they were moving on the next day.

Chapter 7

June, 2003

Florry couldn't help smiling as she watched Mike Styles. This young man, not yet fully grown, tilted the chair precariously where he sat, his jean-clad legs stretched far beneath the kitchen table. He tossed his head and threw back a forelock of fine straight mousy-coloured hair that constantly fell over sleepy, low-lidded eyes. Faded jeans, torn at the knee, were more fashion than damaged. His white t-shirt announced '3 *Gigabytes does not constitute a relationship*'. Mike's easy manner and endless quips could lift Philippa out of her introspective moments more often than not.

"Rhubarb pie, Mike? Florry offered.

"Hey, do cats have fur?"

The past month had had its ups and downs. The rhythm of the house changed as Philippa and Florry danced around each other's personalities. Philippa spent much of her time alone in her room studying or on her computer. She deliberately avoided contact with Florry and when they were together it was with a staged pleasantness. Philippa held her thoughts close and revealed little. Florry busied herself with household chores and cooking.

Philippa fumed when she wanted to get her driver's license and was not able to apply due the fact that she did not have a birth certificate.

"Mr. Evans, what is the problem?" Philippa had all the forms laid out on the kitchen table, all filled in neat clear handwriting. She had called expecting that the birth certificate had been found. She was surprised and somewhat alarmed that it now appeared to be a problem. "I don't understand what the issue is. Obviously, I was born somewhere—surely you can find out where. Isn't there something you can do?"

"Philippa, if we are, and it is likely the case that we are, dealing with an unattended birth, it gets a little complicated. We will have to follow due process and find witnesses willing to swear on oath that you are the child of Patrick and Elaine."

"Of course, I'm their child. Who else would I be? My parents have always been my parents."

"Unfortunately, at this point, it is a matter of filing the required papers and letting due process work. It could take as long as a year before you receive an official birth certificate."

"That totally sucks! I have a car and no way to get my driver's license. What if you can't get witnesses to come forth?"

"Philippa, I'm sure there will not likely be a problem unless we found a serious irregularity."

"Like what?"

"Nothing to worry yourself about—that would only be a problem if something illegal surfaces. We know your parents were law-abiding so please relax and let me handle it. I am sorry that you will have to wait before you can drive, but be patient, we will sort everything out. I will call the minute we resolve this."

Mike and Florry couldn't help but overhear the conversation. Philippa hung up the phone with a bang. Mike let out a long low whistle. Florrry offered pie.

Florry was scooping a large wedge of pie onto a plate for Mike. "You too, Philippa?"

"No thanks. Why did my life have to get so complicated?"

"Hey, gorgeous, new blouse?" Mike winked at Florry trying to change the topic. "Looks fab on you."

"Philippa picked it out for me at the mall." Flattered that Mike noticed, Florry smiled as she reached the plate across the table to Mike's out-stretched hand.

"Here you go, you poor starving thing."

There had been tough challenges and small improvements since Florry's arrival. Philippa's seventeenth birthday, her first without her parents, was a roller-coaster ride. One minute Philippa would be chatting happily on the phone with a friend, then minutes later became morose and sullen. Since it fell on a weekday and Helen had an important event scheduled, she couldn't make it to Ottawa. She sent a bouquet of seventeen long-stemmed roses to keep up the tradition started by Patrick, plus a beautiful vanity case full of Vasanti cosmetics. Florry tried her best to keep the day upbeat but felt Philippa's pain. Late in the afternoon, several school chums arrived with Mike brandishing a pizza. While playing computer games in the recreation room they wolfed it down. Florry ceremoniously paraded a large chocolate cake with flaming candles, one for each year, into their midst.

Throughout the evening, Philippa slipped into deep thoughts and fought back tears. Mike and the others kept the conversation light and silly and finally got her laughing when Mike attempted a handstand and crashed in a heap against the sofa.

"You stupid oaf! You could have crashed into the computer."

When the cake was finished, the teens hurried off to a movie. Later that night, when Philippa returned, she found Florry lying on the couch sobbing.

"Florry, what's the matter?"

"Oh, it's nothing. It's just not a good day for me." Florry, rose, wiped her eyes and turned her back to Philippa and hurried out of the room. Philippa watched puzzled and concerned. Since there was nothing she could do she shrugged and went to her room.

A week later, Philippa and Mike sat together at the kitchen table sifting through camp information. Settling the chair back on all fours, he had a habit of tilting it back on two—Mike rose and strolled over to Florry. "That, madam," he gave her a peck on the cheek, "was the best piece of lemon meringue pie I've ever tasted."

"Oh poo—you say that for each and every bite you eat no matter the flavour," answered Florry, blushing with pleasure. "You're just hoping to inhale another piece, aren't you?" She was already reaching to refill his plate.

The tabletop was strewn with glossy pamphlets and road maps. Philippa had found the payment receipt and information about Popoti Computer Camp in her father's desk. Coaxed insistently by Mike, she decided to go. Together, they now compared lists of items each would take and talked about their traveling plans.

"Dad's driving us to the camp, Florry. It's on Lake Joseph in Muskoka, about a five-hour drive. He plans to return the same day." Mike mumbled through a mouth full of pie. "It's a very picturesque drive. He asked if you wanted to go along for the ride. It'll be an early start. Interested?"

"You tell your dad that he's kind to offer. But Philippa's Aunt Helen's coming up to do some sorting and decorating while Philippa's away. And I haven't been out to the trailer park since coming here so I'm going to take a few days to myself before Helen arrives."

Philippa had reluctantly agreed to allow the two women to deal with the master bedroom and sort through Patrick and Elaine's personal effects but did not want to be there when they went through her parents things. While she was away at camp provided the perfect opportunity to go through everything without interference and decide what to keep and what to discard. Patrick's bathrobe was safely tucked away in Philippa's closet. She would keep it forever.

Mike and Philippa still had several exams to write so between planning for camp and studying, she had little time to mourn. Florry was ever watchful for those moments when Philippa needed to be alone.

During one of her daily phone calls to Joyce she told her. "She's crying less and less but every now and again, she collapses into a miserable heap. Last Wednesday, when we were watching TV, without warning, she burst into tears. The poor darling clung to me—shaking and inhaling great gulps of air. It was the first time she's ever reached out to me. Hopefully, it means she's beginning to trust me. Well, camp might just be the thing to get her mind off missing her parents."

The two weeks passed quickly. Philippa and Mike chatted about their exams and both felt they had aced them. But camp became their primary topic. They selected required clothing, added a few choices of their own and packed favourite CDs. Philippa double checked the camp list against what she had packed and cautioned Mike to do the same. "Be sure to take extra batteries for your boom box."

The morning of departure arrived with assorted luggage

scattered across the front hall floor. Mike and his dad were expected momentarily.

"I packed a lunch for your trip and a few special things to have at camp." Florry set an insulated basket, bulging with food, beside the luggage.

Looking out the living room window, Philippa announced, "they're here." as Style's black SUV pulled into the side drive. She watched Frank in his beige Bermudas and blue golf shirt step out and stride around to the back to open the hatch. Mike, dressed for camp in cut-offs and a yellow tank top sauntered up the walk to gather up Philippa's gear.

"Hey, beautiful," he said to Florry. "Is that just for me or do I have to share?" He reached for the laden basket and blew a 'thank you' kiss to Florry. "You know you spoil me rotten and that's why I love you so much."

A flush of crimson flared down her neck. Up to this time, attention like Mike lavished on Florry had never been a part of her life, and even though she pushed awkwardly at him in denial, she was flattered and captivated by this ungainly youth. She watched as he stashed all the gear into the back of the van.

"Mom's got the car so we have the van with lots of space."

Awkwardly, Florry reached out to set a stray strand of Philippa's hair back behind her ear. "You have a good time and don't worry about Sable and me."

"Thanks, Florry." Philippa kissed her on the cheek.

Flustered, Florry called as she waved goodbye, "you two behave yourselves."

She stood on the porch watching a slim girl in tight pink shorts topped by a sleeveless purple-flowered blouse, her ponytail bouncing gaily from one shoulder to the other, step into the van. "She's easing into my heart," she whispered. "I'll miss her." Florry stood watching until they disappeared from view. The vacant house and silent air made Florry anxious to be on her way.

Hurriedly she gathered up her own small suitcase and some parcels and put Sable on his leash. She stepped onto the veranda, turned and locked the front door. She hummed a little tune as she walked to her car. The bags were easily deposited in the trunk of her Rusty Bucket. She slammed the lid shut and opened the rear door. Sable leapt in wagging his tail. "You're going to have a new adventure, my laddy." After a quick glimpse in the rearview mirror, she backed out and headed south toward her single-wide in Greely. Helen wouldn't arrive for four days so Florry had a short break. Traffic was light and the drive took only thirty minutes.

Joyce spotted the dusty Toyota pulling in, grabbed her pack of cigarettes and hurried across the lawn.

"Flo, honey."

Joyce wrapped her arms around her neighbour as Florry stepped out of the car and gave her a big hug. "What a sight for sore eyes. I missed you gal."

"Well, we talk every day on the phone and it's only been six weeks since I left," said Florry. "My, but it feels good to be back in my own space." Grabbing the suitcase in one hand and a bag of groceries in the other she headed to the door. She propped the case against the jamb and fumbled with her keys, found the right one and pushed the door open.

"I thought you gave those disgusting things up." Florry said. A toss of her head indicated the pack of cigarettes that Joyce held. Holding the door ajar with one foot, she backed into the trailer.

She wrinkled her nose and left the door open to air the trailer. She stood for a minute just looking around taking in the pale blue plush sofa and reclining chair. She noted that Joyce had taken good care of her African violets now in full bloom on the table near the window. White lace curtains on the windows provided enough privacy.

"I didn't have you here to badger me so I slipped back into bad habits, I'll light up outside though—come join me? I want to hear all about everything."

"Give me a minute to settle this stuff and change into something comfortable. Here take the dog."

Florry set the groceries on the counter, picked out items that needed refrigeration, and took the suitcase to her bedroom. She changed out of tailored navy slacks and pale blue sweater into a pair of beige cotton pants and a bright yellow blouse with small blue flowers. She tidied her ponytail and gave a quick look of approval to the mirror. Glancing out the window she watched her friend and wondered why Joyce didn't take better care of herself.

Joyce squatted on the small patch of lawn petting Sable. Her faded green shirt pulled tight against her ample bosom made her buttons gape revealing a washed-to-grey brassiere. Her jeans stretched tight emphasizing deep rolls of fat beneath her stomach and wide hips. Large thighs pressed against the legs of her jeans. Her small pale blue eyes were sunk into a full-cheeked face dominated by an overly large nose. Even her hair seemed fat. Streaked with grey, her mass of tight salt-and-pepper curls framed her head like Brillo.

"I shouldn't judge." Florry grabbed a couple of soft drinks from the fridge and headed out the door. She handed Joyce a Diet Sprite.

"You know I prefer Classic Coke. Why do you buy this stuff?"

Florry laughed, shook her head and reached for two folding chairs from the stack of four leaning against the house. She opened them and motioned Joyce to sit for a good 'catch-up'. Sable was busy sniffing every blade of grass and repeatedly lifting his leg to stake out this new territory.

Joyce examined Florry. "Girl, you look different—better I know, the eye shadow's gone,"

"Not gone, just a softer shade. Helen and Philippa—they know all about cosmetics and fashion. Helen owns a business that puts on fashion shows—anyway, I told this to you already. Well, Philippa suggested my eyes would be prettier with lighter coloured eye shadow, she also told me to use coral lipstick instead of dark pink, even gave me an extra makeup kit she had. What do you think?"

"I think that gal knows what she's talking about," answered Joyce. "You do look a whole lot classier."

"This week, Helen's doing this event for a big fashion house, I forgot the name, I'm not up on those things, but anyway her company organized the show. Designers often let her choose an outfit or two as a kind of a bonus. She asked me if I would like her to bring me one as a surprise. I never had any fancy couturier stuff before. I can hardly wait to see what she chooses. Imagine me, Florry Waters, wearing designer clothes!"

"Now, don't you go getting uppity livin' in that fancy place. By the way, I want to thank you for recommending me to your clients," said Joyce. "That Mrs. Peter sure's a gossipy one, but I like her and everyone seems happy with my work."

"I still go one day a week to the Evans'," Florry cut in. "They arranged it with Philippa and Helen. It gives me a change and frankly, I don't have enough to keep me busy every minute of the day."

"Soft touch eh? How're you getting on with Philippa?"

"Like I said on the phone, I'm really enjoying getting to know her. She's still very sad and keeps to herself too much. I like her friends. They're good kids. They hang out at the house all the time playing video games and talking computer stuff. I've no idea about what gigabytes and micro this and that, are though. It's all gobble-de-gook to me.

"Me too. But these kids can sure work them things," Joyce said.

"Philippa and Mike left this morning to go to a fancy computer camp where they'll learn all about programming."

"Yeh? You can bet your bottom dollar they'll learn a whole lot more. Them summer camps are a hotbed for sex!"

"What? Joyce Hines, you get your mind out of the gutter. Philippa and Mike are just friends."

"Okay, but don't say I didn't warn you." Joyce whispered in a throaty voice as she blew smoke to the sky.

The days at Greely slipped away. Florry cleaned every inch of the trailer, visited with neighbours and walked Sable along the country roads. She and Joyce went to a movie and later stopped off at the local pub for a beer.

"Sure wish you didn't have to leave." Joyce hugged her friend as they parted. Florry was returning to Ottawa early the next morning.

The trip back had Florry fighting commuter traffic so it took longer than she figured. With only a few hours to run around the house and gather up out-of-place things before Helen arrived, Florry quickly set to work. Sable sniffed everything until he was content that all was as it should be. Florry placed several empty boxes and a supply of garbage bags in the hallway outside the master bedroom.

Helen arrived dressed for the job ahead wearing NYD jeans with jeweled pockets, an Alisha Hill top and a pair of Gianmarco Lorenzi boots. She breezed in, threw a casual wave in the air in greeting, then smiled to see a fresh pot of coffee and still-warm brownies.

"We have exactly two days to attack that room." Helen exclaimed as she poured a cup of coffee. "I don't think Patrick and Elaine ever threw anything out so God knows what we'll find. I've got an appointment tomorrow afternoon with an artist who wants to buy the equipment in the studio out back. Did you arrange for the consignment shop to pick up the bedroom set?"

"Yes," answered Florry, "and I also asked a friend to take the mattress to the dump."

"Good. The new set I ordered should be here Wednesday. Then we'll have a proper guest room when Elloit and I visit." Helen refilled her cup and eyed the brownies, "Oh, what the hell." She grabbed two in defiance of her diet and turned toward the kitchen door. "Well let's get at it - no time to waste."

Systematically they sorted clothes and after some discussion decided into which box or bag they each went depending whether they were destined for the Thrift Shoppe or the garbage. Helen waded through stacks of papers and notes that were stuffed in boxes and drawers. She put any sales receipts necessary for tax purposes into folders and threw out everything that was not needed.

Florry sorted medications and toiletries in the medicine cabinet. Elaine and Patrick had separate shoe closets. All the shoes were discarded. They boxed loose photographs found in nearly every drawer for Philippa to organize into albums. The entire task took only one day, far less time than they expected.

Helen took advantage of the extra time and set off the following morning to do some shopping. Florry readied herself to do a thorough cleaning before the new bedroom set arrived. Humming 'Whenever I Feel Afraid', she thought about Joyce's comment. Would Philippa behave herself at camp?

*****

Frank guided the SUV down a long lane bordered by towering pine trees. Rounding a bend, a large wooden arch announced the entrance to Camp Popoti. Straight ahead, clasping a clip board, a smiling youth wearing a Popoti t-shirt waved them to a stop and greeted them.

"Welcome. Could I have your names please?"

Once they were checked off the list and had received instructions about a meet-and-greet and where Mike's and Philippa's cabins were, Frank drove to the camp center and unloaded the van. Hasty goodbyes indicated how eager the teens were to start their adventure.

Wheeling their suitcases along a well-maintained dirt path, they separated at a Y junction where signs pointed them to the Guys and Gals accommodations. A frame cabin, painted bright pink, set among white birches overlooking the shores of Lake Joseph was Philippa's destination. Smells of dank earth and moist air, of woods and lakes, brought to mind weekends with her mother and father in Algonquin Park. A choking sob caught in her throat but she swallowed, got control of herself, and turned into the cabin.

Camp Popoti, an elite camp, offered sophisticated computer programming to jury-selected teens. Fierce competition for placement attracted applications from all over North America. It was unusual for two students from the same city let alone the same school to be chosen, however, Mike and Philippa proved to be the exception. Experts in the computer field volunteered their time and expertise to work with bright computer savvy youngsters over two intense weeks. They taught the elements of computer language and introduced them to gaming techniques. In addition to computer training, the camp offered other activities. Sailing, swimming, kayaking, rock climbing, nature crafts, fishing and archery were among them. It also provided sessions in art, woodworking and music.

"Hello." Philippa shouted through the door.

Pink Cabin was empty. She stowed her gear beside the only unclaimed bed, one of three. Sheets and blankets were folded at the foot of the bed, a bare mattress of blue-striped ticking lay on the metal springs. Noticing camper's items thrown here and there, Philippa tried to imagine what her cabin mates would be like. She decided that the girl occupying the bed next to hers definitely was a bit of a scatter-brain and not the least bit organized. The bed, strewn with belongings, had a suitcase lying open on it and garments hanging off the end. In contrast the next bed, neat and tidy, with everything folded and stored away had a suitcase, neatly closed, tucked under the bed. Philippa did likewise, made up her bed and went back outside. All the cabins were different colours so each camper was assigned a cabin by colour.

Tentatively, she moved away from 'Pink Cabin' taking in the sights around her. Walking along the dirt path, being careful not to trip on tree roots, she headed to what the greeter had called the main lodge. It was really a large canvas tent. An introduction session was slated to begin shortly. She signed in, received an information package and a badge with 'Philippa Snelling—Group G' on it. Following instructions she moved to table 'G' where three boys were already deep in conversation.

Smiling awkwardly, she sat down and looked around the room trying to spot Mike. She noticed that far more boys than girls filed in. She saw Mike arrive and move to table 'B'. He would not be in her group. Philippa felt the presence of someone at her elbow and looked up into a face splattered with freckles.

"Hi. I'm Tracey. God, I'm glad to see another girl in our group. Are you in Pink Cabin? I'm next door in Blue—I saw you arrive. Move over, I'm with this team."

Tracey banged her knee on the bench. "Shit! I'm so GD clumsy. Got more bruises than you can count—definitely not meant to be attractive to the opposite sex—especially with this crop of freckles and flaming red hair."

Philippa took in the star tattooed on Tracey's shoulder, multiple bracelets and ropes on each wrist, army-issue boots and tight khaki short shorts, not to mention a clinging camouflage patterned tank top stretched over a 'DD' bosom.

Tracey reached over the table with her hand outstretched. "Hi guys. I'm Tracey."

A short, pudgy blonde boy stood up and took her hand. "Rick. Hello. This is Mark and that's Ray."

Ray extended a hand and Philippa noticed very pink fingernail beds against chocolate brown skin. His smile spread beneath a broad nose with full lips parted to reveal gleaming white teeth. He wore two gold earrings in one ear.

Mark, wearing freshly pressed beige slacks and a short-sleeved pin-striped shirt, nodded.

Tracey struck up a conversation immediately, rattling on about mosquitoes and snakes. Philippa watched and listened in silence. Tracey finally turned, "and you, do you play Jungle Stump?"

Philippa hesitated, then joined in. "Yep, I just blew my score over the top."

Once the talk turned to computer games she felt at home with the conversation and became animated and fully engaged. A voice from the PA system drew their attention.

"Welcome everyone! Welcome to Camp Popoti. You'll find we operate a little differently here compared to other camps so I'll only say a few words. Nobody acts as the head person at Popoti. We work in teams. Look around you and get to know the people at your table—they're your partners for the entire time you're here. Coming down the aisle are your mentors. They'll take it from here. Have a great experience."

Rhythmic reggae music blared from the speakers, switched to a drum role, then a parade of eleven counselors in various ridiculous get-ups entered the room, skipping, dancing and waving to the beat of *When the Saints Go Marching In*. Spontaneous cheering and laughing broke out, then rhythmic clapping as the characters, in outlandish costumes, scattered around the room performing animated antics. With a final Popoti whoop they rushed to designated tables. Looming above Philippa, Charlie Stein grinned and fluffed his boa in her face. His pink sequined dress glinted as she lowered her eyes to avoid fluttering feathers.

"Team, first—they had to pay me a princely sum to appear in

drag—nothing like whiskers and sequins." He stroked a blonde Van Dyke and cast a scrutinizing look around the table. "Welcome to Popoti! I'm your team leader, Charlie Stein, but everyone calls me Chuck."

Philippa gasped. "Chuck Stein! Not Chuck Stein from ExTreme Games?"

"Oops. Now I'm in trouble." Chuck turned to smile at Philippa. "Someone knows who I am. I either have to live up to a good reputation or overcome a bad one. Which one is it?" Charlie narrowed his soft-blue eyes and stared directly into Philippa's hazel ones.

"Oh, my God, I'm so into your games. I have nearly every one. They're the most challenging and the graphics are amazing! You're the god of gaming! I can't believe *I'll* be working with *you!*" Philippa breathless with excitement clutched her two fists to her chest.

"Believe you me, I'm no god." Charlie sloughed off Philippa's comments and raised his hand for attention. "Listen up. There're no 'I's' at Popoti. We're a team and during the next two weeks we're working together. I repeat—*we* are working *together*." He threw the boa in the air and let it fall on the table. "And by the end of your two weeks you will have designed and created a computer game. You will need to stretch your brain power to the limit. There's a prize for the best game design so that's our goal, working together and aiming for the big prize.

"What is it?" Several 'G. teamers called out.

"Ah, there's no way I'm telling. But it's worth working your butts off to win, I assure you."

Chuck pulled the hem of his dress up so he could lift one hairy leg onto the seat between Rick and Mark. He leaned forward, an elbow propped on his knee. Giving Ray a steely stare he said, "Hands off the merchandise friend" indicating his hairy leg.

When the laughter subsided he continued. "So, team, I want you to huddle and come up with a plan but before you do that, let's get to know each other. You're first." Chuck pointed at Philippa.

"I'm Philippa Snelling."

"Not enough, getting to know each other means giving us the whole scoop, all about you particularly computer experience," prompted Chuck.

"Um, well I, um go to Ridgemount High in Ottawa, grade eleven. I guess I'm known as the local computer nerd. I won the University of Ottawa prize for programming a triathlon challenge game. I just turned seventeen."

"Great. Next." Chuck pointed at Ray.

"Ray Staples, Bass Point, Newfoundland. Also grade eleven. I hold the top marks in school for computer classes. I haven't worked with games much, but I helped design effective traffic movement through our local amusement park. I play championship darts."

"Well, that's interesting, I too, play a mean game of darts — you're on Ray." Chuck pointed to Mark.

"Mark Pepper from Toronto, Upper Canada College grade twelve — Head Boy and tenor in the choir. When I'm not singing or running the school, I've got my nose stuck in complex computer stuff. I've designed crossword puzzles."

Chuck nodded at Tracey.

"Anime, that's my thing. I draw characters and write story plots. I like dark and troubled characters, most with animal features. And, oh yes, my name's Tracey Hutton, I'm sixteen and

I'm from LA, sophomore."

Rick jumped right in. "I'm Rick Cooms from Calgary." He reached a soft hand to shake everyone's. "I'm in grade twelve at Forest High School. I think I was chosen for this camp because of my understanding of algorithms, and yes, I'm a nerd too."

"Frank van Hurst from Hamilton. I'm in grade 12 too. I am just another of you nerds."

Everyone broke into laughter and nodded agreement that group G were all computer geeks. They high-fived all around.

Chuck thanked everyone. "I'm getting out of this dress. Why don't you find a quiet spot to start working on a strategic plan and think about what you hope to design. When I catch up with you we'll determine if it's feasible and how you'll go about it."

G team watched Chuck stride away laughing at his stalky frame clad in shimmering sequins and tennis shoes.

"There's a picnic table under that big elm tree outside. Let's move out there." Ray was already half risen from the bench. Philippa blushed when Mark fell in beside her and offered her a piece of his Hershey bar.

Chapter 8

Gathered together under the lofty branches of the old elm tree, the eager teens, all in shorts, lifted first one bare leg, then the other over the bench to sit up to the picnic table. Tracey edged in between Mark and Philippa hip-bumping one, then the other to widen the space. Rick sat across from her and smiled at her aggressiveness. Ray, seated beside him, stretched his long legs under the table and gripped the front of the seat as he stretched full length.

"Let's design a game based on 'Foreign Spies', the movie," said Rick, arms folded smugly across his red tank-top. "Its action packed and we know the storyline."

"Great idea, but I think the idea is to come up with our own ideas and we've only got two weeks," stated Mark. "Besides, I'm not sure about the legal implications of using someone else's storyline from a film—copyright or some such thing that wouldn't allow it."

Rick stared at Mark, but his eyes were hidden behind dark sun glasses. He ran both hands through his thick mop of shoulder-length hair. "Hey, we're just kids and this is just an exercise at summer camp. You into lawyer stuff?"

"Kinda, my mother's …"

Philippa interrupted Mark. "Tracey, you said you draw anime—is there anything that could be developed into story lines? What have you got that can be used in designing a game?"

Uncharacteristically, Tracey lowered her eyes and whispered with an awkward shy smile. "I might. I do have a few ideas and have drawn some characters that are somewhat way-out, but I like them. And, well, uh, I kinda have a story idea about a volcano eruption and fierce creatures emerging from the bowels of the earth who try to take over the world ..."

"Well get them up there girl—let's see them. We haven't got all day. If they stink we'll tell you right off." Ray's outburst brought a burst of noisy laughter and nods of agreement from the others.

Mark, turned to come face-to-face with Tracey, took off his sun glasses, looked intensely into her eyes and pleaded. 'Puleeeze."

One by one. Tracey laid a few of her drawings on the table eager to share her creations yet afraid of the response.

"Way cool. Have you done any computer programming with these?"

"No, I don't know how, but I've done a pile of graphics. Want to see more of 'em?" Tracey, recovering her cocky disposition, reached deeper into her backpack and pulled out a thick binder.

Chuck, now dressed in checkered shorts and a navy golf shirt, covered the distance between the counselor's cabin and G group in strong easy strides. The group hardly noticed him as they turned page after page of Tracey's drawing just captivated by her talent.

"These are far-out amazing!" Ray turned to Chuck. "Hey man, looking good."

Chuck's normal clothes got cursory nods of approval from the team. Ray turned immediately back to the drawings.

"Do you think we can do something with these Chuck? I mean, this is awesome stuff."

Tracey's freckles glowed golden against the red flushing her face.

"Problem is," Rick said, "in order to work with these we'd need some pretty sophisticated programs and..."

"Okay—guys 'n gals come with me."

Chuck signaled them forward with a wave of his arm. Tracey gathered up her drawings and followed the team. They cut diagonally across the green to the only concrete building on the premises. Upon entering the hushed, temperature-controlled building, Chuck unlocked a solid metal door on their right with his name on it. He beckoned them into a dark room with numerous blinking lights and flipped the light switch to reveal a bank of computers, a drafting table, a padded mat and a huge video screen that dominated the far wall.

"Behold Command Center." Chuck gestured arms extended, both hands palms up and spread them wide in an all encompassing manner.

Mouths fell open, eyes flew from one station to the other, and awe was written on every face.

"Each group, all nine, have their own workroom and access to the best equipment, design programs and expertise—this is a duplicate of what we use at large corporations."

Rick was eagerly bending over a computer station.

"Go ahead, switch them on," said Chuck.

"Oh—my—god! Would you look at these graphics programs—they're the latest thing—I've read about them but never hoped to actually work with them this soon." Rick was watching the icons that popped up on the monitor. He spun around on the office chair in absolute ecstasy, arms raised in triumph. "Tracey, we can load in your artwork and make the characters do anything we want—leap, run, fly—you name it!"

"Really?" Tracey could not believe that this was a possibility.

Exclamations continued as Chuck walked each one through what was available, how they could utilize the programs and explained what they could achieve with his direction.

"Is that an action mat?" Tracey walked toward the center of the room, did a hand-stand on the mat and turned to the rest. "Who wants to be the acrobat?"

"Looks like you have that one captured."

Mark asked, "How does that relate to our game?"

"You don't know! Where have you been?" Tracey looked at Mark her eyebrows raised in surprise. "Someone is filmed doing actions on the mat—then the film is downloaded to the computer, the graphic characters are substituted and they move as the person did."

"Man, that's amazing." Is that all we have to do to get your drawing to come to life?"

"Now to be effective, it's not the equipment that does it, it's working together according to a plan." Chuck said. "You won't have any problem figuring out how to use the programs, especially with your backgrounds. But, I don't care how smart you think you are, nobody strikes out on their own—it has to be a team effort—everyone has input. I want to see everything documented on paper before any of you attempt to enter data. Careful planning will help avoid error. That's what makes the difference between success and failure both here and in the real world of designing games commercially."

Mark looked troubled. "We're just novices. We're bound to make mistakes."

"You're right. This isn't child's play and won't be easy. You'll face many challenges and will run into major stumbling blocks." Chuck smiled. "That's why I'm here. I'll guide you and teach you but it has to be your design, your ideas and your work. Any questions?"

"Just one—how soon can we start?"

Philippa wasn't the only one anxious to work with the software and tools available. Everyone agreed as they moved from one station to another.

Chuck raised his husky baritone voice to get their attention. "Sorry, but we have to leave. Tonight we're having a powwow and camp initiation, so I'm afraid you'll have to wait 'til tomorrow. I'll meet you here right after breakfast."

As they left the Command Center other groups were also leaving and everyone appeared to be as excited as G group. Mike, a head above his companions, waved and came over. Philippa rattled on to him about the equipment and how exciting it was to work with Chuck. Mike gave Philippa a soft back-hand to her right shoulder.

"I agree. We're working with some guy from GOD, Games On Demand. He's awesome. Hey Flip, it's good to see you so happy." Mike grabbed her in a bear hug and lifted her in the air swinging her in a full circle.

"This is way better than anything I expected," Philippa said as she felt the ground under her feet again. "Everyone speaks our language, Mike."

"Yep. Our kind of geeks all right."

Mark hurried to catch up and slid into step beside them making sure he was next to Philippa. "Mind if I walk with you guys?" They were half way across the common heading toward the cabins.

"I'm heading that-a-way." Mike pointed to a path that led toward the bath houses. Philippa turned to Mark and looked into a face that was all smiles. Dark eyebrows arched above grey eyes. Philippa felt her stomach muscles clench and heat flushed up her neck. Mark had his hands shoved deep into side pockets of tan coloured Docker shorts, a too-large tank top's armpits hung nearly to his waist and he shuffled along in flip-flops. Philippa lowered her head so he would not see the rising colour in her cheeks.

"Yeah, sure Mark, I'm heading the same way. I think we have a great bunch on our team, don't you?"

"It depends," Mark answered. "We'll see how we work together. Tracey's work is outstanding and puts us way ahead of where we might be otherwise. It's important we recognize each other's talents and make the most of them."

Arriving at the juncture that separated the boys' cabins from the girls', Mark waved and headed off to Red Cabin. Sleeping cabins were located, a short distance behind the central buildings, in a lightly wooded area; the boys to the left, the girls to the right.

"See you at dinner." Philippa watched Mark's long strides eat up the path. For the remainder of the afternoon she could not get Mark out of her mind.

****

In the mess tent, everyone was filtering in for supper. Mike slipped in beside Philippa who was scribbling away on foolscap. "So what do you think?"

"Well, like I said, this place's totally amazing. Command Center's awesome."

"Not what I meant. What do you think about Mark?"

"He's going to be a real asset to the team I'm sure."

"Boy, you're blind. Can't you see he's hot for you?"

"This seat taken?" Mark sat bottom first, then swung both legs over the bench to settle into the vacant space across from Philippa.

"Hey Mark. Sure—set your buns down." Mike said and gave Philippa a knowing look. She looked away and pretended to be busy with settling the papers on the bench beside her.

A din of excited voices soon filled the mess hall. The entire camp was hyped and ready to take on the challenges of program writing, not to mention sports activities and field trips. Campers continued to talk with their mouths full as they downed corn-on-the-cob and hot dogs.

"If you get to the powwow first save me a place." Mike waved at Philippa as he gathered his tray and left the dinner table.

A sloping hill rose above a wide grassy area to form a natural amphitheatre. Campers straggled across the open field, welcomed by an enormous bonfire that blazed in the center. Everyone headed for a place on the hill. Philippa came equipped with a sit-upon, found a spot to her liking in the middle of the slope and sat down. She sensed him before she saw him. Mark eased down beside her.

"Hey gorgeous, can I claim you," he quipped.

"I don't see a baggage ticket on me anywhere, do you?"

"That Mike got claims?"

"Nope, we're just friends."

"Is he gay?"

"Why do you ask?"

"Otherwise, he's crazy not to be sitting right here when I'm trying to put the rush on you."

Philippa burst out laughing. "I've heard lines before, but never one with such honesty. You sure don't waste time."

"Yeah, well we've only got two weeks—gotta make the most of it."

She wasn't about to reveal that Mike was gay—that was his prerogative. He said little about his sexual orientation. Relationships, at this point, were not an issue for him, but he would have to deal with them sooner or later. Mike and Philippa held long discussions about the difficulties he would face once he 'came out'. He talked about the horror stories he'd heard and said his parents were his first priority. He told her that when they were comfortable with his sexuality he would be more open about them. Meanwhile, school, band, swimming and computers filled his life.

"About Mike—he's the brother I never had." Philippa went on to explain. "He's a little overprotective sometime so you better watch yourself." She gestured with a nod of her head as she watched Mike approach.

The powwow got into lively mode with the theme of just plain and silly fun that involved all the campers and leaders. Six male counselors dressed as women with grapefruits stuffed in oversized braziers and grass hula skirts sang *Nothing Like A Dame* very loudly and somewhat off-key. Raucous skits featured other counselors wearing outsized hats and outlandish costumes. They drew the campers to the front and had them do the chicken dance that ended with campers clasping their sides from laughing so hard. Rubber chickens were thrown into the crowd to much cheering. The campfire elongated body shapes and faces into grotesque shifting shadows as bodies moved in front of it. Whooping and cheering erupted over and over again. Philippa met several other girls and boys when each, dragged from the audience, was forced to the center to participate in games and songs. For the finale, all the leaders stood in a line, arms across each other's shoulders, and swayed back and forth as they sang

Getting To Know You. The evening ended by everyone joining in a Conga line, kicking and singing past each cabin as the occupants dropped off one-by-one.

Pink Cabin's other two girls who Philippa had met briefly earlier, had already dropped off before Philippa greeted them with giggles and wiggles. They continued a small Conga line in the cabin.

"I'm so totally out of breath," wailed Philippa as she dropped backwards onto her bed, panting from laughing so hard.

Exhausted from the day, she barely managed to get into her pajamas and follow the other girls to the bathhouse. But once in bed, sleep wouldn't come. Soft snoring from the other bunks told her, her roommates were fast asleep. Visions of Tracey's characters kept flying through her mind. She saw them in risky situations—racing to beat lava flows and climbing trees to escape voracious creatures. She felt their individual personalities, anxieties and strengths. It was as if she knew each and every one of them. Abruptly she sat up. Characters and plots that appeared randomly started to become orderly. A storyline developed with quests and challenges. Finally, she fell asleep.

Philippa opened her eyes to black lipstick and raccoon eyes staring right in her face.

"Shit, Tracey," squawked Philippa. "You are one scary broad. What a god awful sight to see first thing in the morning. Do you always get yourself up to look like a ghoul?"

"Puts me in a creative mood—and you know what else—lame people are afraid of me so I get my privacy."

"Yes, I agree, some privacy would be a good idea."

"Anyway, I want to get an early start." Tracey was backing away from the bunks and headed for the door.

"What's early?" Philippa yawned and felt around the floor for her travel alarm clock.

"Six-thirty—no one's up yet."

"Six-thirty! Are you nuts?"

"Shh, ya. I couldn't sleep and I wanted to get a jump start."

Philippa eased one foot to touch the floor, mumbling "Okay, I'll be right along."

Fifteen minutes later, seated side by side at a table in the mess hall, they huddled over Tracey's drawings. Philippa explained her ideas of the night before and the storyline she envisioned. She told Tracey how she thought the game could be articulated.

"Do you really think so? This is way beyond what I thought we could do." Tracey whispered, afraid to speak out loud in case someone might hear even though they were totally alone.

They compared ideas and jotted notes until, an hour later, three drowsy males dropped onto the bench across the table. Tracey and Philippa shared their thoughts and soon all five were eagerly throwing out other possibilities and interrupting each other.

"Yep," yelled Ray as he swept his arms in a grand arches, "when the volcano erupts it could flare across the screen. Man, how do we do that?"

"Stop, stop, stop, you guys," hollered Mark. "This is getting us nowhere. We need to organize ourselves, like Chuck said, work as a team."

"Did I hear my name?"

Chuck hastened down the aisle and arrived at the table. He listened as the teens tripped over each other's words to fill him in on their progress and ideas.

"Man, It sounds like you guys need a leader to keep you in

line. One who'll task each person with a specific aspect of the Project."

"Mark should be the leader," said Rick. "He's experienced, being 'head boy' and all. Everyone agree?"

All hands raised. "Oookay, then Mark you're in charge."

"Don't I get a chance to refuse?"

A resounding 'No' erupted.

"Well in that case here's how I see it."

Mark was in his element as he stood up and took command.

"Tracey'll take charge of the artwork and coordinate with Philippa on the storyline. Ray and Rick will dub in the sound and I'll work on the scoring. All of you—write down anything you think of and hand them over to Philippa so she can incorporate them if they work. Philippa, you work closely with Rick and me to design the program to execute Tracey's artwork and the story. Ray, you'll test it each step of the way and bring back the problems. Make sure that all your ideas are documented."

Chuck nodded his approval. "Sounds like a plan, so let's get at it." He dangled the keys to the work room.

Rick set to work and scanned Tracey's drawings into the computer. Ray took video footage of Tracey doing hand stands, flying leaps and twisting jumps. "Man, how can you do that?"

"Years of gymnastics—I hated it but hey, I guess it paid off. Maybe I should thank my parents. Nah, I might look like a nice girl—can't have that."

Rick linked his computer to another station where Philippa took the live-action video and one-by-one dropped in and substituted the anime drawings. The characters started to come alive and move across the screen.

Tracey went ballistic as she watched her creations come to life.

"Show me how you did that. Oh, my God, that's totally awesome." Tracey leaned over Rick watching his every move. The screen displayed Tracey's drawings animated but still not realistic.

"There is a lot of fine tuning to be done but Chuck and I will work on that, but first we need a plan." Rick shut down the computer and glanced at Tracey's pouting mouth.

Huddled with Mark and Rick, Philippa outlined more aspects of her storyline and how the story and game would unfold. A quick vote unanimously adopted Philippa's creative ideas with only a few additions by the group.

Chuck walked them to the main computer. "You'll find it's better to divide up the tasks. The scoring can be programmed separately and added at the last minute." He encouraged and guided them every step of the way impressed by how quickly each and every one grasped the technology.

"With nine groups, each with their own work room, it's important we secure our room." Chuck closed the door as they were leaving, turned the key and checked that it would not open. He explained that, like in industry, the creative work was to be available to only Group G. "Mark, and only Mark, can borrow the key. In other words, there's tight control of who has access. We don't want anyone to steal your program or vandalize your work. Not that it's likely at Popoti, but you never know."

A throng of other campers left the building full of eager and excited chatter about the progress they had made that morning. Conversation buzzed during lunch sounding like bees swarming their nest. It was a hushed drone as teams protected their ideas and kept them guarded. During the afternoon, everyone was deliberately separated into different groups for recreational activities.

In late afternoon, Tracey and Philippa met on the path and walked back to their cabins to change out of their bathing suits.

"During water polo, I couldn't concentrate, not that I'm great at sports in any case, but my head was full of your characters swimming through steaming water avoiding hungry sharks and falling rocks." Philippa swam her arms through the air as she talked. "Do you think we can simulate that in the studio?"

"Hey, we've got these six characters," Tracey cut in, "but they haven't got names. We gotta giv'em names."

This had not escaped Ray—he arrived at supper with a list of potential character names. It was clear the eager team worked well when they were together and evidently they came up with ideas when they were apart. Gathered in a circle sitting on the grass outside the mess tent, they batted names back and forth. Speedz and Letti quickly became the names of choice for the hero and heroine; Galdzak, Hor, Flank and Zatch, the villains. The team decided to call the game Eruptus. With characters named, the format took shape, with believable actors and real challenges. All five G team stood up and gave a high five. "Five for one and five for all" became their cheer and as Mark called it—their mating call.

The dinner bell sounded across the green. Starving, they raced for the mess tent.

A heaping plate of spaghetti landed on the table before Mike threw his long body onto the bench. His eyes locked onto Philippa's.

"Miss me, sweetheart? Your team getting anywhere?"

Philippa nodded with her mouth full.

"We're all guys so everything's crash-and-burn stuff." Mike slid along the bench to give her a hip a bump.

"You clown, stop it. You want that spaghetti down your back?" Philippa spoke sharply, then burst out laughing and reached her hand to mess Mike's hair.

"Hey, Mike," called a voice from across the table. "How about that graphic? Wasn't it amazing how the blood and guts splattered all over the screen when the truck smashed into the sports car? Wasn't....?"

"Holy shit!" Mike rose to tear after Philippa as she fled from the dining room. He found her by the lake doubled over clutching her stomach, crouched in a ball, shaking and mewling.

"What happened?" Mark, who had followed close behind, stood over Mike as he cradled Philippa. "Is she sick?"

"No, just give us a moment, Mark. She'll be all right—won't you Flip?" Mike was lifting a strand of her hair back from a running nose. "Mark, have you got a Kleenex?"

Mark reached into his jeans and handed off a wad of tissue with a questioning look. The sobbing eased to little shudders. Philippa jerked free of Mike, stood up, looked at Mark, turned and began to run along the shore. Mike watched Mark fall in behind her and decided to let him take it from there. Careful not to intrude, Mark kept a few strides behind.

Philippa, out of breath, finally stopped about a two miles along the shore and sat down. Whenever she was troubled she ran, often with Sable, but here she just ran to escape her feelings. She spread her legs wide on the sandy beach and stretched forward to draw in long deep breaths. She let the tears stream down her face landing in dark spots on the sand. Mark reached for her hand and waited.

Releasing a sigh, Philippa swallowed, swabbed her nose and eyes with the bunched up tissues and between sobs explained to

Mark what had happened. "When he told us what their game looked like, all I could see was the accident that killed my parents. Oh, I made such a fool of myself, I'm sorry."

"There's no reason to apologize. I'll bet Mike went back and mushed spaghetti into that stupid ass's face."

The vision made Philippa smile as she looked into sympathetic soft grey eyes. "Oh, now wouldn't that be a sight?"

Mark laughed. "Like you said, Mike's your protector, so God help any guy who upsets you."

A weak giggle escaped as Philippa rubbed her nose with the back of her hand. Mark reached for it, eased it away and gently kissed a tear on her cheek. Sorrow gave way to electric tingling radiating from the spot he kissed. Hand-in-hand they walked back to camp along the beach kicking sand and talking about school and gaming. By the time they arrived at the mess tent, Mark had his arm around Philippa's waist.

Chuck had seen Philippa flee the hall and slipped out to check on her. He watched the scene unfold. When Mark and Philippa started to run along the water's edge he strolled out to meet Mike. He needed an explanation.

The next morning, Chuck sent Mark and Philippa to the office to pick up some supplies before he called the rest of the team together for a small conference. He explained the trauma Philippa had recently experienced and asked them to be sensitive to her fragile condition and to be prepared to report to him if she was having difficulty. The worried faces before him told him that he could rely on them.

Mark returned holding Philippa's hand. Fleeting smiles and glances passed between the team while they worked. Nothing escaped them and soon the guys gave Mark knowing nudges and

Tracey winked at Philippa.

Days followed days. Ray hooked up with Tracey to consult on colour and audio. Rick and Mark took over the design for scoring. Every challenge the characters undertook had to generate points and rewards for the players. Escaping the molten ash became the first challenge. The team conferred regularly and worked at their tasks totally engrossed in each and every entry.

Every day, Chuck had to drag them away for their midday meal and afternoon activities, insisting they would have to wait until late afternoon before they could access the Command Center again.

They always ate supper together and a space was saved for Mark between Philippa and Ray.

Days ended with a sing-song in the mess hall and campers hummed and sang the tunes as they returned to their cabins for the night. Every day became a pattern of working at Command Center in the morning, sports and craft activities in the afternoon and more gaming programming in the evening. However, it was mandatory that each team return to the mess hall after Command Center. Most nights it was eleven o'clock before the tired campers fell into bed. They were asleep within minutes.

Philippa wakened thinking about Mark. She cuddled her pillow pretending it was his warm body. Thoughts of his broad shoulders, twinkling eyes and eager kisses made heat rush up her inner thighs. She pressed her breasts hard into the mattress. She opened her eyes to see black fingernails against her white sheets.

"Shit Tracey. How the hell do you sneak up like that? I never hear you coming."

"Well, mooning into that pillow might be a good reason. Come on get up. We're going to run the graphics with sound effects today."

G team wasn't the only group in a hurry to get to Command Center. The camp was a hive of creative energy. They were well into their second week and the deadline was coming up fast. Each team was sure they had a winner. Day after day, excited whispering and secret huddles became the norm throughout the mess hall, on the common and along the paths. Everyone huddled with their respective teams members, inseparable, except when the scheduled activities parted them. Talk was all about the 'game'. Afternoons disappeared full of sports activities, but the beginning and ending of each day centered around the activities happening at Command Center.

Mornings started with announcements at breakfast. Shrill feedback blasted through the speakers.

"You know, said Rick, "they do that on purpose to get our attention."

"Everyone—listen up—big announcement. Friday's your last day that's only two sleeps away. That means only two days to finish designing your games. Friday afternoon each group will present their result to one person to be judged."

Chairs shifted and campers strained to hear.

"Why one person? Because that person is equal to ten. Ladies and gentlemen, we're honoured that Hunter Plast, of GAMEZ has volunteered to judge your efforts."

A roar went up in the hall. GAMEZ was among the most prestigious firms producing video games in North America.

"Silence! Quiet! Not only has he agreed to judge, GAMEZ has offered to fly the winning team in their private jet to Silicon Valley to tour the company."

Everyone stood up and clapped and whistled.

"Quiet, listen up. QUIET. Hear this. All participants will receive a full set of Trakaliens, GAMEZ's hottest series!"

More cheers, stomping of feet and banging on the tables before the campers stilled to hear the rest.

"Friday evening we're putting on a really big show thanks to Foremost Productions of Toronto but the highlight will be the announcement of our Popoti's winning team! Good luck to you all!"

The campers stampeded out of the hall shouting and cheering, back slapping and punching. Chuck signaled to G team to gather near a picnic table outside.

"Listen up. What does G stand for? It stands for GREAT." High fives were immediate. "Team, you guys're the greatest. If you don't win the prize, it doesn't mean you're not as good as the others. It means that the competition was outstanding. From what I hear in the staff lounge, this summer has brought the brightest and best young minds this camp has ever seen. I want you to know how proud I am to have had each and every one of you in my group."

Mark interupted. "Hey Chuck, when we arrived here we had no idea we'd be so privileged to work with someone of your caliber. Man, are *we* lucky. We learned incredible stuff from you and that'll always be inspiring. Winning would be great. In fact winning would be fantastic ..."

"Yeah, what Mark's trying to say is," Tracey lowered her voice and spoke haltingly. She was having one of her rare shy moments. "Thank you."

Rick grabbed Chuck in a bear hug barely coming up to his chest then turned his back so his team buddies would not see his tears. He wasn't alone. Soon they would go their separate ways and might never see one another again—unless they won. They moved in a unit across the common, quiet and thoughtful.

Mark took Philippa's hand and pulled her away. "I need to talk to you." They climbed the hill and slipped into the woods. As soon as the camp was out of sight, Mark turned to Philippa and drew her close. He stroked her face, leaned in and softly kissed her cheek, then lifted her hair away from her neck and slid his lips up and behind her ear.

Flushed, Philippa dug her fingernails into her clenched palm knuckle-grasping the back of Mark's neck.

"Mark, I can't bear the thought of us leaving Saturday morning, you to Toronto and me to Ottawa." Philippa leaned against his chest and let every muscle and bone melt into him.

"Philippa, God, how can I say this? Over the couple of weeks, you've become part of me. I can't stand the thought of us being miles away from each other." Mark pulled her tighter and felt her heart racing. He slipped his tongue between her teeth and stroked the roof of her mouth. His hands slid along her ribs until they reached her buttocks. He pulled her tighter and felt her soften against him. Philippa cautiously drew back. Then she leapt at him and kissed him hard.

"Stop, Flip." Mark held her at arm's length. "I didn't mean for this ... Wow. Let me take a few minutes to cool off." Mark turned and tried to move away but Philippa pulled him back.

"Philippa, don't.." Mark pushed her away, then pulled her to him and held her tight. He pulled away and headed into the bush. Once in control, he returned and took hold of her by the shoulders. "Now, that was embarrassing. I apologize."

"No need. Boy, it was intense there for a bit. Are you all right?"

"A little blown away, I guess." said Mark.

Philippa's eyes glinted. "Never been that close before. Thanks Mark, for caring enough to be cautious."

"Flip, I don't want to be careful, I want to swallow you whole. I can't bear that we'll not be together. What're we going to do?" asked Mark.

"Mark, I'm a virgin, I don't want to be a virgin forever. But, I don't want to think back when I'm fifty years old that my first experience took place at a camp by the name of Popoti." She released a nervous laugh. "I care for you, more than you could imagine and maybe you should be my first lover. But, I'm not ready, so let's just leave it there for now."

Mark took Philippa's head in his hands and gently kissed her, then blew a falling strand of hair off her forehead. "You're right. I care too much about you to take advantage."

When they got back to Command Center the others had returned. Ray was eager to run the program again and when it executed smoothly, he pumped a fist clenched 'yes'.

"See guys, it all works. Let's plug in the scoring system and see who can beat me."

Rick and Mark clicked away on the keys, merged their files, downloaded them to the game and punched "exe". The screen exploded in a series of lines running randomly from top to bottom. Rick grabbed the mouse and tried to enter a command to fix it but the screen went black.

"Oh, no." screamed Tracey, fists clenched. "We blew it. We fucked the whole damned thing!"

Grimly they stared at the computer, worried eyes drifted from one to the other.

Standing in the doorway, Chuck bit his bottom lip and

ground his teeth. His mind raced through algorithms and formulas. Determined to appear calm he entered the room. "Okay, it's not the end of the world. Let's go at this methodically. Mark, let me see what you and Rick merged before you downloaded it to the game."

He read each entry again and again shaking his head. The air in the room was hushed and heavy. Tracey and Philippa sat on the action mat and held hands, avoiding each other's eyes.

"Here. It's here," Chuck shouted and pointed at the monitor. "See, its right here at the beginning. You should have a comma not a period, the period stopped the computer from proceeding and reading the next command. Whew. Try it now."

Amidst cheers and backslapping, the team watched their efforts of the past two weeks smoothly execute. Tracey could not get enough of watching her creatures move and perform. They swam, they jumped and they flew across canyons. They were real, alive and believable. Ray challenged everyone to play and they did over and over again. They pumped success with clenched fists and bent arms, shouting "Yes, oh, yes" again and again. They left the Center full of enthusiasm.

Mark looked at Chuck. "Can I borrow the key for a minute, I forgot something."

The other members of group "G" waited outside for Mark to return.

Philippa motioned to Mark. They walked toward the lake where it was quiet. "I want it to be Popoti. When I am fifty, I want to remember it happened at Popoti. I want it to be with you Mark."

Chapter 9

Rumblings disturbed the quiet of the dark night. Flashes of sheet lightening strobe lighted the sky and outlined the shoreline in stark silhouette. Strong winds pushed white caps across the water to crash against shore rocks erupting in a shower of angry spray. The storm seized Muskoka.

A deafening clap of thunder exploded causing alarmed campers to tumble from their beds and stumble to their doors. Flashes of white light illuminated groups of campers, huddled outside their cabins, arms gripping their shoulders as if that would keep them dry. Rain that soon followed drove them back inside where they listened to it pound on the roof, a steady staccato rhythm drumming on the steel. Swaying branches moaned and creaked. Pink Cabin's occupants sat up in their beds clutching their blankets for comfort and looking to each other for confirmation of safety. Every time lightning bolted it shot daggers through the cracks in the cabin's thin wooden boards.

Philippa slipped out of bed, as her two bunk mates girls flinched and shrieked. She padded across the cold bare floor and opened the door to peer out. In the eerie light she saw Lake Joseph's waves tossed up and over the docks, she watched boats tug at their ropes and the sky pierced by blinding daggers. Breathing in large gulps of the ozone charged air she watched the drama of the night. Some part of her felt kin to the storm gods. She reveled in nature's intensity, energy and fierceness. Not so her roommates. They screamed at her to "close the damn door."

Dawn's graying light did little to ease the rage of Thor.

Counselors clad in plastic ponchos, moved through the campgrounds and battened down loose equipment, tightened boat moorings and headed up the muddy paths to check campers in their cabins.

A raspy voice called into Pink cabin. "The power's out. Hurricane force winds downed the power lines. But not to worry, we're on the edge of the system and it's supposed to move on within the hour. We want you to gather in the mess hall as usual as soon as you can."

Pink Cabin girls, clad in plastic ponchos dashed to the washroom and shower facilities shaking themselves dry as they entered the building. By the time they returned to their cabin to get dressed, the sun was trying to break through the heavy clouds but gentle showers continued. Dressed, they headed down the path to the mess tent where staff was inside pushing the canvas high with brooms and paddles to force the water to drain off relieving the weight on the structure. The girls drifted apart to join their friends.

Mike arrived and dropped onto the bench beside Philippa slapping down his breakfast plate heaped high with hash browns and scrambled eggs. He was balancing another plate with buttered toast. "I'm telling you, I've never had to run through a raging downpour to take a leak before. What a gullywash!"

Mark, already seated on the other side of Philippa shook his head. "Your bladder's the least of our problems. What'do'ya think's going to happen to the competition when we've no power?"

Worried looks were exchanged between the three campers.

"Listen up," squawked a voice over the PA. The counselor who supervised canoeing was at the mike. "I've been in touch with the weather gurus and the storm should move out in the next few hours. The Command Center building has an emergency generator, so we have power."

Cheers filled the mess hall.

"The bad news is, if your project's not complete, I'm sorry, you can't access the Center. To protect against lightening strikes we disconnected the power source to that building until we deem it safe and that won't be for a few hours yet. The good news is nothing got fried."

A few groans were heard.

"Judging's going to be a little later than planned, but given how forward-thinking our judge is, when he heard about the storm, he left Toronto last night to be sure to be here for you. Please let me introduce Hunter Plast, head honcho at GAMEZ."

A short, slender balding man peering through thick glasses, wearing a GAMEZ sweat shirt and jeans rose and waved. Cheering and foot stamping welcomed him.

"Right now, I suggest you gather in your groups and plan your strategy for this afternoon. Canoeing trips are cancelled, swimming too, since a lot of debris has washed ashore. Archery and music are still on but no rock climbing."

A few grunts escaped from avid climbers.

"There'll be a special showing of "Foreign Spies" at two o'clock this afternoon right here in the mess hall. Now as for the competition, your groups will be called one-by-one during the movie. The first one will be called at two. Each group will proceed to the main office where they'll make their presentation. Every entry will be presented individually and in private. A designated person in the group is expected to introduce the team and give an overview of how you worked together to reach your goal. Your group leaders have your presentation order. Good luck to all of you."

Chairs scraped as a herd of campers returned their plates and cutlery to the service area, then settled into their nine respective groups.

Mark held up his hand for everyone to quiet down. "We only get one shot at this, guys. We decided to keep the logistics simple to sidestep problems, thanks to Chuck's advice. My take would be to play up the talent of Tracey's art and Philippa's story line. We tekkies are a dime a dozen around here so our grabber is the *artistic* side of our game. What d'ya think?"

"Maybe we should convince Tracey to get rid of the scary makeup." Ray avoided looking at Tracey.

"Putting on a good appearance would definitely be beneficial," Chuck subtly agreed. "And don't forget you have to do a snappy professional presentation of about thirty seconds. This is called an elevator pitch in industry. Learn how to do that well and you'll know how to get an investor's attention sometime in the future."

By the time they had their elevator pitch ready for Mark to deliver and each team member rehearsed their short bio, the rain had stopped.

Chuck stood and announced they were the first presenters.

"Oh shit, that's bad! First is never the winner," wailed Frank.

"Ya, but I guess someone has to do it," said Ray. "At least we won't be pulled away from the movie."

"Like who's gonna concentrate on a dumb movie?"

"The upside is, we'll be able to kick back and drive fear into everyone else," Tracey piped up.

"Okay, then maybe it's not so bad. First it is." Mark nodded and signaled a-thumbs-up

The group left the mess hall laughing nervously and agreed to regroup at Command Center at 1:15pm.

Wearing sparkling white jeans with a tailored navy blouse Philippa arrived before the rest. She wore small silver Celtic cross earrings that had been her mother's, as 'good luck' charms. She paced in front of the building rubbing her hands together.

Team members arrived one at a time, each dressed in their best. At 1:30, Tracey had yet to arrive and anxious glances passed between the team members.

"Do you think she's having one of her weird introverted moments and not coming?" Ray frowned as he squinted up the path to the cabins.

Minutes later Tracey emerged from around the side of the building, mouth-drop gorgeous in slim lime capris, a simple long-sleeve white sweater and simple wedge sandals. Gone were the bangles and ropes from her wrists and she wore no heavy eye makeup. Her mass of dark curls was pulled into a tidy ponytail.

"One word and you'll be sporting a fat lip." She evil-eyed each member of G team only to see broad approving smiles. "Mom insisted I pack these."

Mark winked.

Chuck announced that Command Center was now open. Sighs of relief escaped because they needed to download the final program onto a disc before making their presentation.

While they waited for the main computer to boot up, everyone went over the elevator pitch once more.

"Good afternoon, Mr. Plast, may I present group G?" Mark continued until he heard a gasp from Ray.

"The program's gone!"

"What do you mean gone?"

"It's been deleted—wiped clean." Ray ran through every possible scenario to retrieve the files. Suggestions were thrown out in rapid succession. "Try rebooting." "Press Exe. Twice." Whoever had hacked into their computer knew what they were doing and left no trace of Eruptus.

"Oh, my god, we're totally screwed." Tracey slammed her fist into the wall and kicked the baseboard.

"Well not totally." Mark stepped forward. "One of my bunk mates let slip that he knew how to hack into the Command Center. I got suspicious."

"What?"

"Yes, I reported it and he's been quietly removed from the camp."

"That's just great. But we're still royally screwed."

"Remember yesterday? I asked Chuck for the keys saying I forgot something—well, I transferred our files onto a travel drive." Mark held his hand palm up with the small device cradled in it.

"When Mark told me about the hacker, Chuck said, "I got all the group leaders to do the same so all groups have copies of their latest work. Then we watched for Mark's cabin fellow to appear. Sure enough, he did late last night."

"Surely there was a safety firewall," Ray exclaimed.

"The staff at Popoti didn't think a summer camp needed to have sophisticated security, so the system that was in place was a little out of date; there was some but what we had he hacked into with no problem."

"Hey, we're all computer savvy. Wouldn't you think some jerk might be tempted?" Tracey, all-knowing, threw her arms in the air.

"This guy's so smart he not only hacked into the Command Center computers but the mainframe as well where all the backup files were stored—wiped them clean too."

"Why would he do that? After all, we're only a bunch of young geeks at summer camp."

Chuck ran his fingers through his tight wheat-coloured curls, frowned and lifted one leg up to the bench, leaned forward, rested his elbow on his knee and cupped his chin in his hand. "Think about it. Success at this camp guarantees scholarships to whatever university you choose. Should you shine here it's a huge stepping stone. There's a lot of stress on everyone to compete and excel. Most take it in stride and handle it very well, but there's always the excess stress, a potential for disaster for someone who can't bear to lose. I think he thought if there were no winners, then there were no losers either."

"Well he's a loser, all right," said Frank slamming his fist on the table. "There's no excuse for what he did."

Chuck looked from one to the other. "This guy was so desperate he jeopardized not only his own integrity but that of his team as well."

"Boy, he's in big doo-doo. Did you call the cops?" Frank asked.

"No. His parents were notified and picked him up early this morning. He's very contrite and has agreed to undergo counseling," Chuck said. "As far as the camp's concerned, the matter's closed. This is the first incident we've ever had. Certainly, in the future more safeguards will be put in place. As for the hacker, I suspect his chances of ever working with a gaming corporation are now non-existent."

"Wow, it only takes one stupid act to screw up your life

forever." Ray, clad in a soft denim shirt, leaned over the computer squinting through his thick glasses. He edged the travel drive that Mark handed him into the USB port. "Thanks Mark."

"Okay. Let's finish rehearsing and get ourselves over to the office." Mark was again, in command of his team.

"Hey, guys, for your information—it's all here." Ray ran the program turned a grinning face to the team and winked. He copied Eruptus onto a disc to use in the projector.

Philippa, with some ceremony, attached the graphic label that Tracey and she had designed and printed the previous day. "Team, Eruptus is now officially ready for trial by jury." Everyone kissed the disc for luck and let out a big sigh.

"Here we go. All or nothing—five for one and five for all." They did the team cheer with hands raised high before handing Chuck the disc.

He escorted them into the main building, where each was presented to Hunter Plast. Hunter stood, smiled warmly and reached across the folding table to shake their hands when they were introduced. He wished them luck, indicated that they could begin, picked up a clipboard and sat.

Mark stepped forward. Frank took charge of the computer and the other three stood in front of a large screen. Mark cleared his throat and spoke.

"First, I want to say that each and every member contributed to the maximum, resulting in a really great team. For our project, we opted to develop anime characters into a rescue style game whereby the h-h-hero and h-h-heroine face numerous obstacles and ad-adversaries...." Mark's heart raced and he tripped over his words. He stopped, took a deep breath and ran his sweaty palms down his pant legs. Imploringly, he eyeballed Hunter Plast, took a deep breath and relaxed his clenched fists, then settled into a moderate paced presentation. "… to save the 'Holy Sphere' from an erupting volcano and evil forces. Tracey, our talented artist, is to be credited for giving us our characters. As a team we developed their actions and designed the trials and challenges they had to overcome to make the game challenging and fun." Mark sucked in another gulp of air after this long sentence. "It was written to allow the player to collect rewards throughout the game. The final quest is to get the Holy Sphere to the Golden chamber at the temple of Or. Frank will you please start the game now." And to Hunter Plast he said, "Frank will challenge the internal computer player."

Five pairs of intense eyes watched Plast for some reaction to their game. He showed none. At the end of their presentation they were thanked and dismissed. G group left the building without any indication of how Plast felt. Deep in their personal thoughts, they walked across the common to the mess hall.

Throughout the afternoon, groups left and returned, some with gloom written all over their faces, some grinning.

Mark and Philippa decided to take a long walk to get away from the tense atmosphere. Arms around each other they wandered along the wet beach side-stepping debris from the storm.

"What's life like for you in Toronto? We've never discussed it—our conversations have always been about camp, Eruptus and school. When you really think about it, I don't really know who you are." Philippa looked inquiringly seeking Mark's eyes hidden behind Raybans. "We're friends and lovers, but apart from Popoti who are you?"

"Quick rundown—I live in a bloody big house in Rosedale, attend a private school, both parents still together. Dad owns an import/export business, Mom's an immigration attorney." Mark rapid fired. "I'm being prepped to take over the 'company' so I work at Dad's office when I'm not in school or busy with other things like this camp."

"So you don't plan on doing computer programming as a career?"

"Nope, but I want to pursue this on a business level, perhaps as an investor or as a sideline. Nothing says I have to stick with furnishings and household items—I plan to expand the company into other areas."

"So tell me, what does an immigration lawyer do?"

"Fairly straight forward, I'd think. She helps people gain permanent resident status in Canada. Mostly she handles reams of paperwork, but occasionally she gets an interesting case. Right now, there's a real odd one."

"Really?"

"In the mid 80's several babies were secretly airlifted out of Romania during the political upheaval that ravaged that country. It was a clandestine operation whereby a group of daring young people with strong ideals and too much family money flew into a private airport in Romania and rescued several babies from an orphanage. They brought them to Canada, landed at a private landing strip outside Halifax and handed over the babes to waiting Canadian families. There're no records registered with the authorities. The children are now our ages. The whole thing has become a nightmare for one family. The kid needs a Social Insurance Number to get a job. The parents came forward to see if Mom could get legal status for their son."

"And can she?" Philippa thought about her own lack of birth certificate. Was she a Romanian orphan?

"It's a can of worms because there's a distinct possibility that the case could turn on its head with charges being laid against the rescuers and the orphan kid be deported. He was only six weeks old when he was brought to Canada. And, I understand there're at least four more children involved. Can you imagine?"

Yes, she could imagine.

"Have any of the other orphans gotten legal status?" Philippa traced a circle with her foot and stared at marks on the ground.

"None of the others have come forward but mom's case has opened a criminal investigation that well may be far-reaching." Mark tightened his hold around Philippa's waist and felt her body tense.

A ripple of fear ran up Philippa's spine. She clenched her fists and closed her eyes.

"Oh, my God – I might be one of them!"

"What are you talking about?"

Philippa explained the missing birth records. Could the fact that there was no record of a birth certificate for *her* be because she was one of the Romanians orphans? Could that be why her parents never told anyone Elaine was pregnant? Could it be she was not their child at all? Her parents said she was born in Nova Scotia. The Romanian children were delivered to Halifax, the timing was right. And Philippa certainly did not physically resemble either parent. Would she be deported? She shivered at the thought.

"Mark, I don't know who I am. I have this weird thing that whenever I look in the mirror the reflection will be someone else. What if I *am* one of those orphans?"

"Hey, lighten up. It is probably a simple case of incorrect registration. I'm sure your lawyer will get everything sorted out."

"I sure hope so, but it is disconcerting to say the least."

Come on, you're getting chilled. Let's go back." Mark wrapped his sweater around Philippa's shoulders, left his arm possessively there and directed her toward the mess hall.

The tent was hushed yet intense, campers spoke in whispers. A shroud of anticipation draped heavily over every table where thoughtful team members munched on a late afternoon feast of hamburgers and fries. They quietly swilled soft drinks never taking their eyes off the entrance.

"Plast left the Command Center." Frank informed Philippa and Mark as they approached G Group.

"When?"

"Bout a half hour ago."

"How long do you think it'll take?"

"Don't know," said Chuck, "but I expect he'll review all the entries and his notes before he's comfortable with his decision."

"God, I'm dying here." Ray rubbed his hands up and down his twitching legs.

A low conversation buzz grew agitated and started to build as time crawled toward late afternoon. Heightened tension, already guitar string tight, tested everyone's nerves. Finally the camp director and Hunter Plast entered the hall and approached the PA system. Anxious eyes followed every step. A loud shriek of back-feed blasted from the speakers causing every face to wince.

"Everyone, over the past two weeks we've made new friends, learned new sports, and had fun. You worked like mad to hone your programming skills and the results are outstanding. You're an amazing bunch of talent and I want to thank you for making history. This is the very first time ever in the life of Popoti where we haven't had to rush someone to the hospital from either an allergic reaction or an accident caused by some silly bugger playing stupid. I applaud you."

This broke the tension and as expected, foot stomping and cheers rang through the hall. Shoulders relaxed a little and hands unclenched.

"Our councilors, all volunteers from industry, tell me you've set high standards for future camps – both with your sports agility and computer knowledge."

More cheers and table banging accompanied by nods and knowing glances between friends.

"And speaking of high standards, I have to say that the gaming competition was far and away beyond the quality of anything we've seen here in previous years. Now, I know you're all eager to know who won so, I'll turn the mike over to Hunter Plast."

Hunter looked out over the gathering and cleared his throat.

Tracey grabbed Philippa's hand and whispered in her ear. "God, I'm wet-my-pants nervous."

"First let me say, we have no losers here. Each and every team took on a formidable task—the results prove that you rose to meet it. The variety of ideas and the quality of programming were above anything I anticipated. Nobody expected perfection—that's not possible in such short a time, but, I did hope to see creativity and technology applied in a way that demonstrated that you could work as a team, had a handle on computer programming and understood the complexities of gaming." Pause. "You blew me away!"

Applause exploded.

"Each and every entry deserves recognition. But, as in the real world, only one in hundreds of games makes it to the best-seller list. So I had to make very tough choices."

Trophies, lined up across a table at the front of the hall were made out of empty CD cases with Camp Popoti engraved on them and mounted on birch bark logs. They were labeled 'Best Action,' 'Best Storyline,' 'Best Effort,' and 'Best Graphics.' A gold one emblazoned with 'Best Game' stood separate.

Hunter Plast spoke to each and every game. He pointed out their strong points and noted how they could be improved. He praised the overall teamwork and imagination of every game. Campers began to fidget in their seats. There was still no indication which team won—then holding up the coveted trophy, Plast announced "G team is the winner of "Best Graphics".

Tracey was pushed to the front to accept the award accompanied by loud wolf whistles. Mike's team walked away with 'Best Effort'. Continuing in order, the awards were announced until the last one remained on the table.

"Teams, once again, I want to commend you on your dedication and the fantastic results you achieved." Hunter Plast reached for the gold trophy and held it high. "It is my pleasure to invite G team to come forward to accept the Best Game award."

The campers roared and clapped. A few groaned. Hands reached out and slapped the backs of G members as they made their way forward. The team stood in a line, their faces flushed with grins stretched from ear to ear. Hunter Plast talked to each member and shook their hands. Frank, not able to stand still, shifted his weight from one foot to the other and rubbed his sweaty hands down the sides of his navy shorts.

"Eruptus not only had unique graphics but a complete storyline, solvable challenges and great characters. It's my pleasure to congratulate all of you on your accomplishment."

Chuck came forward to join his team. He shook the boy's hands and hugged the girls. Flushed with success, they finally left the hall. Tracey wandered away and with her back to the group punched in numbers on her cell phone. "We won, Pa, we won! You won't believe it but Hunter Past was the judge and we get to go to Silicon Valley to tour GAMEZ."

Philippa grew quiet and motioned Chuck aside. "Do I need a passport to cross the border?"

"No, your driver's license or school picture ID will be enough. We'll send you home with documents outlining all the details. It looks like the trip will be two weeks from now. I'll be going with you." Chuck turned to the group. "Does anyone have a problem getting away?"

"Tracey gets cheated," said Ray turning sharply to Chuck. "She only gets to go from LA to San Fran, that's a bummer."

"Why don't you stay in Canada for the two weeks and fly out with the rest of us?" Philippa's hazel eyes bore into Tracey. "You could be my house guest. I'd love it!"

Tracey quickly punched "redial" and after some back-and-forth, nodded. Both girls, arms wrapped around each other jumped gleefully up and down.

"Hey, Flip," asked Mark with a mischievous smirk, "can I stay with you too?"

The following morning, luggage was strewn along the front of the mess hall in semi-organized piles. Campers hugged, choked back tears and promised to stay in touch. Mike waved at his dad when he saw the SUV pull in. He motioned him to the stack where he, Philippa and Tracey had stashed their gear.

Mark held Philippa close reluctant to let her go. He kissed her softly and whispered in her ear, "in two weeks then."

Philippa had phoned and warned Florry to prepare for company.

****

The guest room furniture and new bedding Helen had ordered arrived on schedule. A mahogany Shaker-style suite with a queen-sized bed was tastefully decorated with a counterpane in shades of green accented with raspberry tones. Maroon mini blinds provided privacy and heavy apple green drapes puddled to the floor. A forty-two inch TV dominated the new entertainment center.

Florry had already scrubbed every corner of the room except one small storage closet. Everything had been removed from it but somehow she had not gotten around to washing it. Now she carried a bucket and rags from the bathroom to the bedroom. After wiping down the walls and shelves she stood on tiptoes to reach the top shelf. Not quite tall enough, she retrieved the two-step ladder from the kitchen and returned to finish the job. Briskly, she attacked the shelf and hit something wedged in the back. Reaching her arm in as far as she could, she caught the edge of a package, wiggled it but couldn't dislodge it. It simply wouldn't budge. Stepping up one more rung on the ladder, Florry got a good grip on the edge of the wrapper and with determined force she yanked it loose.

It was a sealed padded brown envelope. Florry hesitated to open it, but shook her head knowing it was her job to sort though

Patrick and Elaine's effects so went ahead anyway. If there was a question, she'd call Helen. After getting down from the ladder, she dropped the cleaning rag into the bucket and rubbed her damp hands on the seat of her faded jeans. A sigh escaped as she plopped into the upholstered comfy chair. She tore open the package and pulled out its contents. Her breath caught. She paled, gasped and clutched the contents to her chest.

Chapter 10

July 29, 1985

Patrick and Elaine pulled into Jasper, Alberta, as the setting sun, a majestic golden globe lay cradled between mountain tops. Jagged peaks punctured the soft hues of fading light and the Miette River caught the glow undulating it like a ribbon dancing from shore to shore. Scruff timberline trees ended abruptly before the mountains rose boldly like Atlas holding up the sky. Jasper lay nestled serenely amid the forests of Jasper national Park and boasted only one main industry, tourism.

Entering the town on Connaught Drive Patrick eased the van into a parking space in front of the Visitors Center and came to a stop. Papers in hand, he and Elaine went in search of Mountain Adventures.

A lonesome cowboy type, dressed in a plaid shirt and jeans, no doubt geared up to appeal to tourists, greeted them and pointed them in the direction of Patricia Circle. They drove past the address several times before they realized that a small, white frame house was their destination. Three buzzers at the door, were labeled "Jasper Dry Cleaning", "The Copy Centre" and "Mountain Adventures." "She'll be Comin' Round The Mountain" rang out when Elaine pressed the button.

"Pure western hokey," grimaced Elaine.

Patrick nodded; a big foolish grin on his face. "Yep, bet they come to the door in spurs."

The door opened and a small woman in a jean skirt and a

simple pink blouse ran her hand down a flowered apron and smiled at them. "I'll bet you're Elaine and Patrick. Please come in. I'm Vincent's mother. We've been expecting you. Vince will be right with you, he's on the phone.

Patrick and Elaine were lead to a large open room that smelled of dust and wet dog. A stuffed elk's head watched them from above a scarred log mantelpiece straddling a massive fireplace. Hunting scene fabric themed the over-stuffed furniture and invited them to sit. As soon as they settled, a long-eared basset hound meandered over to sniff them before he offered his rump for a good scratch.

Within minutes, they heard footsteps and a tidy small man in his early 50's entered the room with brisk short steps. His eyes magnified through bottle-glass spectacles peered at the new arrivals. A small bony hand reached out to grasp Patrick's freckled one.

"Vincent Price—"

"Really?"

"No, not that one, have to answer to that all the time—just call me Vince. I see you met our furry greeter, Sadie, sure hope she wasn't a nuisance."

"No, she made us feel welcome."

"Sure am glad you made it. I arranged rooms for you over to the ranch and if you're ready, I'll hitch a ride and show you the way." Vince spoke in a deep voice that seemed to come from the wrong body. He squinted and rubbed his palms together as he spoke. "The ranch's only fifteen minutes up the valley."

Patrick suppressed a giggle as he glanced at Elaine. Not the cowboy image they had imagined; this short man looked more like a desk clerk from a B movie. The ride to the ranch was filled with Vince's bass voice recounting expedition mishaps. Elaine was quickly becoming apprehensive about the whole idea of a trek through mountainous terrain with this odd little man.

They rounded a hillock and spread out before them was an impressive horse ranch. The timber-frame main house loomed in the foreground. A deep pitched roof sloped well beyond an imposing front porch, designed to carry a snow load in the winter and ensure cool shade in the summer. Festive gardens bordered the walkway and splashes of brilliant colour continued around all the buildings. Timber barns topped with silver metal roofs towered beside corrals where horses of all shades hung their necks over the railings watching the Dodge Caravan as it approached. To the extreme left two tidy cottages stood facing Pyramid Mountain.

"There's a meet-and-greet planned for six o'clock. That gives you nearly an hour to settle in." The deep western accent was all business. "The other two couples arrived earlier and I think they're belly-up to the bar. That's over at the lodge, the main house, we call it the lodge. First drink's on the house—anything after that goes on your tab—turn right, into this cabin, the one with the yellow pansies."

Patrick turned the wheel and coasted to a stop.

"The Fosters' are in the one next to you, purple pansies, and the Notzias' are staying at the lodge." Vince rattled on as he stepped down from the van careful where he set his sparkling white runners, skittered up the walkway and opened the door. He handed Patrick the key and gave them a quick tour of the cabin. "See you up at the lodge." He waved as he set off across the lawn.

"This is mighty cozy," said Elaine, feigning western lingo. She rolled her suitcase to the bedroom and commandeered the stall for a hot shower. Patrick took advantage of the time to shave away his afternoon stubble, load his camera and check the backpacks to make sure everything was ready for morning. Refreshed and changed, Elaine, joined Patrick. "We've time for that drink on the house before the meet-and-greet." She gave Patrick a quick peck on the cheek and headed out the door. He was quick to follow.

Entering into an impressive open hallway they heard laughter from a room to the left that suggested they head in that direction. Bare log walls and heavy beams created a warm club-room atmosphere. Directly ahead, a wall of windows framed the mountain. Over-stuffed brown leather furniture, grouped around a large stone fireplace, drew them forward. Patrick did an about-face when over his shoulder he was beckoned by a rustic, well-stocked bar made from grayed western cedar.

Stunned by the beauty of the woman working the bar, he almost forgot his thirst and stared unabashed. Unpainted bronzed skin glowed, highlighting sharp cheek bones that accented a face sculpted to perfection. Sleek black hair hung to her waist and shot blue glints as she moved beneath the light. Looking up, her black eyes smiled in greeting.

"Hey, you must be the Snellings. Welcome. Meet the Fosters and the Notzias."

Patrick nodded to shapes in the room.

"What can I get you? I'm Shelly Price, by the way, Vince's wife."

Vince was not what they had expected now Shelly was certainly not who they expected him to have married.

"Two chilled dark beers would be great," answered Elaine from mid room.

A tall, rotund man with ruddy features and graying hair, rose from one of the sofas and approached Patrick with his hand outstretched. "Dan Foster; this is Ami, my wife." He said pointing to a head that peered above the cushions. "This here's Clyde and Edith Notzia from Toronto" he indicated to the shapes that rose from the couch. "Ami and I are from Saanach, BC."

Hands were extended all around. Shelly handed Patrick and Elaine chilled glasses of local micro-brewed beer. The smell of sweet malt made Patrick lick his lips as he clinked glasses all around in a traditional toast of greeting, then downed the cool drink in one draught. Conversation flowed easily until a signal from Shelly indicated that everyone take a seat.

Vince arrived, clipboard in hand. Standing, back to the fireplace, he officially welcomed everyone. Activities of the three days on the trail were quickly dispensed and he gave them an indication of what they would be seeing and doing.

"Most of the trail's above the tree line offering fantastic views. Make sure you've got lots of film for your cameras. If you're short see Shelly we always keep a supply. On a clear day you can see Mount Robson. You'll be travelling up the The Notch, a steep, challenging slope, to reach Amber Mountain summit ridge. There's a good chance you'll see marmots, big horn sheep, mountain caribou, white-tailed ptarmigan, any number of critters. We'll continue on up Maligne Canyon and camp the first night at Berg Lake."

"Will you be our guide?" Elaine asked cautiously hoping not.

"Naw. We've got real cowboys for that job. I'm more the accountant type."

Smiling heads nodded in approval.

"The boys 'll've gone ahead to set up camp so you folks can

just enjoy the ride and food," he continued. "Day two, you'll be heading along the park's northern boundary to Moose Horn Lake. You'll do 6 hours a day for three days in a row. That'll be plenty. You city slickers will be begging to get off you butts well before quitting time."

A few chuckles rippled through the room.

"The weather looks promising but you need to know that freak storms can move in unexpectedly, that's why, I've asked you to pack rain gear. Anyway, I'm happy to see you've all met. The rest of the gab, I'll save for Harv."

Furrowed brows questioned Vince.

"Tomorrow morning, you'll meet him; he's your trail master. He'll introduce you to your mounts, give you a rundown on horse culture and be your guide. Shelly and I'll meet you at 'camp' at the end of each day—once again, welcome, and happy trails."

Shelly handed Vince a short beer, that he threw back in a quick toss, then indicated that the group move to the dining room. A long harvest table laden with overflowing bowls and platters enticed the guests to scramble for seats. Without ceremony, the ravenous bunch reached eagerly for the offerings.

"I'd no idea I was starving until I stepped in here." Elaine grabbed the closest bowl to her and started filling her plate.

Heaped dishes passed from one to the other as did the conversation. Mountains of mashed potatoes, mounds of shaved beef, and bowls of steaming vegetables were sloshed with savory gravy. After dinner everyone returned to the lounge and raised their glasses in anticipation of a successful trail riding experience. Stuffed with hearty food and sleepy from chilled beer, the trail riders left the lodge to get a good night's sleep before an early morning start.

Elaine, for the first in a very long time, fell into a deep dreamless sleep. She was nudged awake at morning light by a smiling Patrick.

"This country air's good for you." Patrick lifted the duvet and eased in beside Elaine.

"Hey! Don't let that cold air in here," shrilled Elaine.

"Well let's see about warming you up then." Lifting Elaine to sitting position he handed her a steaming cup of black coffee.

"Mmmm, so good. What a perfect start to a day." Elaine rubbed sleep from her eyes and gave Patrick a kiss on the forehead. "Guess we have to soon mosey on over to the big house."

"I think we have enough time for a little private moseying before that."

When they arrived at the lodge, Shelly encouraged everyone to "load up" from the selection of steaming trays spread across a large antique oak server. Patrick indeed did load up with pancakes, bacon, sausages, hash brown potatoes, poured syrup over the whole plate and grabbing an orange juice and sat to enjoy every morsel. Elaine picked a blueberry muffin and a bowl of fruit.

Their attention was soon drawn to a new person in the doorway. Harv sauntered in all smiles.

Patrick pinched Elaine and whispered in her ear. "Spurs! Now, here's our cowboy, bowed legs and all."

Harv indeed, portrayed everything one would expect a man of the west to be. His faded denim shirt was tucked into jeans that clung to long slim legs. Dusty cowboy boots with ornate designs burned into them and spurs at the heels jangled as he walked. He even clutched a soiled Stetson by the brim with both hands. Harv placed his hat on the back of a chair and grabbed a plate. One expected a 'howdy', but instead with a thick Scottish burr he introduced himself. The place broke into uproarious laughter.

"I dinna know why everyone does that!" He said impishly as he straddled a chair and set his heaping plate on the table. "You folks all rrready to hit the trrrail? You dinna want to keep eatin' too much to bow your horses back, do you?"

Everyone chuckled and instantly knew they were going to enjoy the company of this ruddy Scotsman.

After breakfast they gathered at the barn as instructed. Six horses hitched to the railing snorted in anticipation. Harv galloped toward them, riding high on a gleaming chestnut mare. His tourist riders stood in a group to one side with admiring looks. This is what they had signed on for, a real western experience.

"Ye'll be saddlin-up their own steed. I want you t' talk to 'em and begin the bondin' necessary between rider and horse." As he spoke he guided each person to a specific horse and introduced the animal.

Elaine met Flick, a handsome gelded bay. He immediately nuzzled her when she blew softly on his nose. Running her hands along his neck she cupped his ears. Without fear she moved her hand along Flick's side, rubbed his flanks and eased around his hind quarters making sure she maintained body contact with her hand until she circumvented the rear end. By the time she returned to Flick's head, horse and rider had established a mutual trust. Harv nodded in appreciation at least he had one person who knew horses.

Patiently, the animals allowed the saddles to be slung on and cinched by inexperienced hands. He then came along and smacked the horses' under bellies and tightened the belts. "They fill their gut with air so ye canna get 'em tight—just give 'em a smack and they let the air go." Harv tested each one then gave the rider instructions on how to put their left leg in the stirrup and lift the right one over the saddle. Elaine mounted without assistance then sat back to watch Harv help Patrick swing up. It took several attempts and finally Harv warned Patrick he was going to give him a heave.

"Just put your foot in my hands."

A surprised Patrick landed in the saddle. Harv did a last minute check of the stirrups, rode to the front of the line and signaled them forward to the hills.

The grey dawn gave way to brilliant sunshine but the mountain was shrouded in a low thin vapour cloud. The riders could not see the tops of even the lowest trees. Curious ravens circled overhead alerting wildlife in the area of the intrusion. Riders followed behind each other silently savouring the morning, smelling the dank earth, and sensing the rhythm of their mounts. Several rabbits scurried into tall grass bordering the trail. Two Stellar Jays flew from tree to tree following the horses and breaking the silence by screeching warnings to all ears within hearing range. The riders rode for nearly two hours steadily uphill before the mist lifted.

Elaine leaned over to Patrick who just started to relax on his steed and no longer held his reins tight and high. Patrick's horse, Cole, fittingly named, purposely misspelled, sauntered at a steady pace. His gleaming black coat ended at a single white legging that, when he walked, created a peculiar optical illusion giving the appearance he had only three legs.

"Paddy, look behind."

Patrick gave Elaine a dubious glance. He had become

comfortable with sitting on Cole and looking straight ahead, but turning to look back—he had his doubts. Holding tight to the saddle horn with one hand and the other on the back he slowly eased around.

At just that moment, Harv told everyone to stop. They had been gradually climbing along a trail bordered in tall pine. Now they had reached an elevation above the lower trees. The view over the valley spread out like an intricate tapestry for miles. The silence was audible.

"Damn." Clyde slapped his upper arm. "Mosquito took a chunk out of me."

"Yessir, we grow 'em mighty big in the west. Hungrrry little buggers. You'll wanta slather on that rrrepellent stuff," Harv advised. "We'll take a little rrrest at the edge of this clearrring comin' up. Ye'll see two wee trails off to the side, one for the lassies and the other the laddies."

The exercise of dismounting appeared as comical as getting on the horses. Elaine helped Patrick, giggling as she braced her shoulder against him. Staggering and off center, the boys headed into the bush walking with very stiff legs. Elaine and the girls headed down the other path.

"Oh my God!" She exclaimed upon return. "The wind blows right up your arse!"

"Ey, it's a wee bit of an experrrience." Harv laughed. "The thrones are 'open pit'. That means they run down a crevice inside the mountain, howeverrr the wind does rush up a bit."

Everyone chuckled. Granola bars and steaming hot coffee were distributed all around. Nobody sat. They strolled, chatted and munched. At Harv's command they mounted their now familiar and trusty steeds and headed out.

The trees thinned as they picked their way along a rocky path. Conversation was at a minimum. Everyone was just content to hear the soft tread of horse hooves on fir needles. Shortly before noon, Harv halted and explained that they would break for lunch around the next bend. Once again, the white pine and spruce parted so the riders had a view of the Athabaska River stretched below them, a long ribbon of bluish green. The edge of a glacier peeked through the mountains. Cameras clicked and exclamations abounded.

"I'm already dealing with visual overload and we're still on our first morning out," announced Elaine. She wandered away from the group and settled on a log overlooking the valley. Patrick joined her.

"I feel Roger with me," whispered Elaine, "and it's a good feeling. Thank you Paddy, you always know to do the right thing. This trip is such a healing experience. How could one not be happy? Look at that amazing sight." She pointed down the valley.

The call of a bell from the clearing rang and rang.

Harv yelled. "Chow time."

Everyone was more than ready for the feast of baked brown beans, Kaiser rolls and butter tarts washed down with strong coffee. The horses grazed close by, blowing greetings to each other. Elaine smiled. "Horse gossip," she nudged Patrick's arm and pointed.

Glossy black ravens cruised the perimeters of the camp waiting for the riders to leave so they could clean up any scraps. The horses were only on the trail again for another couple of hours when groans of discomfort were expressed by Dan and Patrick.

"My balls are pounded to smithereens."

"God, my back's broken!"

Harv laughed and assured the group they were near the end-of-day camp sight. Elaine sat tall and smiled at the others. Trail riding was one of her passions and why they had chosen this adventure. She rode often when she and Patrick spent weekends in Algonquin Park but Patrick always declined and used that time to wander off with his camera. He was paying for it now.

The crew had been there and set up camp. Vince and Shelly greeted them with mugs of cold beer.

"Perfect," uttered Don. "Did you two bring all this up here?"

"No," laughed Shelly, "we have a crew who do this but they headed on back, as we will. We just like to greet you at day's end. We cheat. There's a road up the other side."

"Ay, they like their four wheelers to get here and their wee feather beds at the ranch to return to." Harv explained. "They're not the roughing it type."

Harv designated duties to each rider and Patrick was amazed that within minutes, a table set with a full-course meal, invited the riders to a hardy feast. Forgetting his sore rump he dug in and washed everything down with more malty cold beer. Harv warned everyone to gather up all scraps and deposit everything, dirty dishes and all in a large steel box.

"Dinna wanta invite those pesky bears to dinerrr."

"Bears!" Ami Foster cried out in alarm. "There are bears here?"

"Oh, aye, and we have to honuh the fact that they were here first and we'rrre the intrrruders," Harv answered. "But nevu you mind, they'rrre not hungrrry this time of year – lots of fish and food available in the wild. But they do like a trrreat every now and again and will rrrip a camp to pieces of they smell people food. That's why we take extreme caution."

Once the chores were finished, Harv built a campfire. Elaine and Patrick walked to the edge of the clearing and sat on an outcropping. The night sky was black velvet studded with star diamonds. They sat, Patrick with his arm around Elaine's shoulder, quietly—each lost in their own thoughts. Soft chords from a guitar drifted to them soon joined by a sweet lilting voice followed by others. Patrick and Elaine wandered back to the fire. Little time was spent around the campfire because the weary riders simply wanted to crawl into their sleeping bags and sleep. Elaine, though, felt the opposite. Wide awake and inspired by the wilderness surrounding them she took Patrick's hand and returned to the outcropping. A groaning Patrick, dragging a blanket, staggered to an open space in the trees. Spreading the blanket they lay down and tried to outdo each other by star naming.

"Paddy, I'm such a pill to live with. Sorry I get so melancholy and introspective. I struggle and try to control those dark moments. But here, for the first time in a very long time, I'm beginning to feel a little lighter, less depressed."

Patrick, occupied swatting mosquitoes, barely heard her. Getting into deep discussions late at night was not what he wanted to deal with right now. He knew Elaine could drag on for hours. He wanted to return to their tent and talk Elaine into giving him a massage.

"Elaine, sweetheart, my back hurts, the ground's hard, my ass hurts and I just want t' go to sleep before these damn critters eat me alive." With that Patrick jumped up and pulled Elaine to her feet and pushed her gently to their tent. They changed and slipped into their sleeping bag.

"The air's so still. I just can't settle." Elaine punched her pillow and shifted her legs.

"Shush woman. Your man must sleep."

Sleep did come finally, for both of them.

"Paddy!" Elaine's scream jolted Patrick upright. "What's that? Can you hear it?"

Screeching winds and loud thunder set Patrick scrambling. He grabbed a flashlight and saw the sides of the tent bellow and collapse. Cautiously he peered outside into the black where sounds of cracking trees and howling gusts were all around. Quickly he closed the flap to avoid being pummeled by flying debris and soil. Everything that wasn't secure was airborne. He and Elaine had seen many storms in the wilderness of Algonquin Park but nothing like this. A flashlight beam slid along the side of the tent.

Harv, struggling against the blow checked the tethers and called into each tent. "Stay put. We've got a wee bit of unsettled weather out here. Not to worrry, it will blow itself out in a bit."

"A wee bit unsettled! Shit, it is crazy out there," Patrick screamed over the wind.

Dan and Ami Foster's tent lifted and blew away. They scrambled to catch their personal belongings that were flying everywhere. Harv rushed to their side and helped them gather the loose items before they disappeared into the forest. The Fosters moved in with Patrick and Elaine whose tent had been carefully staked nestled against a rise, it was a solid testament to their camping experience. At that moment a sound like a cannon being fired indicated a tree had given up its hold on life and split in two.

First they spoke in hushed tones as if to appease the storm gods but found they had to shout to be heard even in such close quarters. The screaming winds finally stopped followed by a deadly silence. Then the thunder gods spoke again to announce torrential rains. It teemed for the rest of the night.

At dawn, a sleepless Harv wandered through the sodden camp and along the trail. He stayed up all night with the horses calming them during the storm. Now he was evaluating the damage. There was no way they could continue. The trails were littered with debris and fallen trees. He reversed and scouted back the way they had come. It was the same story.

"Folks. We've a wee bit of trrrouble. We canna leave here, the paths'rrre all buggerrred. I dinna know what kind of storm that was but it created one hell of a mess. Not ta worry, Vince'll get the rrrangers busy and come to our rrrescue. In the meantime we should gather the bits that have flown about and set them to drrry. Patrick, could you help Dan and me, gatherrr up that tent that broke loose. I found it wrrrapped around a fallen trrree."

Harv and Patrick lifted the weight of the tree that was pinning the tent under it. Dan tugged with all his might and could not budge the canvas. Planting his feet he braced himself to give one big pull while at the same time Harv hoisted the tree a little higher. The canvas released and Dan hurled backward landing smack against a jagged branch. Blood oozed down his neck. Harv rushed to his side and assessed the gash on Dan's neck.

"You'rrre one lucky son-of-a-gun. You've a nasty gash but it could be a lot worrrse. Just sit therrre and I'll get the medical kit." Harv turned to Patrick and asked him to stay with Dan.

"You mentioned you were from Saanach." Patrick, holding bunched up tissue to the cut, tried to distract Dan with conversation. "Did you ever know any Ewers? Elaine's mother, Shirley was a Ewer, from Saanach."

"Shirley Ewer. No, *I* didn't, but as I recall, my uncle Dan dated a Shirley Ewer. I'm named after him. Sad story though. He was killed in an avalanche just shortly after his eighteenth birthday. Rumour has it that because of his death, Shirley had a nervous breakdown and was sent to an institution for nearly a year."

Patrick began to piece this information together with what he already knew. More than likely this Uncle Dan was the father of Shirley's baby. His tragic death prevented any marriage so to hide the pregnancy a nervous breakdown was a clever cover story. Patrick was anxious to learn more when they were in Victoria.

Harv dressed the wound and declared Dan fit for adventure. He suggested a fishing excursion. Patrick leapt at this suggestion. Elaine offered to stay back and wait for Vince and the rangers. Ami and Edith stayed as well. Ami launched into stories about her three children and Edith joined in with comparative yarns about her two.

"Jaime is such a wee darling, He's just being potty trained and he's so cute doing big grunts until his face turns red." Ami demonstrated by puffing her cheeks and holding her breath.

Edith reached for her backpack and produced a small album full of family pictures.

"How many children do you and Patrick have?" Edith passed the album to Elaine who indicated zero with her thumb and forefinger. "Oh, is that by choice?"

Elaine shook her head then excused herself to fiddle with her saddle. She imagined accusatory whisperings behind her.

It was late afternoon before the sound of chain saws and

motors reached them. Vince climbed over a fallen tree and barged into the camp.

"Boy, I'm glad to see you gals. Where are the fellows? Oh, here they come, been fishing I see."

Harv and the boys waved and Patrick held high a generous catch. As they packed up, Vince explained that tornados, winds and floods throughout the area had caused severe loss and damage in forty municipalities. The City of Edmonton and Strathcona County were at a complete halt.

"So far there've been reports of fifteen deaths and they expect that to rise. Phones're out and power lines're down through most of the region. I was just lucky to get to the ranger station early."

Harv nodded in agreement.

"It's a good thing it's your first night and you were not too far away. The lower part of the road wasn't damaged. It is just the last four miles or so that needed to be cleared. Thank God I was able to get this crew right away. Anyway folks, Mother Nature scuppered your plans for the remainder of your trek."

Groans of disappointment passed from one to the other.

"We've made some arrangements for you back at the ranch. Shelly's planning a gourmet dinner and some of our local talent is coming over this evening for some good old fiddle playing."

Back at the lodge sitting around the lounge nursing frosty glasses, the guests recounted their adventure.

"Okay, I know for sure my heart's in good shape because I didn't have an attack when I stepped out of the Johnny hut to come face to face with that elk buck. Holy cow, I was lucky it was after my business!" Clyde recounted.

"I sure hope the elk's heart was in good shape because the yell you let out was loud enough to trip an avalanche!"

"That small-mouthed bass was a challenge to land, but boy, was he a beaut!"

"And I got incredible pictures of stellar jays and a fox toying with a squirrel he caught."

"How about the wild flowers?" Elaine asked. "I was surprised that such tiny delicate flowers bloomed in this rugged environment."

"That's one of the reasons they're tiny," offered Vince. "I just want to thank you all for being so flexible—you're a great group and I hope you come back again. The next time's on us."

All three couples opted to stay at the ranch for the remaining two days and help the crews clear the brush and deliver food and water to the locals. Shelly and Vince served another great meal including the "catch" and the entertainment made the fearful adventure seem far behind. During the following days everyone helped the community by delivering food Shelly and the crew prepared. The men joined the ranch hands to help clear the debris. Before their stay ended, the grounds were almost back to normal and the roads were open.

"Well, Vince, Shelly, it was sure different than we planned but life and disasters happen." Patrick shook Vince's hand as they stood beside the packed van ready to leave. "We had, in spite of the weather, an amazing experience and will remember it forever."

Waving vigorously, Patrick eased out of the driveway and he and Elaine watched the ranch disappear in the rear-view mirror as they resumed their trip west.

Vince yelled after the departing van. "Be sure to get gas!"

"Funny thing to say. I wonder what he meant," said Elaine.

Chapter 11

Using the map spread across Elaine's lap, the adventurous couple headed for the Columbia Ice Fields Parkway that skirted the shoulder of the Great Divide.

"The parkway follows the eastern range of the Canadian Rockies. There are numerous points of interest including three major rivers and two waterfalls noted in the brochures," Elaine said pouring over them.

They stopped at every pull-off, parked and explored designated sites of Western Canada's unforgettable wilderness. Mountain peaks pierced billowing clouds, rivers rushed through gorges and majestic pines towering above them scented the air. Patrick, with a freshly loaded camera, took shot after shot. Elaine gathered discarded refuse.

"Sweetheart, I have a serious problem. These rushing waters have a disastrous effect on my bladder and from the number of tourists roving about I can't simply duck behind a tree." Elaine laughed at Patrick as he shouted over a roaring waterfall they had stopped to admire. Around the next bend they were relieved to see Johnny huts in the trees.

On the road again the morning disappeared. "Shelly packed a lunch. Do you want to eat while driving or find a picnic table?" Elaine was holding up a brown paper bag.

They pulled into a laneway and ventured only a few hundred yards before they found a flat rock beside a fast flowing creek. As soon as they opened the package the ever pesky Stellar jays called out begging for small favours. Respectful of the signs warning people to take their garbage with them, Elaine made one small concession. "Here you noisy birds" She cast bread crumbs about and was rewarded as the jays quickly flew in accompanied by several sparrows. They scurried about collecting the crumbs, fending off their own as they flew to nearby branches. The travelers dangled their feet in the cool waters as they washed down the lunch of ham and cheese wedged between thick slices of home-made brown bread with iced tea. It took some effort to drag their comfortable selves back to the van and return to the road.

Mid afternoon, they reached the Columbia Ice Fields and taking care to avoid wandering tourists, that presumed the road was for their exclusive use, parked the van. After queuing up for a half hour they climbed aboard a specially designed Brewster Ice Explorer Snocoach.

Patrick examined the coach with interest. "This buggy's neat. Did you notice the tires? They're as tall as me and half a car wide."

An interpreter explained the significance of the ice field as they drove up the Athabaska Glacier. The wide tires gripped the frozen surface and crossed the ice slowly and steadily. High onto the glacier the snocoach stopped and everyone disembarked.

"Explore the field but be careful where you walk and stay well back from the crevasses." The guide pointed out a few hazards and made a few suggestions. "Do not drop any garbage or cigarettes."

Elaine smiled her approval. She stepped away from the vehicle feeling the very beginning of life that lay frozen in layers and layers of blue ice. Her warm breath crystallized and was sucked away by a wisp of a breeze. She wandered some distance from the bus to reflect and absorb the intensity of this wondrous place. Patrick spotted a mountain goat on a high cleft watching the tourists. He snapped his picture. "He's definitely posing," Patrick informed everyone as he pointed aloft; with his zoom lens he captured several photos.

"Elaine, comm'on babe, there's a bus 'a leaving." Patrick approached the lone figure standing very still near the sharp edge of a chasm. His heart gripped. He knew Elaine could slip in and out of depression in an instant. Was she contemplating suicide?

He eased next to Elaine and relaxed when he noted her face revealing nothing but sheer pleasure. She clutched his sleeve and bent over to take one last look down the endlessly deep crevasse walled in brilliant turquoise ice.

"Oh, Paddy, this is such a spiritual place. I felt as if I could speak directly to Roger – I did. I wish we could stay longer." She had no choice but to follow at Patrick's insistence to the snocoach.

"Wait Elaine, I want to get a picture of you beside the coach." He carefully directed her to stand beside the tires to create a comparative to their size. She looked a miniature doll next to them.

Back in the van, they headed south with Mount Victoria, a beacon in the distance.

"Elaine, honey, we might just have a small problem." Patrick pointed to the gas gauge hovering at 'empty'. "I think I know now why Vince mentioned getting gas."

"Paddy, I haven't seen a single station the entire day. There must be some, this is a major highway. Oh, what if there isn't? What will we do?"

"Well, we can coast down the hills, but going up's going to be a challenge. Just keep your fingers crossed for a gas station."

The scenery forgotten, they anxiously searched the road ahead.

"I think we're getting close to Lake Louise, if only we can make it." The van sputtered as it licked the last of its fuel from the bottom of the tank. "Well there you go. We're in for it." Patrick glided to a stop and got out on the side of the road waving frantically to an approaching half-ton truck. The driver pulled over and rolled down his window.

"It seems we have a little problem—ran out of gas. Would you mind sending a service vehicle from the first station along the road?" The obliging motorist tipped his peaked cap and promised to send help. The better part of an hour passed before a ranger's vehicle slid to a stop beside the van.

"Get at least two of you a day," the ranger taunted as he poured the contents of a jerry-can into the gas tank. Slightly humbled and definitely embarrassed, Patrick asked how much he owed.

"Aw, we just rack this up to tourist assistance, no charge. You all have a good trip."

"Well, that was western hospitality at its best." Patrick watched as the jeep drove off. He settled into the driver's seat of the van, started it and put it in gear. They didn't find a service station anywhere along the highway.

The next hour more than made up for their delay as Canada's finest scenery continued to unfold before them. Suddenly, the road veered to the right winding through sheer walls of rock, then, without warning Lake Louise filled the windshield. True to all the tourism promotions the lake reflected the mountain, a mirror image that reached as far below as above. No picture could ever capture the surge of emotion that flooded over Elaine. She wiped angrily at tears rolling down her cheeks.

"Damn tears are blurring my vision. Oh, Paddy, it's so incredibly beautiful?"

Patrick slowed the van and pulled over to the side of the road. He reached for Elaine and they clung together until mountain shadows crept across the water and the radiant red sun dropped quickly behind the mountains.

Early the next day, Patrick left the motel early, filled the gas tank and bought two coffees. He waved and called a cheery "good morning" when a sleep tossed Elaine wandered out of the door. Her head was lowered, shoulders slumped forward and she was clutching her upper arms tightly. "Not good," he muttered to himself as he noted her body language and turned with an overly cheery smile.

"Sleep well sweetheart?" He asked.

"Oh, Paddy, I'm such a disappointment to you." Elaine's face was tear-streaked and she wiped her nose with the back of her hand. "I'm a failure. Why can't I give you a baby and a happy home? You do everything for me, plan wonderful trips, look after me and I can't even give you…"

"I'm the happiest man alive," Patrick cut in. "I don't need a baby, you are my sole *raison d'etre*. Now let's get this coffee into you then with a hot shower you'll be ready for the road."

Patrick eased Elaine into the bathroom with lots of reassurance and light kisses and left her soaking under a hot shower. Every time Elaine succumbed to these bouts of depression he felt gall rising in his throat and feared for her life.

Time and time again they had visited fertility clinics that had been recommended. They had checked adoption possibilities. It was apparent that Elaine would never conceive and Patrick's age disqualified them from adopting an infant, and it was a baby that

Elaine wanted. Patrick, too, would have liked a child but was more concerned about Elaine's black moods becoming increasingly dangerous to her mental health. Every month before her period started, she hung on to a glimmer of hope only to be devastated when the flow started.

Water pelted Elaine's back. "Elaine, honey," She could hear her mother's voice buzzing in her head. "This is one of the most important days of your life. Your body has come of age. Now you can make babies." Shirley kissed and hugged Elaine exclaiming over and over again how wonderful it was, she was now a woman. Elaine, barely 14-years old, lay twisted in cramps, a hot water bottle on her stomach and a clumsy pad wadded between her legs. As far as she was concerned, it had been the most miserable day of her life.

The hot water turned cool. She stepped out of the shower and dressed for the day. Her movements were slow, her mood low. After a cup of strong black coffee she got dressed and followed Patrick to the vehicle.

Patrick pointed out all the sights as the highway continued to pass scenic wonders but Elaine slumped against the passenger door still miserable. She had wakened to hear her mother's voice telling her over and over again that women were put on earth to bring babies into the world. Shirley repeatedly lectured Elaine that she could never be a complete woman until she had fulfilled God's will and had children. Once again Elaine heard those words "your worth as a woman will be judged by the children you bring into this world." She could not shake off her despair no matter how many soothing words Patrick offered. She stayed curled into a ball against the passenger door. A mound of damp tissues lay on the floor.

"Elaine, sweetheart, you know it is not you who's to blame. It's simply our lot in life. When we get home, maybe a puppy will help."

He was not prepared for the vicious attack. Elaine launched herself at Patrick, raking her fingernails down his cheek. He managed to hold her off as he eased off the gas and got the van to the side of the road. He grabbed Elaine firmly by the wrists.

"For God's sake, Elaine! Do you want to get us killed?"

"That would be better than this. What's the use of us living when we don't have children? No puppy or cat or any other creature can replace our very own baby. I don't want to go on living without a family."

Alarmed, Patrick reached for Elaine. Never had she expressed this intensity of desperation. He realized that if she didn't improve he would need to get professional help as soon as they got back to Ottawa. He dreaded facing the possibility that this might be the case but her agitated behavior was definitely pointing in that direction. Finally, he got Elaine calmed down and somewhat settled before he continued driving.

They pulled into a motel near the foot of the mountains and after some coaxing Patrick convinced Elaine to go on an exploration hike. Elaine's despondent mood soon turned into one of ranting. She picked up a discarded beer bottle beside a patch of wild lupines and added it to a nearly full bag of garbage she had collected in a half hour. Given a reason, her moods often swung from a depressed state to one of anger then calm.

"How do responsible human beings justify discarding their trash wherever it suits them? They're destroying pristine wilderness. How can we teach them to take responsibility for this planet?"

"You are trying. You make every effort to speak out against it. You advocate and through your art make strong public statements. Your work does educate people."

Elaine's work had yet to reach the audience she strove to engage. "I doubt it. Not enough people see it and I am not well recognized. If only the corporate sector would see how their products are littering the countryside, it's a disgrace."

"Hopefully, the Victoria show will present an opportunity." Patrick took the garbage bag from Elaine and threw it in the back of the van to be deposited in the nearest receptacle.

Elaine, still angry, launched into a two hour rant of how politicians, large corporations and the public in general had no idea the negative impact packaging had on the environment.

"More and more conscientious advocates are appealing to governments and corporations. I've invited several, based in British Columbia, to view my exhibition. But I've no idea if they will come." Elaine hoped to align herself with them so together they would present a strong voice.

The smooth ferry ride from Vancouver to the island calmed Elaine and her spirits lifted. The wind grabbed and slapped strands of red hair against her cheeks. She clutched her royal purple windbreaker tight as she leaned on the stern's railing and breathed in the moist air. The ferry's wake faded away to the mainland. Elaine thought about the show in Victorian and knew it could be a turning point in her career.

****

As soon as booth's display was organized to Elaine's satisfaction, Patrick left the building to meet with Lisa Hopper, the researcher that Don Evans had contacted. Her office was within walking distance from the conference centre.

"Mr. Snelling, I'm so pleased you made it."

"Patrick, please."

"Have a seat. Was your trip west okay?"

"It has been wonderful, thanks—amazing scenery and great weather for the most part. I'm dying to know if you found anything further about Shirley Ewing."

"Yes, I have, but, before we get into that, Don Evans sent along a letter that was forwarded to him."

Patrick had arranged with Don Evans to receive their mail and forward anything he felt important. Patrick noted the India postmark and knew it was from his sister Helen. He would read it later, but first he wanted to know what Lisa Hopper had discovered.

"Indeed, Shirley Ewing had a baby. She went to Vancouver and was admitted to a home for single mothers. She is listed as the birth mother, but no name for the father."

"Miss Hopper..."

"Lisa, let's keep this on a first name basis."

"Lisa, I think I inadvertently discovered who the father was and the reason she gave up the baby." Patrick relayed the story about Dan's uncle.

"Oh, that's unfortunate. She did put the baby, a little girl, up for adoption and a family by the name of Vatars adopted her."

"What happened to them? Do you know? Are they still in British Columbia?"

"No, as a matter-of-fact, they moved to Belleville, Ontario. They called their little girl Florenzia. I understand they are of Slavic background. Florenzia left school and moved away when she was quite young. She didn't finish high school. I lost all trace of her from there. I'm sorry."

"No, don't be. You did an amazing job. I was certainly hoping, that while we were in the west, to find a sister for my wife. She has suffered several losses and has some disturbing esteem issues. I just thought this would be an incredible boost to her moral."

"What will you do, continue the search?"

"Do you think you can find out more?"

"Not me personally, but Don Evans suggested a private investigator in Kingston who would be prepared to take on the case. What does Elaine think about having a half-sister?"

"I don't know. I haven't told her. Right now, I think I will just let it rest. I have a feeling Elaine is not in the right frame of mind to deal with this. I don't want to introduce something that may end up being another disappointment in her life. If I am successful finding her sister then I'll tell her."

"Well, best of luck. I'm glad I was able to shed some light on the case." Lisa ushered Patrick to the door and they shook hands.

A small park across the street offered an inviting bench. Patrick dusted off the slatted seat and pulled Helen's letter from his hip pocket before he sat to read it.

Helen, his kid sister, was thirteen years younger than Patrick. The age difference created a distance in their relationship when they were young, but, in the last few years, since their parents had both passed away, they each made an effort to keep in touch. Helen specialized in event management and had secured a job with a recruitment firm to organize job fairs in foreign countries. She was in Delhi, India. Her letter was lengthy and recounted daily adventures. She was spending a great deal of time with a certain young man, Elliott Ravi.

"Helen's in love!" Patrick announced to Elaine when he returned to join her. He handed her the letter to read.

"Where did you get this?"

Prepared for this, Patrick explained that he had had Don Evans forward it to a general delivery address. It was a small lie but it quelled Elaine's curiosity.

The art show was well attended and Elaine did have some environment advocates drop by her booth. She was pleased with the contacts she made and together they vowed to keep in touch and put pressure on the media and corporations. The final day of the show, she was introduced to the president of a large oil refinery. Just as she was about to attack him about pollution issues berating companies like his as prime contributors, he made a point of congratulating her on raising environmental awareness. He then purchased two major pieces for his corporate offices. His company supported environmental initiatives and provided schools with educational programs on public responsibility.

Elaine was a little guarded about her feelings on receiving accolades from one of the sources of her nemesis, but, a sale was a sale. At the end of the final day, she was breaking down her display and packaging the remaining sculptures when a voice with a slight British accent spoke over the loud speaker.

"I want to thank all the artists for participating in this show. The judges did an amazing job of bringing together diverse talent from across Canada. The show was indeed most successful with a record turnout. Sales were brisk and I hope each and every one of you benefitted by this. I have to note that this year we were impressed with the remarkable variety of creative work. We do now, however, want to single out and recognize three artists for their attractive displays and outstanding work."

Elaine froze when she heard her name. She turned to see a trio of officials descending on her partially dismantled booth carrying a plaque. The client from the oil company was with them. Following were reporters for the Vancouver Sun and the Globe and Mail. Elaine was surprised and excited. This award was very prestigious and an amazing affirmation of her work. She cornered the corporate buyer and teased him that he needed to anti-up more for her work because she was now an award winning artist.

The next morning still bubbling with enthusiasm, she gathered up copies of the newspapers and raved about the success of the show. Patrick was happy to see her elated mood and praised her accomplishment.

Between a scheduled Alaskan cruise and several art shows the next few months flew by. They drove back across the Rockies to Calgary Then to Banff where they each took the course they had enrolled in.

Patrick received another letter from Helen, this time Patrick did have it directed to the post office. Helen wrote that she was getting married and that she and Elliott would be moving to Montreal in July. Since Patrick was her only family in Canada, she and Eliott decided to be married in Delhi where he had numerous relatives. Afterward they would fly to Montreal. Elliott has been recruited by an accounting firm and she would find a new job when they were settled.

Pleased his sister would be so close and anxious to meet her choice of husband Patrick suggested to Elaine that they should have a private wedding celebration for them. The timing was right as they would be back in Ottawa by July.

"Of course! What a great idea." Elaine was checking their next show. It was now well into December and she was anxious to get out of the Prairie Provinces to a kinder climate.

Patrick had arranged for them to spend Christmas and New Years in Niagara Falls. They crossed into Montana intending to head south and avoid winter storms. They were fortunate and managed to keep one step ahead of a major snow system and beat it to their destination. They stayed below the Great Lakes, explored the mid west and crossed back into Canada at Niagara Falls just in time for the holiday celebrations.

The outdoor festivities were crowded and noisy. Loud music drowned out the roar of the falls. Celebrities pumped the audience into frantic action, dancing and waving, to keep warm and hype the mood of great expectations for the incoming year. On the stroke of midnight, fireworks exploded over the falls.

"Paddy, love, I just know that 1986 is going to change our lives. I just feel it." Elaine hugged and kissed Patrick.

Patrick thought about finding Elaine's sister and agreed.

Upbeat and rested they went on to Toronto after the holiday. Through an agency, they had rented a furnished studio apartment near College Street and settled in for the rest of the winter. They planned to produce more work and take advantage of some local shows. Elaine headed off to the Ontario Art College prepared to teach a six-week course they hired her to do.

Two weeks later, while Elaine was busy with classes, Patrick drove to Kingston to meet the private investigator, Bob Smythe. His office was located on the second floor of an old limestone building overlooking Lake Ontario. The lake was foreboding and grey in the bleak winter chill. Patrick shivered as he walked along the street carefully avoiding patches of black ice. He found the address and climbed the stairs to the second floor. The heavy wooden door opened to a small tired reception area with no receptionist. Patrick heard a voice and walked through a door to his right. A small lean man in his fifty's wearing jeans and a tweed suit jacket over a white shirt and v-necked sweater rose from his desk and approached Patrick with an outstretched hand.

"Patrick, I'm Bob, pleased to meet you." They shook hands. "Have a seat."

A beige naugahyde sofa backed against the wall and a wing-backed chair faced it. Patrick settled for the sofa as Bob gathered a file from his desk and sat in the chair.

"Your little lady has been rather elusive, I might say." Smythe placed a buff file on a coffee table between them. "I was able to find an old school chum who was only too happy to talk about Florenzia."

"Is she still in Belleville?"

"No, but I have traced her to a village in northern Quebec. It appears she was far from happy at home. Her parents were strict and critical. They were old world and wanted Florenzia to adhere to their ways. She ran away when she was seventeen."

"Where did she go and how did you find her?"

"It certainly took some sleuthing. She went to great lengths to put some distance between herself and her parents. I tracked her to Montreal where she was working as a nanny for an English family. Luckily, they were still at the same location. I learned that when she completed her contract with that family she left no forwarding address. But I was able to track her."

Smythe went into detail of how he had a friend in the federal government who traced her SIN number. "That's totally irregular but he and I have a special relationship and I pulled in a favour."

Smythe proceeded to fill in all the details and provided Patrick with a thick file with the results of his investigation and where Elaine's sister was currently working. She was in a small town in eastern Quebec.

Patrick drove back to Toronto thinking and rethinking what to do with the information he now had. He decided to speak with Elaine's sister first. If she made such an effort to conceal her whereabouts, she might not want to meet a sister she did not know existed. He studied the road map and decided that he would take a side trip in late June while Elaine worked a large show and convention in New Brunswick.

Chapter 12

July 2003

Philippa charged through the door yelling "we're home!" She held the door open and motioned Tracey forward. Laden down with two oversize suitcases, Mike followed, caught the closing door with his shoulder when Philippa let go and bumped it all the way open with his hip. Once inside he pushed it closed with his foot. He dumped the bags on the hall floor, placed his hands on his lower back and stretched. He turned to the hall mirror lifted his sunglasses and took in his tanned round face with faint marking from his glasses. He reached to touch one angry pimple on his right cheek then withdrew his finger. He frowned and at the same time noticed an ice cream stain on his camp Popoti shirt, they had stopped in Barry's Bay for lunch. "Slob." He muttered. Turning away too quickly, he stumbled over Tracey's red suitcase.

"Hey, careful," cautioned Tracey, "you might damage my delicate undies."

"Like, I can see you wearing anything delicate," Mike retorted. "More apt to be Jocky shorts and Ts—nothing delicate about you."

Philippa and Tracey exchanged knowing looks. Philippa had never seen such beautiful lace underwear as Tracey wore, a complete contradiction of her public persona.

"Florry where are you?" Philippa stepped around the staircases and peered down the long hall lined with shelves of her mother's and father's art work.

"Hey, these are way cool." Tracey was admiring Elaine's work. Philippa smiled at her friend and called again. "Florry."

The question was answered by enticing smells wafting from the kitchen. Mike elbowed past the girls, his long legs carrying him in a beeline for the swinging door to the kitchen. He found Florry bent over the sink scrubbing baking pans. He threw his arms around her giving her a peck on the cheek at the same time. Over her left shoulder he eyed a double layer chocolate cake decorated with 'Welcome Home'.

Florry untangled herself from Mike's grasp, turned and gave him a playful slap on the shoulder.

"They didn't teach you any more manners or respect for your elders at that fancy camp, did they?" She grinned as she ruffled his hair then pushed him aside. She reached for the refrigerator door to grab a carton of milk. The shelves were stocked to overflowing. "Welcome home."

"Florry isn't happy unless she's feeding you," Philippa pushed Tracey through the doors. "Mike's her favourite person because he can eat non-stop and flatters her all the time so she'll continue to feed him glorious food. Wait 'til you taste her blueberry pies. Florry, meet Tracey—Tracey this is Florry."

Florry took one look at Philippa's new friend and was startled by the black lipstick, and nail polish, spiked hair and army boots. She forced a weak smile, and nodded. She turned her eyes to Philippa and examined her as if she had never seen her before. Gently she reached out and stroked Philippa's face, noticeably emotional, then abruptly pulled her hand back as if it had touched fire. Quickly turning away she busied herself cutting each of the teens a large slice of cake. She reached into the cupboard directly above her head and took out three glasses and filled them with milk, hardly uttering a word. She set the food and drinks on the table and abruptly left the kitchen with the excuse of having to check the laundry.

"What's with her?" Asked Mike. "She's as jumpy as a cat."

"Absolutely no idea. You'd think I'd risen from the dead or something."

"Maybe, she freaked at the sight of me. You did warn her about me didn't you? Or maybe she simply missed you," said Tracey.

"Naw - something's gotten into her." Mike's words were muffled by a mouthful of cake.

"Weird, she's never been demonstrative before. I mean her touch was like a kiss — and for her to leave the kitchen when Mike might want another slice of cake — never. This is way too weird — really weird."

"Well, maybe she was worried about you and was afraid to say so."

"Can't imagine. We're talking about Miss Super Efficiency here, the no fuss madam. I mean she's all about organizing the house, cleaning every little nook and cranny and having a schedule. Hmph, oh, well, something got her all shook up — could be Tracey's boots on her polished-to-the-highest-shine floor.

"That would do it." Mike was reaching for the cake server to replenish his already empty plate.

Philippa motioned Tracey to a chair. "Who cares? Let's dig in."

Cake and milk took precedent and after each consumed two pieces, they rinsed their plates and forks and put them in the dishwasher. Philippa ushered Mike to the door.

"Soon as you make your parents happy to have you out of the house again, come on over. Tracey and I'll likely be gaming within the hour."

"That should be just about the right timing," said Mike. He bumped into the door jamb as he turned to go. "Tell Florry to save me some of that delicious cake."

"Klutz." Laughing, both girls grabbed their gear and headed upstairs.

"Wow! This is amazing!" yelled Philippa over her shoulder. She and Tracey had lugged Tracey's bags into newly decorated guest room. "Florry, did you and Aunt Helen do this?"

Florry, wearing a tailored short-sleeved apricot shirt and well-worn jeans, appeared in the bedroom doorway. She watched the two friends unpack Tracey's case. Philippa's tidy cotton shirt and short shorts were a direct contrast to the khaki cargo pants and over-sized t-shirt Tracey was wearing. She searched Philippa's face taking in every detail of her soft brown hair now lightened from exposure to the sun, her slim frame with a small but rounded bosom. She noticed how tanned her legs were and for the first time was aware that Philippa seemed relaxed and happy. Florry was not. She hugged her elbows and leaned back against the doorframe.

"You don't have to shout, I'm right here. Well, I can't take any of the credit. It was all your Aunt Helen's doing. She's got an eye for this kind of thing. Check out the TV."

The girls opened the entertainment center to excited exclamations.

Florry watched. She stroked her upper arms rubbing her bare skin as if she experienced a sudden chill. Slipping out the doorway she left the girls to their own devices and went to her room and quietly closed the door.

Philippa hung clothes in the closet while Tracey put her neatly folded items in the dresser drawers "Have you ever wondered who you are?"

"Yep all the time. I'm always coming up with this crazy broad who likes to startle people." Tracey reached for the pants Philippa held, grabbed a hanger and clipped them on. She handed them to Philippa.

"No. I mean did you ever question if your parents were your real mother and father."

"When you meet my father you'll know I couldn't be anyone else's. Flip, what's this about?" Tracey sat on the edge of the bed and patted the new green comforter to motion Philippa to join her.

"Oh God, Trace, since my parents were killed, it's been a nightmare. They can't find any reference to my birth. It's as if I was found under a bush." The changes to her parents' room brought back all her fears. Philippa spilled out the whole story including the fact that there was no record of her birth and how Mark's mother was dealing with Romanian orphans. "I think I'm one."

"Holy shit! You've got to be kidding." Tracey grabbed Philippa's shoulder and turned her to be face-to-face. Philippa gave her a weak smile.

"No, I'm not. At camp, I was so busy I was able to put it out of my mind most of the time, but now, that I'm home, its front and center again."

"What're you going to do?"

"The lawyers have tried everything from this end. I guess I have to tell them to call Mark's mother."

"Do you think we could research it on the web? I mean lawyers do things one way but computer geeks have a whole different way of accessing information." Tracey jumped off the bed and pulled Philippa toward the door.

"Do you think we could? Oh, Tracey, I'm scared to death that I might be deported."

"Hey, we don't have to tell anyone what we find out, but you'll know who you are. Let me email a contact I have in LA. He might be able to get the ball rolling."

The two girls abandoned the unpacking and headed for the office and the desktop computer.

"Florry," shouted Philippa as the two girls raced down the stairs, "tell Mike we're in the office when he comes."

Florry hadn't heard through the closed door of her bedroom. She sat on a vanity chair with her head in her hands. Minutes later she jerked upright and crossed the room to her dresser. She opened the bottom drawer and lifted carefully folded jeans to reach the package she had found in the cupboard. She peered inside, held it close to her heart then put it away again. "Florry Waters, you've got to get a hold on yourself." A quick glimpse in the mirror had her fussing with her hair tucking a wayward strand into her ponytail. She frowned at the image shook her head as if to clear it from disturbing thoughts and turned for the door. "I've got to do something about this." She headed for the kitchen and picked up the phone. She dialed Don Evans cell phone.

"Mr. Evans, its Florry. I've got to see you. It's urgent."

Evans walked to the reception desk with the phone still at his ear. "Well, let me see what is available." Turning to his secretary he asked "What is the first available opening?" His secretary suggested an appointment time for the following morning.

"Thank you. Thank you. I'll be there."

Don Evans stared at the buzzing phone. "What ever is bothering her? She sounds really frazzled. Wasn't Philippa expected home today?" He asked an empty room not expecting an answer. He shrugged and picked up a file folder, opened it and grabbed a yellow lined legal pad to start making notes about a case he was summarizing.

The next morning, still puzzled why she needed to see him so urgently, Don waited for his secretary to usher Florry into his office. He selected a new file folder, made sure he had a pen handy and the ever-ready note pad. Nothing could have prepared him for what she shared in their meeting.

Sitting in the straight back black leather chair facing his desk, Florry nervously wrung the handles of a large black purse.

"My dear Florry, I do hope you haven't had a problem with Philippa," Don inquired.

"No."

"Hopefully—not Mrs. Ravi."

"No, no problem."

"Is Philippa okay? I mean did she have a bad experience at camp?"

"No, in fact it was more than positive. It was good for her, she's tanned and healthy. The whole experience helped her deal with losing her parents. I guess they worked really hard to design some computer game. Her team won—it was a competition. The prize is a trip to San Francisco—Silicon Valley. She brought a friend back from camp with her. Really odd girl."

"Oh, so that's what you're concerned about?"

"No, she's certainly different, a little scary, all got up in loose dark clothes trying to hide the fact that she is really very pretty. Don't know what to think of her. If she was mine, I wouldn't allow her to wear the get-ups she does. However, underneath it all she's a nice girl. She wants to camouflage that though. She's from Los Angeles and will fly out to San Francisco with Philippa, then go back home from there. They leave a week Friday."

"Oh, so Philippa needs extra money."

"No. It's an all expenses paid trip."

"Then, since that's not it then, what can I do for you? What was so urgent to bring you here? How can I help?"

"It's a long story. It's about something I found. I don't know how to begin or what you'll think of me after."

"First, let me get you a cup of tea, as I remember you take a little milk, no sugar?"

"Yes, that'd be kind, thank you." He pushed the intercom button on the phone and asked his assistant to bring tea for Florry and coffee for him.

Drawing her chair closer to Don's desk, Florry fidgeted with her purse straps, smoothed her trim navy skirt, shifted in the chair and kept clearing her throat. She was definitely uncomfortable.

Don learned a long time ago that clients with difficult stories just needed to tell it at their own pace. He leaned forward with his arms on his desk pad, his pen poised ready to write and waited. His assistant knocked quietly on the door and entered with a silver tray containing an elegant china teapot, matching creamer and cups along with a mug of dark coffee.

"Is this steeped enough?" Don poured a small sample into her cup. Florry nodded. Evans poured a full cup, handed it over the desk to the seemingly distraught woman sitting across from him. Her eyes were lowered and she was biting her bottom lip.

Florry reached for the cup and saucer and took her time

stirring her tea then turned to Don.

"I overheard Helen mention that there were some papers missing."

Don was immediately cautious. Client information was confidential and he did not want to be caught in a compromising situation.

"I was cleaning a cupboard and came across this envelope." She set her cup and saucer on the desk and reached into her large bag and pulled out the brown manila envelope. She placed her purse carefully on the floor beside her chair.

Don sighed with relief. "You found the missing birth certificate." He smiled and held out his hand.

Florry appeared not to hear. "It's really difficult for me." She was clasping the package to her chest.

"Florry, I don't understand why it would be any concern of yours. No one will be angry that you found it. In fact, I am delighted. It will make everything so much easier."

"I don't think so." Florry placed the envelope firmly on her lap and anchored it with both hands. "When I found it, I knew I had to tell Philippa. But I can't. It's too complicated. That's why I need you. Someone else will have to tell her. You'll have to do it."

"Okay. I can do that. But first, I want to know why her birth certificate is causing you so much stress."

"It's not her birth certificate." Florry straightened, leaned forward and handed the package, held with both hands like an offering, to Don Evans.

He opened it, looked at the contents. He took off his glasses, took a tissue out of a box on the desk and cleaned the glass. "Florry, what is this?"

Chapter 13

April, 1986

Winter eased into a grey wet spring typical for Toronto set on the shores of Lake Ontario. Elaine's teaching months were coming to a close. She demanded excellence from her students and for the most part, they rose to the challenge. Over and over again, she placed emphasis on how art could be instrumental in expressing social issues.

"Nothing needs to be thrown away. Everything can be recycled or composted. To express this she held up a delicate sculpture. "My art turns the most mundane articles into exquisite art pieces. Well, not everyone thinks them exquisite."

Several chuckles were heard.

"This sculpture is made out of pop cans. The point is—I make a statement that everything has beauty." She described how her work helped save the environment by using only scavenged material. By using recycled items, she eliminated the need to produce more and kept them from going to landfill sites. She told her students how she searched for refuse cast off in the wilderness. "You can find hidden beauty in just about anything."

"How about cigarette butts?'

The question from her student brought more chuckles. Elaine had to agree that not everything had artistic appeal but then compost used in a garden undeniably produced beauty and bounty and tobacco was very useful for keeping earwigs away. She demonstrated numerous ways to turn refuse into imaginative creations. She encouraged them to express a point of view and promote controversy. Garbage pick-up days became their mining days.

Within weeks, Elaine was pleasantly surprised as she watched her classes bring life to things she least expected they would mold into art. They grasped the concept wholeheartedly and came up with ideas that delighted her, resulting in outstanding artistic creations. Somehow she had to find a way to publicly show what these young people had accomplished.

Elaine met with the President of the Toronto branch of the Sierra Club and through him convinced the executive to sponsor a showing of the student's works at the Eaton Centre. The Faculty Dean at the Ontario College of Art was more than pleased with her outreach idea and got Board approval for the showing.

The studio space provided by the college was humming with activity during class and after. Elaine and the students worked there during class time and had been allowed access after-hours. Elaine and Patrick both were given permission to take advantage of it to produce work of their own. Brisk sales at the Victoria show and the extra ones they attended in the Toronto area left Elaine short of significant works so having workspace was an unexpected, but much needed bonus. The innovative efforts she saw in the classroom inspired her to incorporate new ideas and materials in her own work.

Many of the students dropped in after hours to complete their projects. They took a keen interest in both Elaine's and Patrick's skills who soon became confidants and substitute parents to about seventeen young budding artists.

Near the end of the semester, Elaine stayed late to put the finishing touches on a large whimsical creature in chains.

Beautifully executed, it was made entirely from discarded pop cans. The delicately twisted slivers of metal were polished to catch light and charred to absorb it. It was an eye catching, masterful piece that expressed the horrific plight of how discarded containers endangered wildlife by injuring them or choking them. She was the only person working in the studio with the exception of one other.

Sophie, a promising student had missed the previous three days of class and stayed late to catch up and complete a sculpture she was creating from Styrofoam cups. All of a sudden she doubled over and let out an agonizing scream. Elaine spun around in time to see Sophie slump to the floor.

"Oh, my God! Sophie, what's wrong?" Elaine rushed to Sophie's side and cradled her head. She looked down and saw blood oozing through Sophie's khaki jeans and down her inner thigh seams, spreading bright red on the floor's white tile.

She eased Sophie's head to the floor muttering soothing words as she rushed to the phone, dialed reception and asked them to call an ambulance. She returned to cradle and comfort Sophie.

"Please, don't call my parents," Sophie whispered.

"Why, for goodness sake!"

"I had an abortion. They'll kill me. I'm Italian."

"Whatever the devil does that mean?" Elaine was alarmed at how much blood there was.

"I didn't go to a regular doctor." Sophie was getting weaker and then fell silent.

When the ambulance arrived Sophie was unconscious and her skin looked transparent. Elaine told the medics what she knew, watched as the stretcher was carried away, then went to Administration to fill out a report. The school called Sophie's parents. Unnerved, Elaine left the school and went home to Patrick.

It had been three months since Elaine had gone off on a tangent about her inability to conceive. Sophie's situation threw her into an emotional vortex. Her breathing was shallow and she was agitated beyond consoling.

"She just let some whack cut away a life. He killed a baby. Sophie might die! I don't understand why a kid—a kid can get pregnant as soon as she drops her pants and I can't no matter how hard I try!"

Elaine banged hr fists on the counter, punched a wall kicked at a table leg and finally fell into the far corner of their apartment curled into the fetal position. She gnawed at the back of her hand and rocked back and forth as tears rolled down her face.

"I don't want her to die. Patrick, I don't want her to die. Dear God, it should be me who conceived. I would never have let that butcher take a life. Why, why, why when I want so desperately to create a life?"

"Sweetheart, I'm sure Sophie'll be okay, I'm sure you got help in time. She'll be fine. She will be back to class in no time." Patrick's soothing words didn't penetrate Elaine's dark place. Patrick knelt in front of her and reached his arms toward her.

She slapped him hard across the face and started to push him away with her feet. Patrick grabbed for her arms but she swung to the side and evaded him. She flailed her arms wildly thrashing at any part of Patrick within reach. He managed to duck most of the blows but the few he caught were feeble and only smarted. What did hurt was seeing Elaine tormenting herself again. Her face was distorted with despair; she tore out her hair and wailed agonizing cries.

At this moment Patrick loathed Elaine's mother. No matter how hard he tried, he never could convince Elaine that her mother was insanely wrong and having a baby was not the reason she was put on earth.

"I'm useless as a human being. I can't even fulfill my designated purpose. Oh, I wish I'd never been born."

"For God's sake," Patrick soothed. "You're not useless at all. The message you deliver with your art is most important. What you're doing will make life better for generations of babies."

"Most important! How can you say that? How can it be important when I struggle to save this earth for who? No one. Why do I even care, I don't have a single child to inherit this screwed up world!"

She got to her feet and started hurling anything within reach. The one-and-only alarm clock smashed into little pieces when it hit the door jamb. Patrick grabbed the lamp before it hit the floor. Elaine fell to the carpet and pounded it with her fists. She lay on her back and kicked at air. Finally, Patrick was able to calm her enough to get her to her feet and ease her into the bedroom. Exhausted, she flopped onto the bed and burrowed beneath a pillow. Patrick cradled and stroked her until she fell into a deep but troubled sleep about four in the morning. He tucked the comforter around her, kissed her on the forehead and slid out of bed.

He shuffled into the living room wearing sheepskin slippers and a short robe. He crossed to a small closet near the front door and picked up a large brown leather case where his knives and all his carving tools lay pocketed in special pouches, clean and in exact order. He carried it to the beige tweed sofa, set it on the arm, sat down and lifted the lid. Sliding his hand behind the pocket section holding sand paper he lifted out a black file folder.

The following week they would be in Quebec City and he hoped to find time to slip away and check out the information he had on her step-sister. Patrick prayed the woman would be agreeable to opening up her past and welcome a new-found sister, but he had to be sure first. Elaine was fragile enough without enduring another negative emotional shock. However, a positive one might be the very boost she needed. Patrick heaved a sigh and looked through the bedroom door where Elaine, buried deep in the comforter, slept fitfully. Muttering to himself he closed the case and returned it to the cupboard. "I hope she's alright tomorrow. She just has to be. The students only have four days to get their stuff ready for the big show. Now, how am I supposed to wake up without an alarm clock? I'll have to buy a new one tomorrow."

****

The show at the Eaton Center was a huge success. The Sierra Club turned out in force as did a good number of the general public, her students' families and the fifth estate. Everyone congratulated the young artists on their innovative and creative work. To show their support, family and guests purchased numerous items. Grins were flashed from one to the other. The media loved the concept and interpretations. A reporter from a local TV station was exuberant about the environment messages emphasized by the unusual pieces and interviewed a number of the students and executive members of the Sierra Club. It was to be aired on the late night news the following day. Elaine was applauded over and over again for instilling important ideals in others.

Patrick pondered how this beautiful woman, smiling so confidently at everyone in the room, could have been lying in a tortured heap, only days before. Now, she appeared radiant, her unruly flaming curls danced across her shoulders as she turned this way and that to be congratulated, hugged or have her hand shaken. She wore a brightly coloured caftan that swayed when she moved emphasizing her already natural grace. Patrick shook his head in wonderment and smiled with pride.

After the show, Elaine invited the students to Lychee Gardens where they celebrated with the endless buffet of Chinese food. Sophie now recuperated, presented Elaine with flowers and a charm bracelet designed and made by the class from bottle caps. Each charm was different and signed by the student who made it. Elaine was noticeably moved and hugged each of them.

The following day, Patrick and Elaine left Toronto and followed Old Highway 2 east along the shores of Lake Ontario. Elaine was still exuberant telling Patrick that the faculty had invited her to return the following winter to teach again. They stopped for lunch in Port Hope and wandered the historic center of the town. Lake Ontario lay to their right as they drove and the dark water shot blinding flashes when the early April sun caught a wave. Trees were greening and earth was being coaxed back to life. They spent the night at a Bed and Breakfast in Brockville. The night air was damp and raw but regardless they wandered along the waterfront and admired the majestic homes. The aftermath of the previous day left both equally tired so bed time was early and welcome.

In the morning, refreshed and ready to explore a new day, Patrick was delighted to see Elaine radiant and smiling. They continued their journey to Montreal. Old Montreal was bustling with traffic along Catherine Street, horns blared and pedestrians talked loudly with animated gestures.

"I don't understand a word, but don't you feel a special energy here?" Elaine asked as she spread her arms wide to encompass the scene.

"You're catching on, Sweetheart. Quebecers are famous for using their hands as much as words to get a point across."

Patrick had promised his sister that he would check out several apartments. Helen and her fiancé, Elliott, were being married in three weeks. They were then taking a month's honeymoon in Australia, returning to Delhi to wind down their lives in India before flying to Montreal on July third. Helen had contacted a rental agency and was considering several options. Patrick would be her eyes on the ground. He had to attend to it while they were in Montreal because he and Elaine were scheduled to be in the Maritimes at the time Helen and Elliot arrived.

Elaine was pre-occupied with her entries for a juried show and spent her evenings designing her display drawing one diagram after another, then mentally imagining the effect. She had done a tour of the space, met the coordinator and noted the theme of the show. Her booth had to impress prospective buyers and to do this it had to be carefully thought out. The show opened the following week and was known to be well attended.

Even though Elaine's work got a lot of attention at the show, she sold only one piece to a rather eccentric professor. She found the clientele in Montreal very different from the one in Victoria and she struggled with being unilingual English. Victoria's location had been in a bright open setting, informal and exhibited a sense of freedom. Montreal's was in an old stone storehouse on the waterfront. The booths were cramped for space, the lighting less than desirable and the clientele very eclectic. It seemed everyone had a cigarette in their hand or mouth and the air reeked of second hand smoke.

While Elaine was at the show, Patrick busied himself by visiting several of the many artisan shops in the old part of the city and was able to place his work with some high-end specialty stores. Half of them sold before their two-week stay passed. He spent enough time with the real estate agent to feel confident in recommending to Helen and Elliot a choice of two apartments. He telegraphed Helen and signed the lease on her behalf after she responded with her choice.

When the show was over, Elaine and Patrick packed up and drove directly to Quebec City where Elaine attended a small two-weekend show. Once again, Patrick was able to place some of his better pieces in good venues. Carving was highly sought after in Quebec, quite opposite to the reaction to Elaine's art.

Patrick decided to take time to find Florenzia Vatars. She was working a day's drive north of Quebec City. However, his plans were derailed due to freak snow storms. It was late April but winter refused to admit it was spring. On the heels of the snowstorm, it rained then froze. Roads were impassable. The city came to a standstill—even walking was treacherous on the ice-coated hilly streets.

Nature prevented Patrick from driving north but gave him a wonderland of subjects for his keen eye. The city was transformed into a frozen fairyland. Armed with his camera, Patrick shot rolls and rolls of film capturing the lime-stone buildings huddled beneath mounds of white snow capped with ice. He photographed icicles, glistening with rainbows, hanging from crumbling walls. He caught shots of a snowy owl balancing on an icy branch as it scrutinized tourists slipping and sliding down the ice-coated cobbled streets. Three cats shivered in the doorway of a tavern that showed promise of a warm fireplace inside. It was one of his favourite pictures and destined to be the template for a carving.

Horses with frosty beards pulled calechès and snorted breathe clouds. They became the topic of photo after photo. Patrick was itching to carve these amazing images. He could just feel his knife bringing each subject to life in various types of wood.

After leaving Quebec City, they took their time and finally arrived in North Sydney, Nova Scotia where they caught the ferry to Newfoundland. They both were eager to see the most eastern Canadian province, but their greatest wish was to see the famed icebergs. Aboard the ferry they watched the shores of Nova Scotia slide into the distance. Smells of the salt water and the ever present gulls that screamed the promise of adventure raised their anticipation. They landed at Port aux Basques in south western Newfoundland amid the hustle and bustle of cars, people, cargo and animals being offloaded. Fish smells mingled with diesel fuel. Dark waters of the ocean slammed into jagged rocks as they reached shore spewing spray high into the air. Everything seemed to be in motion.

"Watch yer step," a voice called as Elaine stepped ashore. She laughed as the dock seemed to heave beneath her feet. She opted to walk off the vertigo sensation and let Paddy offload the van. Vendors called out for tourists to try their fresh seafood, trucks honked their horns as they crept through narrow roads overly busy when the ferries were in port. Traffic was reduced to a crawl. She was somewhat skeptical at the very thought of trying the vendors' wares at this point, the smells and the unsteady sidewalk made her feel a little queasy. She found that if she placed one hand on something stable it eased the sensation. Walking close to the buildings steadying herself on their solid frame structures, she examined the port.

Built on solid rock, Port aux Basques was noted for its winding roads and small wooden houses. Elaine's first impression was how bare and stark everything appeared.

"Pard'n mai by, Miss."

Elaine had taken a tentative step onto the sidewalk away from the security of the buildings just as a man pushing a bicycle edged by her. She smiled inwardly at the heavy accent that was such a brunt of jokes on the mainland. The language was a mixture of English, Patois, Scots and years of isolation.

Elaine wandered up a narrow street where she could look out over the harbour. The port was not only the arrival destination for the ferries it was very much a fishing community. Many of the small frame houses had nets draped over a drying frame.

Patrick pulled alongside and motioned for Elaine to get in the van. "I got directions to our hotel and I'm anxious to settle in and find the best restaurant in town for the day's catch. My mouth's watering for a fish feast, so hurry lass."

Well feted after eating far more than they should have, the two mainlanders set off to investigate the shores of Port Aux Basques. Elaine was pleased her queasiness was gone and the cool salt air felt refreshing. Patrick, ecstatic to spot a pelican with an enormous fish in its mouth, got reasonably close with his camera. He got several pictures of it before the fish was tucked away to swell the birds pouch.

"I know how you feel old boy, I'm stuffed too."

The following day they meandered across the island, the van going at or less than the speed limit, heading for Iceberg Alley. Even though the countryside held sparse vegetation, it was dramatic and interesting. They had reservations in Fort Amherst and had been told that bergs had been sighted the previous day.

"Some icebergs can tower as high as five stories. Incredible! Just consider that only about one eighth of the iceberg appears above the surface." Elaine shared her new-found knowledge from a brochure she read while waiting for dinner. "That's the kind that sunk the Titanic, not far off the coast from where we're going."

"Great, but would you just check the map to make sure we are heading the right way."

Elaine nodded then continued. "There are different kinds, "growlers" which ride low in the water and are very unstable, small floaters are known as "bergy bits", and "slob ice" consists of small and slushy ice pieces." Elaine was now reading from the brochure.

"My God, this is a barren land," exclaimed Patrick. There's nothing here but scruff and rock."

When they pulled into St. Johns, late in the day, both Patrick and Elaine were ravenous. The heavy sea air had that effect. They grabbed a hamburger and a beer intending to sit at a picnic table to eat, but it was too damp and the chilly air crept into their bones. They found a motel and devoured their food while snuggled under warm blankets.

Slowly coming awake, Patrick reached for the clock then sat bolt upright when he saw it was ten o'clock. They had slept twelve hours! He eased out from under the warm covers, went to the window and drew the curtains to—nothing. The world beyond was blanketed in dense fog. "Well, that's that." There was no point in getting up so he crept back across the cold floor and slid beneath the covers and warmed himself against Elaine's buttocks. She did not even stir.

Finally, they surfaced hungry and in time for lunch. The fog had lifted somewhat but still hung close to the shore. The mournful moan of a foghorn followed them to a family café, inviting in its simplicity. It offered island fare of pancakes with blueberry syrup. Patrick wolfed down his portion and half of Elaine's. It was mid afternoon before they reached Fort Amherst and they were not disappointed. Silent ice flotillas in every shape and size hugged the horizon.

"Cathedrals of ice" proffered Elaine. "I read that somewhere and it is so fitting."

"Oh, aye," a voice of another observer answered. "We are really lucky. Apparently this is the first year in a long while that the bergs have come down this route."

They spent the rest of the afternoon watching the play of light on the icebergs. The afternoon sun reflected colours ranging from snow-white, to the deepest aquamarine. Spray from the sea crowned the bergs with rainbows, sunlight made water diamonds dance across the never-ending ocean. However, there was only so much iceberg watching one could do so Patrick and Elaine set off to explore, walking the rocky shoreline.

When they returned to the motel, Elaine gathered their dirty laundry and headed for a laundromat and Patrick wandered off with his camera.

While she was stuffing the darks into one machine and the lights into another, a friendly local person chatted away. People from "The Rock" were noted for their friendliness. However, Elaine did not understand a word she was saying her accent was so thick.

The afternoon slid away and once again they felt the penetrating chill of evening. "Ye gads this place chills one where I've never been chilled before." Patrick drew Elaine close to share her warmth. They were both ravenous from the sea air and searched until they found a restaurant perched high over the town where they had a view of the lights of ships moored at sea. A full moon caught the froth of cresting waves beating their way to the craggy shore where they split into cascades of water that sprayed high into the air; then spent, rolled back to the sea.

Patrick and Elaine studied the menu.

"What the heck is brewis?" Patrick looked into the clean-scrubbed face of a lanky teen wrapped in a white floor-length apron.

"That'd bey our mos' popular. It'd bey seaf'd 'n hard t'k. th' best p'rt is th' scrunchions, real tasty."

Elaine looked away hiding a chuckle behind her menu. Dubious about that choice she continued to read the menu. She leaned over to Patrick and whispered. "Oh, my God, I have no idea what half these things are or if they are safe to eat! Listen—they list Jigs Dinner, Lassy Mogs, Figgy Duff Cod tongues and cheeks."

"Oh, aye, m'am," the waiter was quick to cut in. "and we're un'f the few sp'ts in toon th't off'r britches, a real delicacy in these h're p'rts."

After consultation, Patrick settled for Jigs Dinner—salt beef and boiled vegetables, after being assured it was a true Newfoundland culinary tradition. It was served with pease pudding, yellow spilt peas boiled to a paste in a linen sack.

The chef sent out a taste of britches for an appetizer named so for its resemblance to a pair of pants but it was Newfoundland caviar, cod roe. The main course arrived steaming and smelling delicious.

"For goodness sake Patrick, you can't eat that! The potatoes are blue!"

"Aye," the hovering lad announced yet again. "Special t' th' 'land."

Elaine started to giggle and the meal became an adventure of tasting sensations and laughing at the unusual names pronounced in a distinctive accent. They were still laughing when they arrived back at their motel.

"Whoah, I ate way too much."

"Did you have to top it off with a huge piece of blueberry pie?" Elaine patted Patrick's bulging tummy. You look like you're eight months along."

Patrick held his breath but Elaine sauntered into the bathroom seemingly happy. They spent the rest of the week exploring the island then boarded the ferry from Argentia to Sydney, Nova Scotia. The first two weeks of May showed promise of spring as the air softened and warmed.

Chapter 14

The evening air tasted of salt and the brisk frivolous wind stung her cheeks. Elaine leaned into the rail of the ferry inviting the breeze to lift her happy spirits to the gods. Scattered clouds slid across the never-ending sky and screeching gulls circled the ship then flew away and disappeared in the distance. A sharp line defined dark water from waning light and a reddening sun balanced like a tight-rope walker on the horizon, another day drawing to a close.

The fourteen-hour, two hundred and eighty mile trip, left Argentia in the evening and arrived in Nova Scotia late the next afternoon. Patrick joined Elaine and slipped his arm around her waist. Together they watched the afterglow. Shades of pink and purple spread wide, an artists' palette on the still water, churned to a pastel froth in the wake of the boat.

Patrick lifted Elaine's hair from her neck and whispered into her ear. "Our cabin awaits us. The rhythm of the waves suggests soft music and candles—perhaps a glass of Pinot Noir. Are you up for one? Or if m'lady would rather, there's good old maritime entertainment and great food on board..." He drew her close easing his hand beneath her wind jacket and heavy knit sweater. He guided her along the gangway to their cabin.

When they emerged, the dim light of wall sconces cast soft long shadows that suited their mellow mood. Patrick and Elaine followed muted sounds of fiddle music until it became loud. They pushed open a heavy wooden door to find energetic, foot stomping musicians that had everyone tapping their feet and clapping their hands. Caught up in the rhythm and infectious exuberance of the music, Patrick and Elaine joined in a few jigs when their energy moved them to the dance floor. Falling breathless on their seats laughing, they held their sides and struggled for breath. Later that night they turned down an invitation to watch movies and instead, donned warm jackets, returned to the deck, found two deck chairs and watched brilliant stars fill the night sky.

"Patrick, have you ever wished you didn't marry me."

The words brought Patrick to his feet and in one long step he knelt beside Elaine's chair. "No, emphatically no! You are what completes me. How can you even ask?"

"You're the only person who would put up with me." Elaine was chewing on her knuckles. "I'm such a failure. You would've been the world's best father and now you will never hold your own sons or daughters because of me. You'll never dance a jig with your daughter."

Patrick watched the familiar tension rise in Elaine's face, her clenched hands, her knees drawn up to her chin. He tried to direct her interest to the stars and the sounds of the waves but she curled deeper into a ball and started to keen. A couple walking the deck stopped to inquire if everything was all right. After reassuring them, Patrick pulled Elaine from the deck chair and gently ushered her to their cabin. By the time he got her into bed she was shuddering as if cold to the bone. Patrick held her and spoke soothing words until she fell, yet again, into a troubled sleep.

The episodes were becoming more frequent and Patrick paced the floor mumbling. "I don't know enough about nervous disorders. I sure wish I knew more. I'm so concerned for Elaine's

sanity. She has to get help. I'd do anything to make her better."
He reached over her and pulled the sheet that had slipped to the
floor to her chin. She suddenly jerked awake and threw up.

"Oh, Paddy, I'm so sorry." Elaine's mood shifted to one of
embarrassment and anger at herself. She dashed about stripping
the bed and used the small sink in the corner of the room to rinse
a wash clothe. This episode had been short. But what and when
would there be another?

Left with only a blanket after the sheets were thrown into a
hamper on the deck provided for passengers affected by vertigo,
they drew it over themselves and settled into a calm sleep for the
rest of the night.

The van was the second vehicle to disembark so they were
away from the dock in good time. Following the scenic coastline
road they took their time and spent the afternoon stopping
wherever and whenever something caught their attention. A few
kilometers out of Halifax they spotted a Bed and Breakfast sign
on a bleached-to-gray wooden fence. The house, also grey, from
salt air and lack of paint, stood tall behind a tangled garden
flashing the biggest, reddest poppies Elaine had ever seen. An
unkempt lawn, solid with dandelions, was a brilliant yellow
carpet to its doors. Patrick and Elaine looked at each other and
even though no words were spoken knew this place called to
them.

After a considerable wait, the doorbell was answered by a
woman in her early sixties wearing a leather apron and rubber
boots. She was drying her hands right up to her elbows with a
striped towel.

"We saw your sign and wondered …."

"Come in. Come in. Yes, I've a room available," With a

waving arm she directed them through a long hallway to a spacious kitchen. "Marnie," she said. She dropped the towel and extended a handshake, a broad smile welcoming them.

"Patrick and Elaine Snelling from Ottawa."

"Give me a moment to shed these boots and apron." Marnie slipped into a back hall and when she re-emerged her red plaid shirt and overalls were clean and crisp. Marnie was anything but a small person but she moved with the grace of a dancer. Her maritime lilt made words sing. She reached for a kettle and turned the tap to fill it. "Tea or coffee?" She was pointing them to a seat at the table. "What brings you to Halifax? On a holiday?"

"We're both showing at the annual artisans market this weekend."

"No kidding! So am I! So what'll it be?"

"I beg your pardon"

"Tea or coffee?"

"Oh, coffee for both of us."

They watched as Marnie reached for a bodem on the counter and into the cupboard for coffee beans. The noise of the grinder stopped conversation but sent heavenly smells throughout the kitchen. The room in mellow tones of apricot and off white was welcoming. The counters, a deep maroon arborite, held every modern utensil imaginable neatly aligned along the backboard.

"What are you doing?" Patrick yelled over the grinder then dropped the volume when the coffee was ground.

"Making coffee."

"No, I mean for the show."

"Oh, I do art on paper. Got a nice little clientele—make and dye my own paper. That's what I was doing when you rang the bell—making paper. And you?"

Conversation flew across the table as they sipped several cups of coffee and shared stories of attending shows. Marnie insisted on giving Patrick and Elaine a serious rate drop because they were participating in the same show and invited them to stay for the duration.

"I'm parked on the street. Is that all right?"

"Nobody'll even notice. It's fine."

"I'll get the suitcases and lock up then." Patrick strolled off on his mission returning with two small cases. He followed Marnie up a steep winding staircase to a room at the back of the house. He dropped his load in the bedroom. A brass bed with a white eyelet duvet stood against a burgundy wall. Pillows stacked at the headboard were beautifully crafted and full of vibrant shades of every colour appliquéd in abstract designs. A bouquet of wild flowers, tastefully arranged, sat on a small pine table beneath a large casement window.

Elaine who had followed smiled with approval.

Marnie pointed out the window to a steel shed in the backyard. "That's where I was when you rang the bell — making paper. As soon as you're settled come out and join me. I'd love to show you my work."

It didn't take Patrick and Elaine long to unpack and freshen up. They headed for the back yard through the kitchen. The screen door slapped shut behind them. A well-tended vegetable and herb garden bordered the walk on one side and a massive oak tree stood guard from the other. Painted bright orange with clematis vines depicted all over it, the shed door was a work of art in itself. A rusty hinge announced their arrival as Patrick pushed it open.

"Watch your step, the floor's wet." He cautioned Elaine.

A large cauldron was bubbling over a wood fire glowing hot

in a circular pit that was vented through the roof. Benches lining the walls held screens from which water dripped to the concrete floor. Elaine examined one near her and knew she was in the presence of a master craftsman. The paper's texture was smooth and silky, even throughout. Finished framed pieces hung on panels displayed the finished product.

"Marnie, these are exquisite! They're like layered Japanese brush work but three dimensional. I love how you use texture and different materials. However do you keep the full depth of colour and bleed it to the faintest of shades?" Noting Marnie's sly smile, Elaine knew she wouldn't get an answer. Every artist has their secrets.

Happy to have fellow craftsmen and ones who appreciated the quality of her work, Marnie offered her guests carte blanche of her workshop to do any last minute changes to their show pieces. By the time supper was in the works, the trio had become fast friends. Elaine offered to help with cooking and Patrick said he would be happy to mow the lawn.

"No. Thanks. I just love dandelions. Not only are they one of nature's most intricate blooms, I harvest the leaves for salads and wine. Speaking of which, may I pour you a glass? Kitchen maids work better with a glass of wine at hand."

Nursing his wine glass, Patrick mulled over the unusual musky flavour but nodded his approval. Excusing himself, he walked around the property. Marnie was a blessing. She was so exuberant and flamboyant. Elaine and she had hit it off so well that there was no sign of the depression of the previous evening, and there were no babies here. "Soon, I'm going to have to deal with Elaine's irrational behavior and mood swings but right now, it's good to feel relaxed. Marnie's a blessing."

****

The craft show went well and both Elaine and Patrick made impressive sales and contacts. Marnie sold out and came away with future orders. The new friends closed down their booths and headed for a nearby pub to celebrate.

"We had hoped to catch a cruise down the coast." Elaine was explaining their immediate plans. "But there doesn't seem to be anything available at any of the tour offices.

"Tomorrow morning, I'll call in a special favour I'm owed and I might be able to get you on a very special boat."

Marnie's connections went far beyond anything Patrick and Elaine expected. They were invited to join the crew of the Bluenose II for two weeks. Due to visit Halifax before going on to ports in the Bay of Fundy then south to Boston, the Bluenose would dock the following morning.

Patrick grabbed Marnie in a big bear hug, lifted her off the ground and swung her around.

"Put me down you idiot. I'm no light weight and you don't want to damage yourself before the voyage."

"Marnie, my gal, what a once-in-a-lifetime opportunity! The Bluenose and Bluenose II are carved into Canada's maritime heritage. Do you have any history books on her? I need to do some research before we board."

"The original tall ship was built in Lunenburg to compete for the International Fisherman's Trophy but she was a working vessel as well, and earned her keep, when she wasn't racing, through fishing. In October 1921, the Bluenose won her first race and for the next seventeen years, she defeated all contenders." Marnie spoke with pride and knowledge. "In 1928, she beat the Thebaud in the final race series and was named Queen of the

North Atlantic. She was, and still is, the pride of Nova Scotians and Canada. In 1937, the Canadian dime was changed to include an image of the mighty ship. In 1946, the Bluenose struck a reef off Haiti and sank."

"So this isn't the original?"

"Bluenose II was built from the original plans of the first Bluenose, in the same shipyard, and by some of the same men who had constructed her mother ship. Today, she is crewed by young Nova Scotians that live and train aboard her for six months of the year. That's who you will join."

The trip was a fraught with foul weather and heavy seas, unusual for early June. However, being part of the crew more than made up for any disappointments. Given light duties, Patrick and Elaine felt a part of the team and took pride in hoisting her sails and shining her brass. The Bay of Fundy cast up high waves that both Elaine and Patrick found invigorating. Holding tight to guide ropes they put complete trust in the Bluenose as she rode the crest of the waves then dipped low in the water. When she sailed out of the Bay and headed south to Boston the seas calmed. Approaching Boston Harbor dozens of tall ships were moored, their crews polishing every piece of metal and swabbing already spotless decks getting their ships ready for the annual regatta of tall ships.

"I feel like I'm living in another century." Patrick pointed to the masts of ships carrying mighty sails and waved to everyone as they passed.

The snap of the canvas and rush of the water followed by the calm warm evenings seemed to sooth Elaine. She slept soundly and peacefully the entire two weeks on board.

"I wish I could keep her on the water. With the exception of that night on the ferry she's more relaxed and sleeps well. Perhaps it's because we're away from normal every day life." Patrick spoke over the waves to his inner gods.

Both Elaine and Patrick glowed with ruddy cheeks eager to share their stories of sea faring life when they returned to dry land.

When the cab pulled up to Marnie's they were astounded to see the grass recently manicured, not a dandelion in sight. They were met at the door by a young man dressed in cut-off jean shorts and a maroon muscle shirt.

"I'm sorry to be the bearer of sad news," he said. "Marnie was rushed to the hospital two days ago. She suffered an aneurism and is in intensive care. I'm her nephew Ryan."

Devastated and worried, Elaine asked. "What hospital is she in? Can we visit?"

"I'm sorry but only immediate family is allowed. I'm afraid the prognosis is not good." Ryan led the way to the kitchen. "I've arranged for accommodation for you at another bed and breakfast a few blocks away. Sorry, but it is the best I can do." He handed them a slip of paper with their new address.

Marnie died that night. Patrick and Elaine stayed in Halifax long enough to pay their respects.

"We've lost someone who would have been a good friend. I miss her already." Elaine sighed.

"The art community has lost a great talent as well," Patrick added. He presented Elaine with a gift wrapped parcel.

"What's the occasion?

"You forgot? I'm offended." Patrick faked a sulky face. "A wicked woman came into my life twelve years ago."

"Oh, I did forget. It doesn't seem that long ago since that art show in Ottawa. Paddy, you are a pet to remember. What's in the parcel?"

Carefully peeling away the gift wrap, Elaine threw her hands to her mouth and choked. "Oh, I shall treasure this forever. You couldn't have given me anything better." She held up the appliqué pillows from Marnie's B&B. "I miss her, but having these and the art piece we bought from her, will keep her with me always."

Needing to get to the Miramichi in New Brunswick, they left Nova Scotia the next morning early. Elaine had been accepted and booked into an additional and exclusive artisans show specific to environmental issues. She was also invited by the Rotary Club to speak at their national convention taking place in Miramichi.

"Well, Pet, your success in Victoria and Toronto is sure giving you some well-deserved recognition."

"I know. This is an incredible opportunity to address some of the leaders of Canadian industry. A chance like this doesn't land in your lap every day." Elaine was adamant that she would be able to impress the Rotarians and use their connections to promote environmental issues. "I want them to undertake campaigns that would draw attention to the general public about reusing and recycling. They do amazing programs with children and I want more than anything to convince them to incorporate environmental guardianship. First and foremost, I intend to target the tourism industry and point out how garbage or stubbed cigarettes strewn at scenic sites are a blight to all their glowing promotions and a detriment to their industry."

"I'm booked to present three seminars as well." She was totally engrossed and pre-occupied in preparing her speech, seminar notes and a slide show.

"Sweetheart, would you object if I slip away and go on a picture-taking expedition up the coast and inland along the St. Lawrence?

"Why, Paddy, I think that's a brilliant plan. I'll be up to my ears and exhausted by day's end so I'll hardly know you're gone."

Chapter 15

Patrick sped along the highway heading northeast driving a few kilometers over the posted limit. As he munched on a granola bar, he rehearsed over and over in his head how he would approach Florenzia Vatars. She worked as a home helper and her last listed address was near Rimouski, Quebec. Moving inland and heading away from the sparkling water of Miramichi Bay he drove west toward the Gulf of St. Lawrence. Patrick followed the map to Bathurst then along the coastline of Chaleur Bay. Even though his thoughts were elsewhere, he took advantage of the surroundings. The Gaspe Peninsula abounded with scenic sites and wildlife, and invited exploration. His camera loaded and ready, he photographed everything from coastal scenes, picturesque cottages, fishing nets hanging from boats, a few fancy yachts and, of course, animals and birds.

Three days later sitting in a booth in a coffee shop in Rimouski he traced his finger along a secondary road on his map spread out across the yellow laminate table. Patrick squinted out the window. The house where Florenzia Vatars was supposed to work was located on the outskirts of the town. Patrick drummed his fingers on the map and sipped his coffee—a drop fell from the rim, a stain seeped over the river. Slowly he set the mug aside, folded the map, picked up his take-away coffee, threw coins on the table, and left.

"So how do I approach this woman and tell her who I am?" He sat in the van talking to the windshield. "Not to mention how to tell her who she is."

Patrick rummaged through the glove compartment for a tissue to mop up a spot of coffee that dripped onto the steering wheel before it slipped onto his jeans.

"How in the blazes do you tell someone they have a sister they never knew they had? And ask her if she wants to meet her? Then, I'll have to do it all over again with Elaine." Patrick had a habit of talking out loud to himself. He looked at his hands. They were shaking. "Oh, for God's sake, Paddy, m'boy, get on with it. The worst that can happen is she'll throw you out." And with that he crumpled his empty cup. Threw it on the floor of the passenger side, started the engine and drove off.

The number of the house, freshly stenciled on the mailbox left no doubt that he was at the right place. Patrick pulled over to the side of the road, took a deep breath and stepped out of the van. At that moment, the door of the house opened and a carriage was pushed through by a slim, ginger-haired woman. She edged the pram to the rails of the sweeping porch that stretched across the entire front of the grey brick two-storey house. Unaware she was being watched she stood for a few minutes jiggling the carriage then went back into the house.

Patrick watched the scene as it unfolded on the veranda. "That must be Elaine's sister. She doesn't look like Elaine but that coppery hair was a dead give away." Muttering to himself seemed to give him courage. Rubbing his hands down the seam of his jeans, he took another deep breath and headed up the walk.

The house sat back from the road some distance from its neighbours. One could easily drive by and never know it was there. Obviously the owner wanted privacy and acreage. The gardens spilled over with petunias and geraniums, a testament to someone's love of flowers. Well manicured lawns spread around the relatively new and impressive house.

Patrick walked up the steps, hesitated, bent over and peered into the carriage. A tiny bundle was snuggled in a pink quilt. Patrick pulled an edge of the blanket away from its nose and without knowing why he reached down and lifted the baby.

"You are so beautiful and so incredibly tiny." He whispered as he laid her against his chest and breathed in sweet smells of powder and milk. "Wouldn't Elaine love to have a wee one like you? I can just see her face radiantly beaming, full of love and joy." He was about to place the baby back in the carriage when impulsively, he turned and quickly strode to the van and drove off with the baby laid on the passenger seat.

Trancelike he steered the van along the paved road, performing mechanically. A mile down the road his heart pumping wildly, his head pounding at the realization of what he had just done filtered through the daze and slammed home. He pressed his palm hard against the steering wheel and drove blindly until a short time later he pulled over, stopped, stepped outside and leaned against the van. His stomach seized and tremors shook him right to the bone.

Shouting to the sky he yelled, "My God! What have I done? I've just committed a federal crime. I could be sentenced to life in prison!" Crossing his arms he clutched his waist and crouched into a ball, holding himself as tight as he could to stop shaking. A shrill cry drew him upright. Choking back saliva, he rubbed his upper arms to ward off a chill and peered into the van.

The small bundle on the seat was moving and howls of discomfort emanated from it. Patrick opened the door, lifted the blanket and saw a wee face flare red and then relax. It cooed and smiled.

"Oh, well, that part of you works little lass. Now, I guess I'd better tend to that—it's a wee bit smelly. Regardless of what I've done, you're not to blame and need my assistance."

Slipping into the driver's seat Patrick, now focused on the immediate need, started the motor and drove until he saw a shopping mall. Cautiously, he parked at the farthest point from the store, checked that the baby was secured with the seat belt and would not roll off the seat, locked the van and went into a drugstore. He bought disposable diapers and wet wipes. Nervously looking around he returned to the van, changed the baby, dropped the soiled nappy in a garbage bin and drove off. Near Riviere-Du-Loup he left the main roads and cut across country.

"Paddy you dumb fool, you bloody well kidnapped a baby. Jesus, did I think for one minute—no—I always go off half-cocked and react without giving a single sensible thought. I'll darn well go to prison for the rest of my life. I've got to take her back. But god in heaven, they'll arrest me no matter what. It's too late! I'm for it." Patrick's words flew through the van as he shouted in panic. "There's no out now, I've done it. No matter what, I will be arrested and convicted."

The baby, alarmed by the shouting started to scream. Patrick again pulled off to the side of the road. He stepped out and placed his hands on the roof of the van for several minutes then held his chest to settle his panicked heart. The pitiful screams from the baby moved him to action. He returned to his seat and lifted the tiny infant.

"Wee one. I've done a terrible thing. Love can make you crazy. I love Elaine more than life but it shouldn't make me insane. What kind of person would do what I did? Whatever will

I do?" He whispered his fears as he cradled her—his speech becoming soothing nonsense sounds. Once again he thought about Elaine and how this baby could cure her emotional state. Barely any weight in his arms the trusting wee face eyed him and smiled. Patrick found a small bottle with formula tucked in the folds of her blanket. He touched it to her mouth teasing it along her lips. Eagerly she drew it in and sucked.

"Well, there. You see we're in luck, at least you're not expecting a breast." Captivated he watched her cheeks compress and relax as she sucked the bottle dry. Holding her over his shoulder he rubbed her back until a clear belch told him she wouldn't spit up. His hand as big as her back, he held her until she fell asleep.

As he laid her back on the seat, Patrick spoke to her softly. "Seeing as you and I will be together for a wee bit, I'd better find a few things to manage the situation."

Patrick approached Riviere-du-Loup and purchased a local paper and town map. Fortunately it was Saturday and he scoured the classified ads. Several garage sales later he accumulated a car bed, a couple of changes of clothing, a baby sling and nursing bottles. He had to be careful not to be seen with the baby so left her concealed in the locked van. At another drugstore he purchased formula and an electric kettle.

He returned to a main road near Edmunston checked into a moderate motel. He was careful not be seen carrying in the car bed which now held the baby. She slept on peacefully, every now and again sucking sounds emanated as she attacked her fist. Patrick watched every breath she took. The magnitude of what he had done overwhelmed him and his chest was so constricted he feared he might go into cardiac arrest.

"God, what will Elaine do when she finds out what I've done? She's going to kill me. But she'll know how to solve this predicament. In the meantime I now had a small charge that totally relies on me." He boiled the kettle, made formula following the instructions on the box and placed the bottle in water to cool.

"Well, Patrick, my lad, you've got the makings of a father in you." Patrick said as he admired his work, tested the temperature on his wrist and poured the results into newly sterilized bottles. He cradled the baby in the crook of his right arm and held the bottle to the little bow of a mouth with the same hand. Automatically he swayed from one foot to the other. With his left hand he reached the TV knob, turned the power on and channel surfed all the news broadcasts. Not one station carried a story of a missing baby. Patrick sat down to think about this making sure the nipple stayed between the little pulsing lips.

"Don't know why I'm concerned you'll lose it—you grip that nipple like an ironman." His greedy wee charge sucked back all the formula and let out a loud burp when her back was rubbed. "Well, well, aren't we doing a fine job?"

Throughout the evening he checked local and national broadcasts and still there was no mention of a missing baby. He checked the little one tucked into the car bed wrapped in clean receiving blankets and her quilt. Exhausted, Patrick fell into bed. After a restless night, He switched on the news again but there was still no mention of a kidnapping.

"I would have thought there'd be a nation-wide alert by this time. I wonder why not."

He filled the sink with tepid water and gave the baby a bath. "You're a slippery, wee, lass, but never you mind, I've got a good grip." A small hand slapped the water. He lifted her onto a towel and patted her dry. Patrick gave her a loving kiss on the forehead.

"Oh, little one—you've stolen my heart just as I have stolen you."

He waited for an updated broadcast but found nothing had changed.

"Well, this'll make it easier to move about," he said to the baby. "Now my next obstacle's Elaine. She'll know how to help me. She's used to my stupid irrational behavior. She'll explain to the authorities how I go off without a thought to the consequences." He knew her busy week would be finished by mid-afternoon and he planned to be at the hotel when she returned. He arrived an hour before Elaine.

"What have you done?" Elaine screamed, her face contorted in disbelief when he told her. "They'll put you in jail forever. No, no, we have to take her back."

Patrick nodded and sat disparate holding the babe who stared at this ranting red head in motion. She wrinkled her tiny face about to burst into tears at the loud noises. Patrick shushed her and gently jiggled her up and down. With a small gurgle and a quick intake of breath, she settled, trusting and relaxed. Patrick smiled and held the bundle out to Elaine.

"No Patrick. NO. Oh my God, I'm just flabbergasted that you would do such a thing."

"I don't know what came over me, I—I just looked at her tiny face and knew that you would love her." Patrick searched Elaine's face for some indication of empathy. "I over reacted when I held her. I couldn't put her back in the carriage. I wanted to make you happy."

"Oh, Patrick, this is an impossible situation, whatever will we do?" Elaine reached for the baby.

"I've thought about what a crazy thing I've done every minute since I drove off. But the weird thing is Elaine—nobody's looking for her—there's nothing on the news. We could keep her and nobody'd be the wiser."

"Patrick, are you out of your mind?"

"I don't know why there's not a big kerfuffle over her missing. I can't explain it. It doesn't make sense unless... Do you want to know what I'm thinking?"

Elaine lifted her eyes from her small charge and stared at Patrick, "I'm listening," was her curt reply.

"The family must not have wanted the baby and for some reason haven't reported it missing. My actions must have solved their problem."

"Otherwise how do you explain that there're no news broadcasts about a missing baby? Maybe its God's way of giving you your baby—you—we want one so desperately and it's apparent that she wasn't wanted where she was."

"Do you suppose?" Elaine cooed and hummed.

"Well, it's possible. Not everyone wants a baby as much as you do—we do."

"But, Patrick, it's impossible. How'll we tell our friends and family?"

"I've been thinking about that. Listen to me. We can announce that you had a baby. We've been gone a year—nobody'll suspect. She's a tiny wee thing, small enough to be a newborn." Patrick started to pace back and forth speaking rapidly as his thoughts unfolded. "We don't have any family except Helen and she's in India. With us being gone a whole year it's possible to return with a baby without anyone thinking it's strange. Everyone knows how badly we wanted one and they'll think this trip was exactly what we needed to be successful"

Elaine sat on the edge of the bed listening to what Patrick was saying. "You've stolen a baby girl and now are suggesting we keep her? Are you daft?" She glanced into the soft eyes that were watching her with intense concentration. "Heaven knows my heart wants it to be so."

"So then it's settled."

"Oh, Paddy, it's not that easy. Darn you—you just never think before you leap. How deeply you must love me." Elaine started to cry. "Even if we return her, they'll lock you up forever. I couldn't bear that. I'd absolutely die without you. Whatever are we to do?"

"We need to keep her." Patrick stated firmly looking directly into Elaine's eyes. "We have to check out right now before anyone sees her then check into another place with her. They know here that we didn't have a baby when we checked in and that could catch us up."

"Did anyone see you bring her in?"

Patrick stopped pacing and turned to hug Elaine. "No, I was extremely careful."

Within a half hour they checked out and headed down the coast toward Moncton, the baby, in her new car bed, gurgled and made happy noises. They planned to become lost in a large town for a week then head back to Quebec City. During that time they devised one plan after another until they decided to announce that Elaine had given birth in Nova Scotia. They even planned a baptism party and compiled a list of guests to be invited. The occasion would mark not only their new addition, but would celebrate the arrival of the newly weds, Helen and Elliot. Every day they concocted more to their story and fabricated a believable tale. They continued to watch the newspapers and TV daily but there was not a mention of a kidnapped or missing baby. Committed to parenthood, they left Quebec City and six hours later were the other side of Montreal heading toward Ottawa.

Tiny hands clasped Elaine's finger, bright eyes now recognized her. "Paddy she's so beautiful. She's captured my heart and soul. It's supposed to be—I've accepted that this child was meant to be ours, our special gift. For the first time in many years I feel whole."

Patrick smiled, kissed his two fingers and placed them against Elaine's cheek.

"She needs a name." Elaine tucked the sleeping baby into the car bed on the back seat. "What do you think they called her?"

"We'll never know. It's for us to decide. She's ours now."

"I like Lynne."

"I've always thought I'd have a son one day and in my fantasies he was Philip." Patrick switched on the signal lights and eased into the right turning-lane onto the highway to Ottawa, their year-long trip almost at an end.

"Philippa—Philippa Lynne. What do you think?"

Patrick turned to smile at the back seat. "Hello, Philippa Lynne Snelling."

CHAPTER 16

July, 2003

"I like to sew."

"Pardon, what did you say?" Don Evans leaned forward and stared at Florry.

"I like to sew."

"Oh, dear don't tell me you're planning to leave Snellings and open your own dressmaking business ..."

Florry pointed to the brown paper package she had placed on Evans desk.

Don looked at her inquiringly, opened the package and pulled out a small, beautifully made quilt. The whimsical design portrayed butterflies and flowers in pastel colours on a pink background.

"I found it." A sob escaped and Florry reached into her small brown handbag and pulled out a tissue.

Still very confused, Don raised his right hand palm up as if to stop Florry. "I think I must have missed something. Let's just start at the beginning."

"Yes, well, I'll start at the beginning then." Florry blew her nose and concentrated on the wide gold ring on Evans finger. "I lived in Belleville with my parents until I was seventeen. They were old country—Eastern European—and insisted on their old ways. I wasn't allowed to mix with kids my own age or go to school dances. I was like a prisoner. One day, I decided I couldn't take their controlling any more and left. Packed a bag and walked out. When I look back, I must have broken their hearts. But I was strong willed and determined to have a life of my own."

She rolled the tissue into a tight ball and stuffed it into the pocket of her beige cardigan.

"Yes, go on."

She grasped the arms of the chair and continued. "I worked at housekeeping jobs in Montreal for thirteen years and ended up in Quebec City. There, I took a job as a nanny with a family that had a three-year-old boy, Guy, and a nine-month-old baby, Roy. It suited me fine. It was in a pleasant part of the city with a beautiful park and lots of trees. I'd walk the children each day. Guy loved to play on the slide and I'd sit with Roy watching him."

Florry shifted in her seat and searched in her purse for another tissue. Don reached into his drawer and handed her a packet.

"The children's mother often worked late, she was a pharmacist, and I found myself in the company of the father on many an evening. He was attentive and I was lonely and vulnerable. The inevitable happened and I became pregnant."

"Oh, Florry."

"Well, that having happened, I couldn't stay there could I?"

"So you left?"

"Yes, I was terrified. There was no going back to my parents I'd been away so long. I had kept in touch though. However, they were so strict they'd disown me. I didn't know where to turn. But I wasn't stupid so figured out that a church might help me. Rightfully so. One of the nuns, a sister Amelia, at a center city Catholic Church found me a place to stay in exchange for light housekeeping at an orphanage run by nuns. They were very kind while I dealt with morning sickness. When I started to feel better they found me a job near Rimouski. The lady of the house suffered from lupus disease and migraine headaches. The poor lady needed care. She lacked energy and spent most of her days in bed."

"But, what about you?"

"The family didn't mind that I was pregnant as long as it didn't interfere with my work and even said I could stay on after the baby. I changed my first name to Florry and my last name to Waters. Not officially, you understand just to make it easier. People don't like foreign names."

"Well, I could disagree with you on that one." Don sat back in his chair and encouraged Florry to continue.

"The poor lady took a fair amount of care. She had strange ideas, got upset easily and was somewhat stressful. My having the baby became a topic that she dwelt on a great deal and not in a kindly way. She didn't really approve that I was keeping it, you see. I'd made up my mind that there was no way I was giving my baby away. When Babs was born, I was only off from my duties one week."

"Where did you go?" Don Evans still was having trouble understanding why Florry was telling him her life story.

"Well, nowhere really, but I didn't have to look after the misses. Her husband was kind enough to hire another helper while I had a little rest. I'd my own room and he bought me a lovely cradle. His misses was some miffed, she berated me for keeping Babs and wasn't too happy her husband was supportive."

"Did he have designs on you as well?"

"Oh, no, he was a gentleman and devoted to his wife,

although she did not make it easy for him. Even though she was difficult, I decided to stay."

"So what happened?"

"I took money from my savings and found an old fashioned pram—found it second hand, good as new. It was lovely to tuck my baby girl in for her naps. We soon settled into a routine, wee Babs, I called her Barbara Alice, Babs for short. She was a good baby so I had no problem carrying on with my duties."

"But things changed." Don glanced at his watch. He didn't mean to be hurried but he had documents that needed attention and he could not understand why Florry was telling him her problems. "When did all this happen?"

"Babs was born May 24th, seventeen years ago."

"And what became of her?"

"That's the problem, you see."

"No, I don't see."

"When she was near six weeks old, on June 28, I was going about my duties and as was my custom, I set her on the front porch for her afternoon nap. She napped most of the time, being that young and all. I liked her to have a bit of fresh air so I'd put her on the front porch—a big veranda they had." Florry started to choke up and blew her nose.

"It's okay. Relax. Do go on." Don looked at the quilt.

"Well, this particular day, I put her out and set about doing the laundry. The misses called and I'd to change all her bedding, poor thing had a delicate stomach. Then after I got her settled and all, I went back to the laundry since I had more of it then."

"The bedding?"

"Yes. Then I went to gather in Babs and she was gone!"

"Gone, gone where?"

"That's the question. I bent to the carriage and it was empty. No worse feeling could ever be. My insides turned hollow and my throat was choking."

"Did you find her?"

"Knowing the misses was unpredictable I got hold of myself thinking she may have slipped downstairs while I was putting her linens into the machine and taken Babs back upstairs with her. But that wasn't the case when I ran up to check.

I was ever so frightened at what might've happened to my baby and called the police. The Surete du Quebec car arrived and the police were very intimidating. They kept at me demanding I tell them what I'd done with my baby. I told them over and over again what had happened but they wouldn't believe me. There was no convincing them that I had not gotten rid of her."

"Why would they think that?"

"The misses was no help by telling 'em that I was an unwed and not happy about being a single mother. She kept telling 'em how hard it was for me to look after her and the baby too. Even when I contradicted her, they listened to her not me. Suspicion was written all over their faces. I spent hours and hours at the station going over and over every detail and being repeatedly asked the same questions. I pleaded for them to find my Babs. They were convinced I disposed of her because it would then be easier for me."

"But eventually they believed you surely."

"No. They made little effort to confirm my story. They just saw me as a desperate distraught woman. They talked to a few neighbours, asked about at hotels, motels and bus stops. Nothing else was done. Nobody saw anything. They went right back to accusing me of doing in my baby. Mr. Evans, you know me.

There's no way I'd harm my own wee baby. I loved my Babs above anything and there's no way I'd hurt her."

"Couldn't they see how distressed you were?"

"Yes, but they took it as play acting. Another thing was I didn't speak French well and half the time they talked over my head in their language and I had no idea what was going on."

"I can see where that would be a problem."

"Even though I was inconsolable I couldn't make them understand that I would never, never injure my baby. Eventually, after days and days of sleepless nights, I was exhausted from the constant interrogation and lack of sleep. They defeated and crushed all the energy right out of me. Drained me of all emotion and strength—I went into a deep depression and refused to talk to them." Florry rummaged frantically in her purse, shut the clasp and opened and shut it again.

Evans asked her to continue.

"Nobody believed me. They searched and searched for a body and, of course, none was found. They couldn't find any evidence to take me to trial so I was finally released after six months. Of course, I'd lost my job. I was alone and deeply depressed."

"Whatever did you do?"

"I returned to my family. There was no baby so they'd never know. I became Florenzia Vatars again."

Don Evans shook a niggling thought that he had heard that name before from his head. He urged Florry to continue.

"Well, I wasn't home long before my mother took quite sick so it was a good thing I was there to look after her. She lingered for seven years needing a great deal of care. She was no sooner put in the ground than my father had a stroke that left him paralyzed. Once again, I became a caregiver. He lived for four years before a massive coronary took him away. I inherited the house, sold it and moved here."

"Yes, and bought your single-wide in Greely, right?"

"That's right. I started looking for work here and that's when I started working at your house. At that time, I also, officially changed my name to Florence Waters."

"Florry, I don't know what to say. I wish there was something I could do but I don't understand why you're telling me this now."

"It's the quilt."

"Oh, the baby blanket?"

"Yes. It was taken with wee Babs when she was picked from the carriage."

"What? Where on earth did you find it?"

"In the upstairs closet—the Snelling's closet. Philippa is Babs!"

"Come again."

"Philippa is Babs. We, Helen and me, cleaned out the closets but I hadn't washed the last one until Philippa was on her way home from camp. I wiped it down with a sponge and all-purpose cleaner, to make it smell fresh. A package was stuck at the back and it finally let go—that package. That package had the blanket stuffed in it. I'd know it anywhere—the quilt. I made it. I made it for Babs. I appliquéd the tiny roses and butterflies in the old European manner my mother'd taught me."

"Could you be mistaken?"

"No, it wasn't from a pattern. I designed it myself and edged the center rose in white because I wanted it to look like it was frosted. No one else would've done that. I'd know my own work anywhere. Mr. Evans you have to believe me. Philippa is my Babs."

Don Evans rocked back and forth in his chair trying to absorb what he had just heard. It would certainly explain the fact there was no birth certificate for Philippa. But it was just too far fetched to believe.

"What do I do now, Mr. Evans? Philippa's my daughter. The Snellings kidnapped my baby."

His lawyer instincts brought Don erect. "Now Florry, we need to think about all of this. You need to consider Philippa. We'll have to work it through and find the best resolution. I don't think it's in Philippa's or your best interests to brand her parents as criminals."

"But they are! They stole my baby." Florry started to fidget getting quite agitated and got up from her chair.

"All right, Florry, calm down. I need to understand this whole situation. First, let me assure you, I'll act on your better behalf. You may have grounds to investigate the Snellings. But if you can just leave it with me for a few days, I'd like to think about the best way to deal with it."

"I want to tell Philippa right now, I want her to know I grieved for her for seventeen years."

"I know Florry, but you have to remember that she loved her mother and father. You can't go about this without considering the impact it'll have on Philippa. She could refuse to believe you, become extremely angry and demand you leave her alone. In fact, she could turn against you and never want you near her again. As I see it, it has to be handled with care, very delicately considering the impact on all parties involved. Please, you must trust me to handle it. Let me consider it for a few days."

"I don't know how I can go back to that house and not tell her. I just know she's my daughter and I can't hold back any longer.

She has to know I'm her real mother."

"Florry, you've lived with this terrible situation for seventeen years—a few more days won't change anything."

"I know Mr. Evans but now I know where she is—I want her to know I'm her mother."

"Is she at home today?"

"No. She went to a movie with her friends—I expect she will get home about five."

"Isn't her Aunt Helen due to arrive this evening to see Philippa and her friend off to San Francisco tomorrow? Why don't I call Helen and tell her that you've encountered a small legal matter and must return to your home for a few days."

"That would help. I couldn't bear seeing Philippa, Babs, and not telling her. You promise me you'll look after it?"

"By the time Philippa gets home from Los Angeles I'll have sorted it out, I promise. In the meantime, I'll double check everything and decide the best way to broach this. Can you meet with me before then?"

"Of course. Will you tell her that I'll take Sable with me so he will be looked after while she is in California?"

Florry left the law office picked up Sable and a few personal items then drove to her single-wide. Once in the house, she carefully put away Sable's dog food and sorted her sundries in the bathroom. She returned to the kitchen and looked in the refrigerator to take stock. She would have to make a quick trip to the convenience store. She reached for the pad and pencil she always kept close at hand on the counter. She picked them up and stared at them as if not knowing why she held them. All of a sudden she spun around and threw them across the room.

"I hate Philippa's parents. They ruined my life. They're the worst kind of criminals." She was shouting and pacing up and down in front of the sofa. "I wish they weren't dead so I could kill them myself." She did not hear the screen door open then close.

"Florry, what is going on? Calm down. I've never seen you like this. Whatever is the matter?" Joyce reached for her friend.

"Don't touch me. Leave me alone."

"But Florry, honey, I just want to help."

"No one can help. I can't even see justice done."

"Whatever is going on?"

Florry turned and looked at her friend's concerned face, sucked in a big breathe of air and flopped on the sofa. Joyce tentatively eased in beside her.

"Oh, Joyce, I'm in such a mess. I've never told you who I really am and what happened to me. Now everything is coming at me full force." Florry looked at Joyce. "I'm scared Joyce, really scared."

"What of? You in trouble with the law?"

"No. But I was. It's a long story."

"Well, you calm yourself while I make a pot of tea then you tell old Joyce all about it."

Florry, nursing the cup of tea, told her story to Joyce, who uncharacteristically did not interrupt once.

"Now, I'm frightened that Philippa will turn away from me. I won't be able to even talk to her without showing my hatred for Elaine and Patrick. And I do hate them, hate them, hate them." Florry's voice rose to a scream.

"Oh, boy, this is one mess." Joyce was rubbing Florry's left arm trying to calm her. "How could they have done such a thing and ruined your life?"

"Joyce, I don't want to lose my Babs again. What am I to do?"

Joyce sipped her tea as they sat in silence. "Florry, something must have driven them to steal a baby."

"Helen told me they had tried to conceive for years without any success and that Elaine suffered deep depression as a result. They went on a year's trip across Canada and returned with a newborn. Everyone assumed that the trip had been therapeutic and they had a baby girl. But, Joyce, Elaine didn't birth her—she was stolen—stolen from me. They fooled everyone."

"I once knew a couple that were faced with the same problem. The wife became more and more depressed and finally committed suicide. Maybe Elaine was like that and Patrick felt helpless. Maybe they saw this as a way to save Elaine."

"They committed a crime—they're kidnappers."

"I know, but you have to find room in your heart to forgive them or Philippa will never accept you."

"They ruined my life!"

"They certainly made you change your life and it was a cruel thing to do. But you have to accept that this happened and you now have the opportunity to start a new life. Yes, you lost the years of Philippa growing up ..."

"Babs."

"Okay, Babs, but she will not want to change her name so you have to rethink this."

"Joyce, I'm scared stiff. What if she refuses to have anything to do with me? I can't stop being angry with Elaine and Patrick and she loves them. I want that love, it should be mine."

"Okay, here's another thought." Joyce heaved herself up off the sofa and paced the floor. "They're gone, dead. They'll never see their daughter fall in love and get married. You will. They'll never see their grandchildren. You will. Florry honey, for you, life starts now. And as for that love—Philippa will learn to love you."

Florry stood up and walked to the sink with her cup and saucer. She turned and looked at her friend, bent over and patted Sable's head. "Oh, Joyce, thank you. You're right. You've made me focus on the future. I have to let go of the past. I've managed to make it through these years without my Babs, now I should be able to find a way to enjoy being with Philippa. Somehow, I'll try to find it in my heart to forgive—how I don't know."

"Like any tragedy, time heals. Getting through the first few days will be the toughest. Come on let's take that dog out for a walk."

Florry knew when her friend needed a smoke.

****

After Florry left the office, Don Evans phoned Helen's cell number and explained that Florry had gone home for a few days to attend to some personal business. He sat and mulled over the incredulous circumstances. Something kept trying to surface, something he knew he should remember and he wasn't sure what it was. A rap on the door drew his attention.

"Mr. Evans," his assistant spoke around the door. "What do you want me to do with this file of Mr. Snelling's?"

"What file, Susan?"

"We always had a combined file for both Mr. and Mrs. Snelling, but you kept a separate one for Mr. Snelling. I found it listed in the back of the files as I was preparing the legal documents for the insurance company. It was filed under a different number—so I thought you should know. It's old, I think."

Don suddenly remembered Patrick sitting across from him handing him a manila envelope.

"Don can you keep this on file and don't reveal its contents unless something happens to me, then Elaine should know about her sister."

That had been when they first returned to Ottawa. Don had totally forgotten it existed.

"Susan, can you bring it here, please. I need to see it."

It was all there. Patrick wrote the whole story. Now the detail that was stuck in the back of his head jumped forward. Her name Florenzia Vatars, of course, Elaine's half sister. It all fitted and Don now knew that Florry told the truth. Angry with Patrick, Don yelled to the ceiling. "How could you do such a stupid, stupid thing?" He thought about how Florry had suffered all those years without her child. She hadn't watched her grow and had been branded a killer to boot just so Patrick could appease Elaine's emotional lapses. It was a selfish and despicable act.

However, the most surprising thing was the fact that Florry was Elaine's half sister. This placed a whole other perspective on the situation. Don picked up the phone and called his wife.

"Darling, I need a stiff drink. I'm coming right home."

It was Don's wife who put it in context and told him that Florry needed to see Patrick's file.

A few days later, Florry once again sat across from Don Evans. Slowly, she read the papers spread across Don's desk. She read then re-read it a paragraph at a time, pausing to think then continued. She read about the pain Patrick experienced watching his wife fall deeper and deeper into depression. She knew what that was like.

"Elaine was my sister?"

"Yes, and this makes it very awkward," said Don. "If we call in the police, the Snellings, your sister and brother-in-law, will be found responsible for a kidnapping. It is a federal crime. They'll be branded criminals and that would never go away. Regardless of how awful the crime they committed and I'm not excusing them, Philippa enjoyed a happy, safe childhood and loved Elaine and Patrick dearly. Do we shatter that?"

"Whatever are we to do? Philippa did love them. She would never forgive me if I have them branded as criminals."

"There's no doubt whatever that we must tell Philippa and Helen. But, with your permission, I think we can avoid police involvement. As your lawyer, I can represent you and notify the Surete du Quebec to close the file. I'll explain that you were a scared single mother, terrified of what your parents would think of you having a baby. I'll tell them that you arranged for Barbara's aunt to raise her as their own. I can create a plausible story."

Finally looking up with red-rimmed flooded eyes she nodded. "Yes, that would be best. It's too late for justice anyway."

"Florry, how can I express how sorry I am and that you endured all that pain? You need to know that Patrick was a good man and loved his wife, so much so that he committed a heinous crime to save her sanity. They convinced themselves that you did not want the baby. They gave Philippa a good stable life."

"I know. She's grown into a lovely young woman. I am terrified I'll lose her again."

"I'll tell Philippa without you being present—she needs to know the whole story. I've no idea how she will accept this, so it's probably better that an outsider tells her in an unemotional way and deals with facts only. Whatever her reaction, whatever happens, it'll require some time before both of you adjust.

Philippa arrives home this afternoon and I've asked Helen if I might speak with them this evening."

****

Don dressed in beige slacks and a striped navy, short-sleeved shirt arrived at the Snelling house armed with two large files. Helen ushered him into the kitchen.

"I've still got some of Florry's brownies—best in the world and a fresh pot of coffee. Don, we don't regret for one minute, our decision to hire her, she's a jewel. Have a seat." She sat the plate mid table as Don sat across from Philippa, the brownies in easy reach for both of them. Helen poured mugs of coffee for her and Don and a glass of milk for her niece. Don stirred in three lumps of sugar and streamed a generous amount of cream into his mug. He turned his mug around and around, seemingly admiring the intricate floral design. He took a sip and sat back with a big sigh.

He couldn't help noticing how fashionable Helen looked in her slim coral slacks and filmy Monet print blouse. In contrast, Philippa wore denim shorts and a red halter top. The still night hung humid and warm, the faint smell of flowering nicotine drifted through the screen of the open patio door.

"How was San Francisco?"

"Totally, incredibly amazing, Mr. Evans! It was such a privilege to be there and Hunter Platz not only gave us admission to some of the high security areas of his company, he treated us to a tours of the city, Alcatraz and the harbour at night."

"I think Mr. Evans came to discuss some business. Am I right?" Helen looked from one to the other.

"Yes, but I also wanted to hear how Philippa made out."

Don placed the files on the table and braced his back against the chair. His muscles were taut. He took a deep breath, fanned through some papers and spoke in a calm steady voice. He told them everything.

Philippa remained very still, hardly breathing. Don handed over the manila envelope Patrick had left in his care. He found it difficult to look either Philippa or Helen in the eye when he finished; the weight of the moment was crushing him. He coughed quietly into his hand simply to break the silence. He looked from one to the other.

Philippa placed her hand on the envelope and slowly drew it to her. Trembling she drew out the contents, held them with outstretched arms as if to protect herself from them, as if they held her broken heart. They did.

"I'm shocked! How could Patrick have done that? It's totally ridiculous but not unbelievable. I had no doubt but that woman would drive my brother to the brink." Helen said. "When they arrived home with a baby, it was the last thing we expected." She ran her hand through her dark hair and looked toward her niece.

"Aunt Helen, please shut up."

Philippa holding the sheet of paper written in her father's handwriting and spoke in a small shaking voice. "You mean that I was stolen from my mother's half sister—that she is my natural mother?"

Don Evans looked Philippa compassionately in the eye and nodded.

"I thought I was a Romanian orphan."

"What!" Both Helen and Don exclaimed.

Philippa explained how she was beginning to have doubts when her birth certificate couldn't be located and there seemingly was no record it. She explained how, through Mark, she learned about the orphans.

"So my birth mother was really my aunt." Philippa murmured. She mulled over the information. "How weird is that?"

"Your father loved your mother so much—too much. He committed a crime to save her from falling into deeper darker depression, perhaps one she wouldn't return from. And it worked. You were the best thing that ever happened to Elaine. She was a wonderful mother. Both your parents were devoted to each other and to you. You couldn't have had a better childhood." Don Placed his hand over Philippa's that still rested on the envelope.

"Well, this is a fine how-do-you-do. It will be a horrific scandal." Helen stood up and paced the kitchen. "The media will just eat it up, it'll be all over the front pages. Elliott'll be furious."

"Mrs. Ravi, Helen, I think it can be handled discretely and need not involve the press. I firmly believe it can be kept in the family. There's more."

"More. What more could there be?"

"It's about how I learned all this."

Sable pushed against Philippa's hand sensing the tension in the kitchen, he wanted to comfort his own. Her fingers automatically scratched his head.

"Florry found out."

"Florry? Our Florry?"

Don related the rest of the story as he watched carefully for reactions.

"Since this now is a family matter, I'll handle the legal side, including a birth certificate for Philippa. Frankly, there's no need to involve the police since the so-called criminals are both deceased."

"Well, that's a relief," Helen announced. "I just don't think Elliott would stand for it otherwise."

At this point Philippa stared hard into her aunt's eyes and raised her voice. "For God's sake Aunt Helen, this isn't about stupid Elliott. I could care less about him so just stop."

She turned to Don. "Mr. Evans, I don't know how I will handle this. I can't simply accept that I have a new mother. But right now I feel awful that Florry has gone through this. I have to help her—she will need me. When can I see her?"

"She's very anxious to see you, but afraid ..."

At that moment, Florry stepped into the kitchen. She had slipped quietly through the front door shortly after Don Evans arrived. No one had even connected that Sable was there when he was supposed to be in Greely with Florry. She had waited pressed against the hallway wall for support and heard everything.

Philippa rose from her chair and moved toward her. Don tensed.

Mother and daughter stood looking at each other. Don could not read the expression on their faces. Sable whined.

A young adult voice broke the silence.

"I guess we take the next steps through life together."

Philippa reached for Florry's hand. "It won't be easy but, you know something, I think we can move forward. Do you mind if I still call you Florry? It would be difficult to call you Mom—I never even called Elaine that."

"Perhaps in time, perhaps in time" Florry gathered her daughter into her arms.

Five Years Later

"Florry, I'm home," Philippa yelled as she threw open the front door. "Florry, where are you? Sable, come."

Philippa left her suitcase in the front hall and headed for the kitchen. "In a way, I'm pleased no one's home. This way I can get these flowers in water and my suitcase tucked away in my room. I wanted to surprise Florry anyway—she has no idea I was coming home. She must be out walking Sable." Philippa muttered to herself as she set about finding a vase and arranging a dozen pink roses she had bought for the occasion. Once done she set them on the table and headed for her bedroom with her luggage. She needed to change out of her traveling clothes, a stylish navy shirtwaist, pantyhose and heels, and get into her black jeans and her 'Canada' sweat shirt.

An hour later, still there was no sign of Florry or Sable. As she was starting to get concerned, Philippa finally heard noises in the front hall. A deep bass voice was offering to hang up Florry's sweater and Sable's leash. As she crept to the banister to peer into the hallway, she saw her neighbour, Mr. Petry, bend to give Florry a light kiss on her cheek.

Puzzled, Philippa stepped away from the stairs and let the couple leave the entrance way. Once she heard the kitchen door swing closed, she went downstairs.

"Walter, how ever did these flowers get here? You didn't do that did you?"

"Nope. Have no idea where they came from."

Throwing the door open, Philippa rushed in and threw her

arms around Florry. "Happy Mother's Day."

It had been five years since Florry discovered that Philippa was her long-lost daughter. Even though Philippa had difficulty calling Florry 'mother, mom' or any other maternal title she decided to honour her on this occasion to recognize how lucky she was to have this special person in her life. Philippa was careful never to refer to Elaine as her mother to Florry. She knew that the seventeen years of suffering would never really disappear. To Philippa, she had two mothers and she held them each in a separate corner of her heart. She recognized that she was fortunate to have been raised by Elaine and Patrick, they gave her a rare perspective on life. It would have been entirely different if she had been reared by Florry, not a negative upbringing but different. When Elaine and Patrick were killed and Florry came into her life, the adjustments were many and not always easy. Over time she bonded with her birth mother and learned to love her deeply. She knew how important it was to Florry to be recognized and honoured on this day.

Florry never got over having to touch Philippa as if it was the first time she saw her, as if to assure herself she was real. The intensity she felt when her fingers touched this precious face was always emotional. Finding her stolen daughter seventeen years after she disappeared was unexpected and awesome. Her daughter was beautiful, intelligent and thoughtful, with a smile that captured her heart. Though she could never forgive Elaine and Patrick for kidnapping her Babs, renamed Philippa,, she did credit them with raising her to be a strong and resourceful young woman—a woman to be proud of. She realized that Philippa would never call her anything but Florry, after all she had never called Elaine and Patrick anything other than their given names.

However, almost a year after their death, knowing that Florry was her birth mother, Philippa paid Florry the ultimate compliment by honouring her on Mother's Day. Tears flowed down Florry's face as she reached over and gave her daughter a hug and a kiss on the cheek.

Walter handed Florry his large checkered handkerchief. Then stepped back as if he was intruding on this scene.

"Mr. Petry, how are you? It's so good to see you. Were you out walking with Florry?"

"Yes, it has become a daily event. Good for the old body to get exercise."

"Sit down you two while I rustle up some coffee and fresh cherry pie." True to her character Florry had been up early and baked before her walk. With her back to Philippa, she said. "There's something I have to tell you my dear. Walter and I have formed a special friendship."

"Well, that's wonderful."

"After you left for university, Walter came over several times to see if I needed help with anything. We found that we had a great deal in common and started to see more and more of each other."

"Do I detect that this friendship goes deep?"

"Yes, we can honestly say that we are now in a relationship. I hope this is not a problem for you."

Philippa looked at the two of them and saw a glow pass between them. "I am delighted! This is great news and the fact that you live next door to each other makes it easy."

"Well, we need to talk about that—you see, Walter has asked me to marry him."

Silence.

Walter stirred, stood up and put his arm around Florry. "I know this is sudden, but at our age, time gets away too quickly. Once I realized that I was smitten, I proposed. Florry wouldn't accept unless you approved. Please approve, she is the light I have been waiting for."

Philippa sat absolutely still. Her thoughts were racing. She had had an another reason for coming home. Last week she had been offered a to-die-for job in Toronto. She would graduate from M.I.T. in a few weeks and to land such a prestigious placement was unprecedented, especially at the salary she had been offered. It meant that she would have to move away for good. She had been considering what to do about the house, Sable and Florry. Her biggest concern was Florry. She saw how wretched Florry had been when she had gone to Boston, but a permanent move would tear her apart. Now this development was going to save the moment.

"This is the best news! Yes, accept. I am so delighted—what a perfect match—and between two of my very special people. How wonderful is that?"

A blush spread across Florry's face as she turned and nodded her acceptance to Walter.

Sable nudged Philippa's knee looking for attention. After Philippa left Ottawa to attend school in Boston, Sable and Florry became very attached which helped both of them adjust to not having Philippa around. As the trio sat at the kitchen table, it was decided that it would be better for everyone if Sable stayed with Florry. He was getting on in years with a splatter of grey around his muzzle. Moving him to Toronto would be traumatic and unwise as he would be left alone for hours, plus finding a place to live that would welcome a dog simply complicated things.

Philippa would travel often between Ottawa and Toronto thus be able to spend time with him and the newly weds.

"Mike drove up from Boston with me and he has decided to continue at M.I.T. and hone some of his programming skills. Frankly, I think he has found a romantic interest too. If you will excuse me, I want to call Mark to let him know that I'm home and I need to talk to him about finding a place to rent in Toronto."

Philippa went into the office and called Mark's cell. Her heart raced in anticipation of hearing his voice. Their attraction had never slackened, in fact, if anything, it had grown stronger.

"Flip, my love, where are you?"

"I'm home and am full of news. I'm still a little surprised but Florry and Mr.Petry are engaged—she consented just a few minutes ago."

"Oh, my, what do you think about that?"

"Outside of solving a small problem I had, I am delighted. Oh Mark, they are so sweet together."

"What problem?"

"Are you sitting down? I have been offered an incredible job and it's in Markham."

"No Way! Did you accept?"

"I couldn't refuse. I start mid-July. It's a little different than gaming, but then we knew that the opportunities there were limited. It is in security. It seems that many of the same skills are required to track down a hacker, it's all about solving a situation and finding a solution and resolution. Anyway, a recruiting team came to M.I.T., I interviewed, was shortlisted, and was hired."

"All sorts of wonderful visions are running threw my head as I imagine you close to me. Since I graduated and am second-in-command at our family business, it has been all work, work,

work. But when you get here we are going to spend every spare minute together. You do know how much I love you, don't you?"

"Mark, I have to tell you, being in Toronto is a bonus, but I likely would have accepted this job if it was in British Columbia. I do love you and do want to be with you, but right now, my career has to take precedence."

"Right. Anyway we are to young to make decisions to decide our future. That being said, will you marry me?"

"Of course, silly, but only after we're over forty."

"Thought so."

"By the way, I got a text from Tracey and she's over the moon with an offer to work with Disney in digital animation."

"How perfect. Isn't it strange how those two weeks five years ago impacted our lives? We made friends that have stayed connected and we fell in love. Before you start working, we should drive up to Popoti just for old times sake."

"Likely won't have enough time. I have to find a place to live and sort out everything here. Far too much on my plate. Can you tap into possibilities of a rental, preferably a townhouse or condo near Markham?"

"Sure, I'll ask around."

Mark and Philippa talked for another half hour. Philippa told Mark that Ray, Rick and Frank, who had also attended M.I.T. were moving forward in the IT world. Ray and Rick both got offers at a gaming company in Montreal and Frank with a small IT firm in Halifax. The fact that their resume referred to Camp Popoti and that they had glowing references from Chuck had opened doors.

After she ended the conversation with Mark, Philippa smiled and wandered out onto the veranda. Much as she missed Elaine and Patrick and still would break out sobbing at how desperately she felt their absence, she counted her blessings. The circumstances that brought her and Florry together were incredible and she was able to continue in a life that, for the most part, was positive. Genetics definitely came into play as Florry and she bonded quickly. Pressured by Philippa, Florry had contacted Philippa's birth father. Although he kept his distance, he did meet Philippa and shared his biological information. She learned about her half- siblings but due to the circumstances never contacted them. She was ready to move forward facing new challenges, she knew her road to the future would be a journey worth traveling.

Author Molly O'Connor

True to her cultural heritage, Molly O'Connor has always been a storyteller. A graduate of Creative Writing courses at Carleton University and Algonquin College. she found her niche in short story writing. Most of her stories can be savoured over a single cup of coffee, but even though she has found a great deal of success within the short-story genre - publishing her own collection of 14 short stories, a creative memoir, a children's book, as well as stories in five of the very popular Chicken Soup for the Soul anthologies-she has truly enjoyed this foray into the world of novel writing.

Living in a Victorian farmhouse in the Ottawa Valley, with her daughter, son-in-law, four grandchildren, a dog, a bunny and two cats-not to mention the various other invasive creatures that like to scurry around inside the walls of the hundred-year-old farmhouse. Chickens, ducks, and turkeys range outside, Molly O'Connor (perhaps understandably) revels in her rural setting and can often be seen hiking the trails with her camera to capture that perfect shot of a wild flower....

CPSIA information can be obtained
at www.ICGtesting.com
Printed in the USA
BVHW071528310721
612760BV00001B/50

9 781590 954300